BE MORE
OCTOPUS

Suzanne Lissaman

For Muffin and Mia

PART ONE
SPRING 2018

1

Em heard a buzzing sound. She checked her phone. Nothing. It must have been someone else's. She went back to looking out the window as the bus slowly made its way into Birmingham city centre through the morning rush hour traffic.

The buzzing sound happened again. It was definitely close by. She looked down and spotted a splash of claret and blue plastic in the crack between the seats: Connor's phone with its distinctive Aston Villa cover. It must have fallen out of his pocket when he got off the bus a couple of stops ago.

Em picked it up. There was a text message notification on the screen. Should she unlock it to check what it was? Connor had given her his passcode months ago when they'd been waiting for an Uber. Desperate to relieve himself of some of the ten pints of beer he'd downed that evening, he'd left his phone with Em so she could track the car while he disappeared behind a hedge.

The text could be from the manager of their wedding venue. He'd promised to come back to Connor about squeezing in four extra guests for their wedding breakfast. But it was unlikely to be him this early in the morning. It was probably Connor getting someone else to text his phone to find out where it was.

Either way, she ought to check. Em tapped in the six-digit code. The message appeared:

See you at 12.30 ♥♥♥

The hearts were worrying. The sender's name simply said 'A'. Odd, but obviously someone Connor knew.

Em clicked on the notification. No other texts, just that one. A's contact details didn't give any clues either - only the mobile number and the single-letter name.

The phone buzzed again - another text from A.

Check WhatsApp

Em did as she was told. There was plenty to read there. So much that Em missed her stop.

2

Em couldn't face going to work. She phoned the office and left a message saying she needed the day off due to a family emergency. She couldn't bear the thought of going back to the flat she shared with Connor either.

After walking around the city centre on autopilot, mulling over everything she'd seen on Connor's WhatsApp chat with A, she found herself sitting in St Paul's Square, working out what to do next.

A pigeon waddled towards her, staring up at Em expectantly.

'I've got nothing to feed you. Sorry.'

The pigeon came closer. Another bird landed nearby and started walking towards it, cooing loudly, its ruff puffed up, and its head bobbing up and down manically - a male pigeon fancying his chances. Em's pigeon ignored him.

'Do you know what a female octopus would do in this situation?' Em said. 'She would throw things at him.'

Em smiled, remembering the school trip to an aquarium when she'd first learned how a female octopus dealt with unwanted male attention by throwing rocks at her potential suitor. From then on, whenever someone was being annoying, her best friend, Lucy, would advise Em to 'be more octopus'.

Em's pigeon tilted her head as if she were giving Em's suggestion serious consideration. But the only potential projectile in pecking distance was a crumpled brown leaf, useless for putting off her suitor. Em's pigeon elected to flutter away down the path, with the male strutting keenly after her. Em lost sight of them as they disappeared behind the church in the centre of the square.

Em leaned back on the bench. She needed to be more octopus too.

She noticed the inscription on the back of the bench. *In memory of Alan and Audrey - together again 20 May 2008.* Did Alan join Audrey in the afterlife, or did Audrey go first? Were they genuinely happy to be reunited? She thought of her parents and the fulfilling life her father was leading now that her mother had shuffled off this mortal coil. If there were an afterlife, he wouldn't be happy to be reunited with his wife and her domineering ways. Not that Em wanted to see her mother again, either.

Perhaps reincarnation was a better option - no annoying relatives and exes to deal with. Instead, you'd get a whole new bunch of people to learn to live with. Or pigeons? Who knew what creature you would be in your next life? She was certain that Connor would be coming back as a snake.

The inscription didn't indicate how long Alan and Audrey had been together, but it was probably longer than the three years that Em had been with Connor. What a pity she hadn't been more octopus when she first met him, leering at her drunkenly at a wedding.

'There you are.' Lucy's familiar voice snapped Em back to reality.

'Where did you spring from?'

'I needed your advice, but you've ignored my texts, so I checked where you were on Snapchat.'

'You're meant to be in London.'

Lucy had spent a good chunk of yesterday evening excitedly telling Em about her prospective new client.

'They cancelled the meeting. I got the email while I was waiting for the train at New Street. It looks like another marketing agency poached them, so I've been consoling myself with shopping for wedding shoes.' Lucy waved an expensive-looking bag in front of Em.

Em sighed. Time to say out loud what she'd been mulling over for the last hour. 'There's not going to be a wedding - not mine anyway.'

Lucy looked horrified. 'Since when?'

'Since I read Connor's WhatsApp conversation with that girl from the cinema.'

'Not the busty one with the nose ring?' Lucy sat down next to Em. 'Why didn't you tell me?'

'Because I only found out this morning.'

'Has he actually cheated on you?'

'Judging by their photos, yes. And from the descriptions of what they are going to do to one another next time they meet, he's planning to continue cheating on me!'

'Arseholes!'

'Those were involved!' Em shuddered. She tried to get rid of the images of Connor and A's bedroom gymnastics that insisted on forcing their way back into her mind.

'What are you going to do?'

Em shrugged.

It started to spit with rain.

'Time to decamp to my place for a strategy meeting,' Lucy said.

Lucy's flat was only a few streets away on the third floor of an old warehouse that had been converted into chic, loft-style apartments.

Em stood looking out of the massive living room window, watching the rainstorm. 'I would get nothing done living here. I'd spend most of my time looking at the sky and how the light constantly changes over the city. It's mesmerising.'

Not that she could afford to live here on her call centre advisor's salary. Connor did well as a recruitment consultant, though. Em had wanted to save for a deposit so they could live in a place like this rather than their rundown rented maisonette in the suburbs. But Connor wanted to get married first, and the cheap registry office ceremony that Em had suggested wasn't good enough for him. He wanted to put on a show for his friends and family. 'We've got plenty of time to saddle ourselves with a mortgage. Let's have some fun now,' he'd said.

Em suspected it had more to do with not wanting to be outdone by his younger brother's lavish nuptials last year. Flynn and Aimee had celebrated with a big country house do, worthy of an upmarket wedding blog. Aimee had been planning it since she was a child. Every part of the venue seemed to be awash with flowers and bunting, a string quartet played throughout the drinks reception, and the five bridesmaids all had Jimmy Choo shoes, as Aimee had delighted in telling anyone who would listen. It was all a bit too extravagant and cliched for Em's tastes, though she had appreciated the flock of white doves released as the bride and groom emerged from the chapel. Seeing one of the birds taking a dump on the father of the bride's morning suit had been the most entertaining part of the day.

Lucy passed Em a mug of tea. 'Come on. Stop changing the subject. What's the plan?'

'I've just spoken to Dad. He's happy for me to move back home. So I'll go back to the flat today and pack my things. That won't take long.' Em took a sip of her tea. 'I should have time to phone around all the wedding suppliers to give them the news that our wedding is off. Then I'll wait for Connor to come home and tell him it's over. When I've done that, I'll get a taxi to take me to Dad's.' It sounded so clinical when she said it out loud.

'Why are you packing up your things? Connor should be the one moving out.'

'The rent would take most of my salary. Plus, his name's on the rental agreement. I moved in with him, remember?' And she didn't want to live where Connor had been shagging his bit on the side. It hadn't taken Sherlock Holmes to work out that the vivid orange and red background on most of Connor and A's soft porn photos was an exact match for the awful wallpaper in Em and Connor's bedroom. Em didn't want to share that part of the sorry tale with Lucy. She felt a big enough fool for not realising what had been going on sooner.

'I'll be able to save up for somewhere permanent to live while I'm at Dad's. And it will be on a quicker bus route to work.' She may as well look on the bright side. It would also be a bonus not having to put up with Connor's snoring. And then there were his smelly gym clothes abandoned in the bathroom, waiting for the laundry fairies to wash them. If she could be bothered, it wouldn't be too difficult to come up with at least twenty benefits to not being the future Mrs Connor Flanigan.

Lucy looked sceptical. 'I couldn't move back home again.'

'Your parents live in Italy.'

'You know what I mean. Look, if you're sure about moving out, I can pick you up this evening.' Lucy looked thoughtful. 'I'll have to Google what a maid of honour is meant to do in this situation. Do you want me to give you a hand notifying the wedding guests? Oh god, I'm going to have to cancel the hen weekend.'

Em hadn't thought about that. She'd been excited about the trip to Cornwall with her besties. 'Can we still go? I was really looking forward to it.'

'I guess. It seems a shame to miss out on all the fun I'd got planned.' Lucy was always up for a celebration. 'We can turn it into a "slag off the stag" party. I'll consult the rest of the hens. Not Connor's sister, though. At least your mother's not around to see all this.'

'Can you imagine? She'd be piling in with 'I told you so' and making out it's all my fault that he cheated on me.'

That thought finally broke the floodgates. Tears started streaming down Em's face. 'Perhaps, it is my fault. I'm sorry. I'll get a grip in a minute.'

She hated breaking down in front of other people, even Lucy, who'd been her best friend ever since they'd combined forces at nursery to evict the boys from the sandpit. At home, she'd learnt from an early age that crying was something you did in private, where her mother couldn't criticise her for it.

Lucy put her arm around Em. 'It's not your fault the bastard can't keep his cock under control.'

3

Em checked the time on her phone again. Connor was usually home early on Fridays. Where was he?

She looked around the flat for something to distract her, but she'd packed up everything that was hers. The boxes and bags were at their next-door neighbour's flat, waiting for Lucy's arrival.

The neighbour, Mrs Lewis, had been very understanding. 'I knew he was a wrong un. My mother always told me to avoid men who wear brown shoes with a blue suit.'

During the two years that Em had lived with Connor, Mrs Lewis had shared many of her mother's words of wisdom, so Em wasn't surprised to hear that she'd had an opinion on how to select a man. But why this particular clothing combination meant a man wasn't deemed to have long term relationship potential was a bit bewildering. Connor did have two blue suits and several pairs of brown shoes so perhaps Mrs Lewis's mother had a point.

Em got up from the sofa and stared out of the window at the cemetery across the road. The evening sun illuminated the large, angry-looking angel in the middle, its arm raised as if it were conducting an orchestra of uneven headstones. Lucy always said it was a depressing view, but Em found it comforting - the perfect reminder that few things in life were important unless they were genuinely a case of life or death. And this wasn't a life or death situation, more an opportunity to start afresh without a lying, cheating bastard at her side, albeit one that she'd thought she'd loved.

She heard Connor's key in the lock.

'What a shit day,' he said as he walked into the living room and threw himself on the sofa. 'You'll never guess what happened.'

Em turned to face him, pulling his phone out of her back pocket with a flourish as if she were a magician revealing the correct playing card to her audience.

'You lost this?' Em had exhausted all her tears talking to Lucy. She'd lost track of how many times she'd rehearsed this conversation over the last few hours. It would be a relief to get the performance over and done with. Remain calm, she coached herself, pleased that she'd delivered the first line of her script without showing her anger.

There was a brief look of relief on his face, which immediately turned to horror when she unlocked the phone and read his WhatsApp conversation out loud.

'It would seem A - I assume that's Astra who we used to talk to in the bar when we went to the cinema - has been missing you. Or, more precisely, your dick. Though she shouldn't be having trouble remembering what it looks like, as you've sent her a gallery of photos of it from every angle. Some of them are quite professional. The lighting on this one is superb.' She turned the screen towards him. 'It emphasises that peculiar little kink it has at the end.'

Connor looked down at his crotch.

'Don't check it now!' she said. He stared back at her like a rabbit caught in headlights.

'Let's see how long this has been going on.' Em scrolled up and up theatrically, pretending to work it out. 'One, two, three, four months, Connor - FOUR MONTHS!' She was in danger of losing control. Deep breath. 'You've been pretending to be a loving fiancé, yet all the time, you've been shagging Astra in this flat.'

'I'm ... I'm sorry. She ... she tricked me.' It wasn't like cool, confident Connor to stutter. She'd rattled him, at least.

'Tricked you? How precisely did she do that? Mesmerise you with her nipple piercings?'

He was looking panic-stricken now. 'Perhaps tricked is the wrong word. Look, it means nothing.' His voice had taken on a pleading tone.

'It means something to her - she's had your initial tattooed above her vag!' Em scrolled through more images and waved one in front of him, showing a naked Astra with a big C in the appropriate place.

'No, that ... that was there before it's short for ....' His voice petered out as she saw it dawn on him that Em knew exactly what the C stood for, and it was probably what she was mentally calling him now.

'I don't care what it means. I wasn't expecting to see it on your phone.'

'I'm really sorry, Em. It won't happen again.'

'I don't care if it happens again because I'm not sticking around. Do you honestly think our relationship can survive this?'

Connor was now running his hands through his hair, staring at the floor.

Em carried on. 'I've called the hotel and cancelled our wedding booking. And I spent the rest the afternoon calling our other wedding suppliers. We've lost our deposits on everything except the makeup artist. She took pity on me because, quote, "I've been cheated on by a lying scumbag too". And you owe the hotel 50% of the balance. Good job I found out today. Another fortnight and you would have had to pay for the whole thing.'

'I owe the hotel?' He looked worried now.

'Are you expecting me to contribute? Seriously??' Em managed to fake a laugh.

'How am I going to afford that?' If Connor's voice got any higher only dogs would hear him.

'You should've thought of that before you started sticking your cock in another woman's orifices.' Em said as she walked over to the coffee table ready for her grand finale. 'But we all make mistakes. So I'm going to take pity on you and give you your engagement ring back. She casually threw the ring on to the table. 'Selling that should help you considerably.'

Connor shifted uncomfortably on the edge of the sofa, looking at the silver metal circle as it settled on the wooden surface.

While searching for all the wedding paperwork earlier, Em had found the receipt for her ring. It wasn't diamond and platinum as Connor had claimed, but silver and cubic zirconia, as fake as their relationship, it seemed. Selling it would probably get him enough cash to pay for one guest's meal if he was lucky.

She carefully set his phone down next to the ring.

'Goodbye, Connor. Have a lovely life with Astra. Forward my post to Dad's.'

He didn't say a word as she calmly picked up her shoulder bag and walked out without giving him a second glance.

4

Em spent the twenty minute drive to her dad's mulling over her life with Connor while Lucy expertly navigated the Friday evening traffic. Had she missed any clues to his infidelity? Had he cheated on her with anyone else? She couldn't think of a single thing. Either she hadn't been paying enough attention, or he'd been an expert at covering his tracks.

'We're here.' Lucy's voice snapped Em out of her reverie as they pulled up on the drive behind a shiny new red sports car. Another example of her dad moving on with his life, whereas here Em was at the age of 29, returning to the house where she grew up. It felt like such a retrograde step.

Her dad appeared at the front door as soon as they got out of the car. 'Hello, love. Welcome home.'

He left the door open and disappeared into the kitchen, while Em and Lucy started unpacking the car.

Em dragged her large, battered suitcase over the familiar doorstep.

Lucy was already in the hall, clutching Em's big box of books. She seemed to be transfixed by something on the wall opposite her. Em followed her gaze to see what had grabbed her attention.

A massive canvas of a male nude, painted in lurid colours, dominated the end wall. It was a lot more eye-catching than the cheap print of Constable's *The Hay Wain* which had hung there for as long as Em could remember.

'I've got the kettle on, love,' her dad shouted from the kitchen.

'Thanks,' said Em half-heartedly, even more distracted by the painting than Lucy. It bore a disturbing resemblance to her father.

'Ah, you've spotted my new work of art,' her dad said, emerging from the kitchen.

'It would be difficult to miss it, Roger,' said Lucy.

'Strictly, it's not mine. It's Cynthia's, but she gave it to me to look after.' Cynthia was his new girlfriend. They had met a few months ago after he had decided to supplement his retirement pension with some life modelling. He'd proved popular with the ladies of the over-60s creativity class, his full head of hair and neat white teeth (nearly all his own) giving him a significant advantage over the other men in the room. But, judging by the picture, he had another asset as well.

'Did your father ever consider a career as a porn star?' Lucy whispered when Roger had returned to the kitchen to pour their tea.

Em sighed. 'I suppose I should be grateful that Cynthia's not a sculptor.'

'I don't know about that. At least you'd have had somewhere to hang your coat.'

Em screwed up her face. That image was even worse than the ones of Connor with Astra. 'I'm not sure that moving back home was such a good idea.'

'I told you, you should've stood your ground over the flat.'

'Have you got much more to bring in?' Em's dad was back, handing them two large steaming mugs of tea.

'No, this is pretty much it.' Em looked sadly at the small

pile of bags and the box, all she'd got to show for living away from home for eight years.

Her dad started fidgeting with his signet ring, which usually meant he was about to impart some bad news. 'By the way, there's something I should've mentioned on the phone earlier. If you could go out for the night on the third Wednesday of every month, that would probably be for the best.'

Em looked at her father, puzzled.

'It's just that I have a few close friends "swing" by then if you get my drift.' He grinned at her nervously, then made a sharp exit into his study before she could quiz him.

Lucy looked at Em with raised eyebrows. 'I don't think your dad means he's hosting the local Glenn Miller appreciation society, does he?'

5

Em looked amused as Lucy returned to the living room. 'Were you chatting up the pizza delivery man?'

Lucy waved a menu in front of her. It had a mobile number scrawled on the top.

'That's a bit old school,' Em said.

'He seemed cute, and I didn't have my phone with me,' said Lucy. 'You should try flirting a bit yourself.'

'I haven't got your charm.'

'You charmed Connor.'

'And look where that got me! Anyway, he was drunk. I didn't exactly use my womanly wiles to get his attention. I just didn't reject his advances.' Em opened the pizza box. 'And I'm off men for some reason.'

Lucy had invited herself back to Em's on Saturday evening. Em guessed that Lucy didn't want her to be on her own.

They'd avoided the subject of Connor, not that there was much to say. Em had blocked him after he sent her a text pleading for her to come back. She'd half expected him to turn up on the doorstep, but he'd never paid much attention to her friends and family, so he probably couldn't remember where her dad lived.

Lucy sat down next to Em and started to tuck in. 'I used to

be worried about dropping food on your mum's precious sofa. Now I'm more worried about what's been happening on it on the third Wednesday of every month.' Lucy turned to look more closely at the sofa. 'This awful flower pattern would be great at disguising any stains.'

'Don't remind me!' Em knew her dad had been widening his social circle since they'd scattered her mum's ashes, but the whole swingers thing was difficult to get her head around. Cynthia was a bad influence.

'Where is our local Hugh Hefner tonight?' Lucy asked.

'Dad? I think he's round at Cynthia's. After yesterday's revelations, I daren't ask what they're up to.'

'What's the plan then?' Lucy settled back on the sofa.

'I thought we could spend an hour browsing our many streaming services without finding anything interesting. Then we'll resort to watching a one-star movie that's only classed as a horror because the acting is so appalling,' Em said. 'Just for a change.'

'No! I meant, what are your plans for the future?'

'I have no idea! I was awake most of last night, mulling it over. I can't stay here. I looked at a room today, but it was a disaster.'

'That one I found online? I thought it looked great. Modern decor, en suite, and it wasn't too expensive.'

'Yes, it looked fabulous in the listing. But it didn't mention the white tiled walls and plastic-covered chairs and sofas downstairs - very serial killer chic with a landlord to match. He really gave me the creeps.'

'Was he covered in PVC as well?'

Em rolled her eyes. 'You're not taking this seriously. He said it used to be a butcher's shop. He was very cagey about why the previous tenant left. I suspect they're still there, under the very new-looking patio.'

'You're too picky!'

'I'll keep looking. I've got a couple of weeks before the swingers turn up.'

6

Em was nursing a bowl of cornflakes as she looked out at the garden from the kitchen window seat. Rivulets of rain were running down the glass. She was used to spending Sunday mornings snuggled up in bed with Connor, but she needed a new routine now.

She heard the front door slam. Her dad walked into the kitchen.

'Dirty stop out,' she said.

'You look like you've been out all night too.' He sounded concerned.

'Lucy was here till 2 am. Then I didn't sleep well. I was going to go for a run to wake myself up, but I'm not keen on running in the rain.'

Roger busied himself with making tea. 'I remembered last night - I've still got a load of things that you left here when you moved out.'

'I thought Mum had ditched all that because it didn't "spark joy".' Her mother's zealous decluttering had upset Em. She'd even consigned Em's beloved childhood teddy to the bin without giving Em an opportunity to rescue him.

But her mother had been unrepentant. 'You should have taken it with you if you were that bothered. I'm not running a free storage service.'

She seemed to have conveniently forgotten that Em's rented room in London would have made a phone box look spacious. The next time Em came home, she was relegated to sleeping in the smallest bedroom, her old room entirely devoted to her mother's hobbies as if Em had never existed.

'Your mother instructed me to take it all to the tip, but I hid it in the loft when she was out. She never went up there. 'It's a filthy, spider-infested hole, Roger.''

Em laughed at her dad's uncannily accurate impression of her mother's high-pitched, rant-mode voice. Bless him for rescuing her stuff.

'I guess I should investigate the filthy, spider-infested hole, then,' she said.

The loft turned out to be an Aladdin's cave of items that had earned Em's mother's disapproval. It appeared to be empty when Em first opened the hatch, but once she got to the top of the ladder and her eyes adjusted to the dim light from the old 40 watt bulb, she could see various containers stashed away in the dark corners.

An old cricket bat handle stuck out of a battered sports bag, presumably put there after her mother had banned her father from playing for the local club because he 'looked too appreciatively' at the woman who made the teas. 'But her baps were delicious,' he'd said, in a desperate attempt to defend himself from his wife's accusations of adultery.

A guitar case lurked behind the water tank. She didn't recognise that at all. Something to ask her dad about later.

Then, in the far right corner, Em spotted an easel and an art portfolio leaning against a pile of cardboard boxes with TIP handwritten on them in thick, black marker pen. She walked over to investigate, crouching under the eaves to reach the smaller boxes. Books, games, ornaments, and even her beloved teddy. She felt tears welling up. Her dad really had rescued everything.

7

'Shall I bring the rest down? There are still five boxes left.' Em's dad was standing next to her in the bedroom after helping her bring the easel and the rest of her art stuff down from the loft.

'No, let's leave it for now.' Em had been wondering when to tell him that she wasn't planning on stopping at home for long. This was an ideal opportunity.

'I am looking for somewhere else to stay. I think you need your own space now. But if you wouldn't mind keeping a few things until I'm settled, that would be great.'

'Of course I don't mind. It's doing no harm up there. I love having you living here again, but I understand. I'm not going to fake falling down the stairs to persuade you to stay,' he laughed.

Oh god, the stairs incident. Em remembered it so well. It had happened on the morning she was leaving for uni. Her mother had made her opposition to Em "wasting her time and MY money"on a fine art degree very clear from the moment Em had first floated the idea years earlier. She'd tried various ways to dissuade Em, starting with dire predictions of permanent poverty and working her way up to Em's early death from drug addiction. When that didn't work, she tried to make Em feel guilty about her selfishness in leaving her to cope with her "challenging" husband alone. 'He's an incompetent fool. How am I supposed to look after him all by myself with my high blood pressure?' An incompetent fool who had managed to work his way up to chief accountant at a large car parts manufacturer, earning enough to keep his wife in the manner which she demanded. Em's mother failed to give her dad any credit for that, of course.

But Em had dug her heels in. She'd always been good at painting, she got an A in her Art 'A' level, and she'd worked hard at the local college in her art foundation year. She wasn't going to give up the opportunity to do something she loved.

Em's mother was not the sort of person who gave up easily when she'd made her mind up about how things were going to be. While Em and her dad were packing the car ready for the drive to London, they heard a shriek and found her mother lying awkwardly at the foot of the stairs.

'I can't feel my legs, Roger,' she screamed as he went to help her get up. 'Call an ambulance.'

While they were waiting for it to arrive, her mother appeared to be extremely calm for someone with potentially life-changing injuries. Presumably, the pleasure of watching Roger unpack the car was taking her mind off the possibility of having to adjust to being in a wheelchair for the rest of her life. Em wondered how this would pan out. Her mother usually managed to pull some stunt to get her own way but this was the most extreme one so far. Then, as always, Em felt guilty about not being more sympathetic, just in case this time it was genuine.

Puzzled by her mother's paralysis, the paramedics took her to A&E, Em accompanying them in the ambulance and her dad following in the car. After various tests, her mother's mediocre acting abilities failed her when the doctor started checking for numbness by prodding her legs with a needle.

Even her blood pressure appeared to be normal. The medical staff pronounced her fighting fit. The atmosphere in the car on the way home was tense.

'I'm glad you're ok, Mum. Nothing stopping me from going to London now.' Em couldn't resist rubbing it in after such a blatant attempt at scuppering her escape plans.

'Yes, we've still got time to get there today, Em,' her dad had added chirpily, leaving her mother to make her own way indoors sulkily.

Em's dad was cooking Sunday lunch in the kitchen. Em offered to help him prepare the veg, glad of anything that might stop her thoughts wandering back to Connor.

She was struggling to remember why she'd ever agreed to marry him. It wasn't as if the wedding proposal had swept her off her feet. The drunken 'I suppose we should get married as well' while they were in the taxi on the way home from his brother's wedding had been underwhelming. Not that Em was hoping for an extravagant public proposal. She'd have died of embarrassment if he'd turned up at work with a choir of singers performing 'It Had To Be You', which was how Flynn had proposed to Aimee.

The more she thought about it, the more she realised she'd sleepwalked into a long-term relationship. Connor's infidelity had saved her from a lifetime of making do. Perhaps Lucy's approach of working her way through Tinder was a better one. Right now, a long-term relationship wasn't on Em's wish list. Was a loving long term relationship even possible?

'Dad, why did you put up with Mum for so long?' she asked as she scraped the carrot peelings into the compost bin.

'Hope, I suppose. Hope that she would turn back into the woman I fell in love with. I got occasional glimpses of that woman but fewer over the years. And there was you. If I'd left, she would have played up to the solicitors and judges and made me out to be too evil to be allowed anything to do with you. We both know how well she could lie. I wouldn't have stood a chance.'

'But once I'd left home .... '

'After 25 years, it didn't seem so bad. I guess I became institutionalised in a way. Being treated like a major annoyance was just the norm. I'd forgotten what a proper relationship should be like. I had no friends left. I'd lost my confidence. When she died, it was like the sun coming out after a storm. I saw our marriage for what it was for the first time. I realised she was never the woman I fell in love with. It had all been an act to lure me in.'

'You seem to have your confidence back now, though.'

'I'm enjoying making up for lost time,' he grinned, then he seemed guilty at being happy. 'I'm sorry about Connor. But better you found out before you got married. There's someone out there who'll treat you properly.' He pulled Em into a big hug, kissing her on the forehead. 'Don't settle for second best like I did.'

The smoke alarm interrupted them.

'Oh bloody hell,' he laughed, pulling the frying pan off the heat and grabbing a tea towel to waft the smoke away. 'Perhaps, your mother was right. I am an incompetent fool!'

8

Em spent Monday evening scrolling through a list of available rooms. Too expensive, in the wrong area, no broadband, unfurnished, smoking household. It was so depressing. How did anyone with a normal job live independently in Birmingham?

Work had been dire today too. Her manager, Cheryl, was hard to deal with at the best of times, but what could you expect from someone who kept a well-thumbed copy of 'Leadership Tips from Atilla the Hun' on her desk? Today she'd been particularly shitty, hauling Em into her office to complain about the number of calls Em was dealing with, or rather, not dealing with. 'I don't care if Mrs Smith's cat is missing. Once she paid for her insurance renewal, you should have got her off the phone.'

'She was upset. She had no one else to talk to.'

'This isn't the Samaritans. You should be getting through 33.5 calls a day on average. Do you know what your average was last week, Emily?'

Em shook her head.

'32.8. That's not even close.'

0.7 calls below target felt close enough to Em. What even was 0.7 of a call? 'If I cut them off, you complain that my customer satisfaction ratings aren't high enough.'

'Other people manage to hit their targets without compromising their ratings. Toby exceeds his targets every week.' Cheryl's expression became dreamy as she pointed to Toby's stats on the whiteboard.

Bloody Toby. Cheryl had the hots for him even though she was married and he was at least 20 years younger than her. And Toby was more than happy to flirt enthusiastically with Cheryl to keep her sweet. Of course his call stats were terrific. God help any customer who got through to him. He got rid of them as quickly as possible by giving them whatever duff information popped into his head. Then the poor souls phoned back days or weeks later, angrily complaining that their issue hadn't been resolved, which meant everyone else had to spend valuable time placating them.

How did I end up here? Em lay back on her bed and shut her eyes. She thought about what she and Lucy had wanted their futures to look like when they were at school. She remembered summer lunchtimes, lying in the sunshine on the school playing field, watching the clouds float by in a blue sky as they fantasised about what they'd be doing in 10 or 20 years' time.

Lucy had visualised a life full of fast cars, impossibly handsome men, and designer boutique shopping funded by running her own business. And she'd achieved all her objectives.

Em's dreams were simpler. She was going to be a professional artist living in London in one of those gorgeous mews properties she used to see in films. Ideally, it would have a studio attached, and she'd have a caring boyfriend who made her laugh and possibly a cat or two to keep her company while she was painting. But Em hadn't ticked off a single item on her list.

Was it because she didn't really want that? No, that life still sounded perfect to her. But she'd stupidly allowed herself to be derailed by other people's wants and needs. So what was she going to do about it?

Time to come up with a plan. Sticking with the same job wouldn't move her forward at all.

Given that she was struggling to find anywhere to live in Birmingham, she ought to look for a job somewhere else. London would be even more expensive, so it was too soon for that part of the dream. And she needed to start painting again before she could consider charging for her work, so that would have to wait too. Em needed something not too challenging that gave her time to work on her art, plus somewhere to live while she saved up for her own place.

Holiday rep, perhaps? But it was May, so they'd all be sorted now. She scrolled through various job websites for ideas. Cabin crew? You could see the world, but the application was for spring the following year. She'd be serving at least 20 years in prison for murdering Cheryl if she didn't change jobs before then.

She searched for 'Live-in jobs'. Most of the links were not live-in at all or only live-in for part of the week. Then one of the websites caught her attention. *The Lady*. Em's mother always kept a copy of *The Lady* magazine on the coffee table, thinking it gave her an air of sophistication on the rare occasions they had visitors. Em remembered it had a section full of jobs working for the well-to-do. That might be an option. She clicked through to their vacancy section. This was more like it.

She scrolled past anything that required a couple.

Cooking was out too - Em was a disaster in the kitchen. Her report from her Year 9 Food Teacher said it all: 'I suggest Emily pursues a career that enables her to afford to live on Marks & Spencer ready meals.'

Gardening was a non-starter - she couldn't tell a pansy

from a petunia.

Quite a few middle-aged or elderly gentlemen were looking for someone to be a companion. Em wasn't sure whether that was code for something else, so she ignored those.

But one vacancy that caught her eye.

```
Live-in, part-time holiday let concierge required
ASAP in North Devon. You will work 20 hours per
week, including Saturdays (Sundays and Mondays
off), managing five holiday lets on-site at our
impressive Georgian manor house on the outskirts
of the picturesque and genteel resort of Dashford-
on-Sea. You will also assist my elderly mother
with housework when the cleaner is unavailable.
You must be computer literate and have a clean
driving licence. You will have exclusive use of a
self-contained, one-bedroomed flat and a car.
Competitive salary.
```

Dashford-on-Sea. That sounded familiar. Em checked on Google Maps. It was a village a few miles up the coast from Ilfracombe. She had visited it on a family holiday years ago. She remembered it being surrounded by rolling green hills ending in strikingly grey jagged cliffs, with pretty higgledy-piggledy pastel coloured houses grouped around an old harbour and a small sandy beach. A lot more picturesque than suburban Birmingham.

The role didn't sound too strenuous. It would give Em plenty of time to work on her art. With no accommodation or car costs, as long as it paid enough to buy food and art equipment with some money left over to save, it might work. Definitely worth a try.

Em logged in, created a profile and submitted her CV, crossing her fingers while she waited for the 'job application complete' message.

9

Em sat nervously in front of her laptop screen, looking at a message telling her the meeting organiser would admit her shortly. The interview was supposed to have started a couple of minutes ago. Please don't let there be a technical problem.

She'd only submitted the application form two days ago, but they must have been keen to interview her as she'd received the email invitation first thing the following morning.

Em had never had an online interview before, so she'd asked Lucy to practise with her. They'd experimented with the laptop in different locations around the house. The best performance was with the laptop next to the Wi-Fi router in her dad's study. And sitting so she was looking towards the window with the daylight shining on her face made her look professional - not silhouetted like someone in witness protection. She'd tried using one of the Zoom background images but it looked like she was hiding something. 'Your dad's mahogany bookcase gives an air of quality and trustworthiness,' Lucy assured her after Em moved the *Kama Sutra* and *Tantric Sex for Beginners* out of shot.

Em was wearing a plain, white blouse. She'd pinned up her long hair neatly behind her head, kept her makeup as natural as possible and removed all her ear piercings in case the elderly mother objected to them. She'd tried to anticipate all the questions they might ask her, making notes in her favourite journal so she had something to refer to if her mind went blank. Her dad had agreed to go out for the afternoon, so she wouldn't be disturbed. And she'd invented an emergency dental appointment to get out of work. She was all set.

At last, the meeting screen sprang into life. A middle-aged man in a formal shirt and tie appeared in front of a view of the Empire State building. Em looked closer. Was it a fake background? It was a very good one if it was. His profile name described him as 'Nigel Farnham CEO'. Then a woman in her seventies appeared with an Aga and a pile of washing behind her. Her profile just said 'Dashford Grange'. She must be Nancy Farnham, who'd emailed her the interview invitation.

'Apologies for the delay.' Nigel had the authoritative air of someone used to giving orders and having them obeyed immediately. His accent was English public school with a slight hint of American. Perhaps the view behind was real then. 'The last interview overran.'

Not a good sign. They must have been very interested in the previous candidate. May as well relax and see it as interview practice, then.

'Mother, can you hear Emily?'

'I'm not deaf, Nigel. The poor girl hasn't had a chance to open her mouth yet.' Nancy didn't give the impression of someone who needed much looking after.

Em thought she better say something before it deteriorated into a full-blown family row. 'I can hear you both. Thank you for inviting me for an interview.'

Nigel explained the role. 'My mother's getting frailer.' Judging by Nancy's expression, she disagreed, but Nigel didn't seem to be the sort of person who picked up on even unsubtle signals. 'I'm looking for someone who can run the holiday let business for her.'

Nigel's phone rang. 'I have to take this,' he said, putting himself on mute and turning off his video.

Nancy lost no time in taking over the conversation. 'Please excuse my son. He thinks I'm going senile. However, I'm perfectly capable of looking after myself and my holiday accommodation. I'm only going along with his plan because it will give me extra time to have more fun.' She had a mischievous look in her eyes as she spoke. 'And Nigel is paying because it helps him feel less guilty about keeping my grandchildren on the other side of the Atlantic.'

Em warmed to Nancy, if not to Nigel.

Nigel reappeared on screen. Nancy gave Em a conspiratorial 'don't grass me up' look.

After several questions from Nigel about her educational background, it was Nancy's turn to ask about Em's customer care skills. She asked several probing questions about dealing with challenging people. Em's experience of being shouted at by unhappy insurance clients stood her in good stead. Her detailed answers seemed to satisfy Nancy though Nigel's attention was wandering. That was until a large canvas started edging into the study behind Em, in direct view of the webcam.

Em tried to ignore it at first, but she could see Nigel's eyes widening as it became apparent that the painting was of a large, nude woman in a pose that left nothing to the imagination. Another one of Cynthia's creations - being pushed into the study by a completely naked Cynthia.

'Hello, darling! Surprise! Happy birthday!'

'Why didn't you turn the webcam off?' Lucy asked when Em told her about it later.

'I was so gobsmacked, I lost the ability to move for several seconds. At least Nancy thought it was funny but poor Nigel didn't know where to look. I can guarantee that's doesn't normally happen on his Zoom calls.'

'Not unless he's paying good money for them,' Lucy chuckled.

'He just said "Thank you for your time" and ended the call.'

'Fancy ruining your dad's birthday surprise!'

'Do you know the saddest thing?' Em said. 'It's not even Dad's birthday!'

10

After Cynthia apologised and went home, Em spent the rest of the afternoon looking through more job vacancies, convinced that the unusual interruption had ruined what little chance she had of getting the concierge position. She ought to be annoyed, but she'd doubted she would get it anyway. If anyone offered her another online interview, she'd lock the door in future. Lesson learned!

Em had just sent off her CV to a couple of agencies when an unknown number called her. She tapped the green button to accept the call. 'Emily Gillespie speaking.'

Nancy's voice came through loud and clear. 'Thank you for being so entertaining. The look on Nigel's face was priceless. I shall be able to dine out on that story for years,' she said. 'If you can remain calm with all that going on, you'll be fine working here.'

'Thank you,' Em said, unsure if it was a job offer or not.

'Do you still want the job?'

So it was a job offer. Em was speechless.

'Well?' said Nancy.

'Yes, I definitely do. Thank you so much.'

'Excellent. When can you start?'

* * *

Just one week later, Em was resting her head against the train window, watching the countryside rushing by, the cold glass cooling her forehead in the late spring heat. She couldn't believe this was actually happening. Birmingham was over 100 miles away already. The sunshine made the bright green colours of the fields and trees feel very appropriate for her fresh new start, far away from Connor, Astra, the suburban swingers and, of course, Cheryl, who could barely hide her delight when Em handed in her notice.

'Company policy is that employees who resign must leave immediately. Collect your things from your locker, and I'll escort you off the premises.' Em had been more than happy to comply with Cheryl's request.

Lucy had popped round with a bottle of champagne to celebrate. She made Em promise to invite her for the weekend once she'd settled in.

There had been some tears that morning when Em's dad had waved her off at New Street station, but now, after a couple of train changes, she was on the final leg of the journey to Dashford, and any sadness had given way to a weird mix of apprehension and excitement.

Beep, beep.

Em was walking out of Dashford's tiny railway station when she heard the car horn. She turned to her left and saw a woman in a British racing green open-top sports car waving at her across the car park. She looked like a 1950s movie star in sunglasses and a headscarf. As Em approached the car, she realised it was Nancy, looking smaller in real life than she had on screen last week.

'Welcome to Dashford. How was your journey?' Nancy leapt out of the car to help Em with her bags. 'There's not much room in the boot. You'll have to keep most of it on your lap.'

Em wasn't too concerned. When she'd checked Google Maps earlier, it said the journey from the station to Dashford Grange should take nine minutes. She could cope with nursing her rucksack for that.

'Hold on tight.' Nancy pulled out of the car park, aggressively turning into a small gap in the traffic, cutting up a coach in the process. 'A rally driver taught me how to drive. They're used to me around here.'

Em could see the coach driver in the wing mirror. Judging by his angry expression and hand signals, she guessed he wasn't used to Nancy's driving at all.

'What happened to the rally driver?' Em asked as they hurtled around a sharp bend on the way out of the town.

'He died young. Disagreement with a tree and the tree came off best.'

Em shut her eyes. For the first time in her life, she felt tempted to pray. Five terrifying minutes later, the car screeched to a halt on what sounded like a gravel drive. She dared to open her eyes and got her first view of Dashford Grange through a gap in the now tangled bird's nest of hair around her head.

'Sorry, I should have advised you to put a hat on,' Nancy said.

A crash helmet might have been a better idea. Em made a mental note always to offer to drive in future.

11

Nancy helped Em to take her suitcase and rucksack into the main hall. The dark wood panelling and the parquet flooring reminded Em of a fancy hotel.

'I'll take you over to your flat later,' Nancy said as she marched Em on a whistle-stop tour of the main house. Nancy seemed to do everything at top speed.

The house was traditionally furnished with quality antiques and expensive-looking rugs. Oil paintings in ornate gilt frames lined the grand staircase. Em stopped to admire a Victorian lady who strongly resembled Nancy.

'My late great-grandmother,' Nancy commented. 'It's thanks to her that we have this house or thanks to Edward VII anyway.' She raised her eyebrows and gave Em a meaningful look. Em vaguely remembered the king had a reputation as a philanderer. She'd have to check Wikipedia later.

A quick inspection of the upstairs revealed six spacious bedrooms, all with gorgeous views over the fields or towards the sea. There were three bathrooms, probably converted from other bedrooms, judging by their generous sizes. It was like walking into the pages of an interior design magazine.

'You have a beautiful home,' Em said as they returned to

the ground floor.

'Thank you. But you haven't seen the most important room in the house yet: the kitchen.' Nancy led her into a huge room.

Based on the view behind Nancy during the interview, Em had expected to see a kitchen that wouldn't have looked out of place in Downton Abbey. Instead, it was mostly a slick 21st-century affair, with stainless steel countertops and charcoal-coloured high gloss doors. A large American-style fridge freezer dominated the far end of the room.

Nancy got two mugs out of a cupboard. 'Tea?'

'Yes, please. Milk, no sugar.'

'English Breakfast, Darjeeling, Lapsang Souchong or Earl Grey? I prefer Earl Grey personally.'

'Earl Grey would be lovely, thank you.'

Nancy filled a teapot from a boiling water tap.

At the far end of the kitchen was a desk with a laptop. Em recognised the backdrop from the Zoom interview.

Nancy noticed Em looking. 'That is where we get organised. Working next to the Aga keeps me toasty in the cold weather. I'll give you a training session on the booking system next week when you've settled in. Do take a seat.' Nancy pointed to the high stools around the island in the centre of the room.

'I can't show you the holiday accommodation as we've got guests in all of them now. But they will be leaving at the end of the week, so you can view them then. Two cottages have a Friday changeover, and the other three are from Saturday to Saturday. But you can see Wisteria Cottage tomorrow as they've paid for our optional twice-weekly maid service.'

Nancy put a mug of tea in front of Em. 'When you've finished that, we'll head over to your flat.'

She went over to the big desk and started rummaging around in a drawer, producing two sets of keys. 'These are for your flat, and these are your car keys. It's the blue Fiesta parked outside the garage. And this,' she said, pulling a folder out of another drawer, 'is our procedure manual. A little light reading for you if you can't get to sleep tonight,' she laughed.

Em flicked through the pages. What had to be cleaned on which day. Standard shopping lists. Checklists for preparing the accommodation. Processes for checking payments and sending out reminder emails. Copies of the insurance documents. Contact details for local tradespeople if anything needed repairing. 'Everything you need to know is in there, and there's an electronic copy on the laptop if you find that easier.'

Why Nigel thought his mother was helpless, God alone knew. Nancy was more organised than any of Em's previous managers.

'It looks daunting, but it should only take 20 hours a week, mostly on Fridays and Saturdays. The rest of the time, there's just admin and the occasional guest query to deal with, so that shouldn't take more than a couple of hours each day. I'll pay you for any additional hours if someone wants the extra maid service or if our cleaner, Mrs Rossiter, is away and I need a hand. Sundays and Mondays are all your own. Any questions?'

'No, that's all very clear. Thank you.'

'Excellent. It's lovely to have you here.' Nancy clinked her mug against Em's. 'Welcome to Dashford Grange.'

12

Em sat at one of the tables outside the tiny cafe that was built into the side of the seafront wall.

After getting the new guests settled in yesterday, it was lovely to spend Sunday morning doing nothing but breathing in the fresh sea air. And it was fresh today. The warm weather had disappeared, and a strong wind was coming in from the north. But Em didn't mind, even though she hadn't expected to be wearing a woolly hat and scarf in May. Big breakers were rolling onto the sands of Dashford beach, and dark clouds gave the view a mysterious, almost threatening feel. Great inspiration for a painting. It was a good start to her first day off.

Em took a few photos on her phone, then got out her sketchbook and pencil to draw shapes and textures, making notes of the colours, scents and feel of the wind. She'd use her paints to capture the scene and the atmosphere on paper when she got back home.

Home. That was interesting. Even though she'd only been here a few days, it did feel like home.

The woman who ran the cafe came out and plonked a steaming mug of hot chocolate in front of Em. She looked like she was in her late 50s, with short, fluorescent pink hair and the ruddy complexion of someone who was regularly outdoors in all weathers. 'There you go, my lovely. I don't think I've seen you before. Are you here on holiday?'

'No, I've moved into the flat at Dashford Grange to run the holiday lets.'

'I'd heard Mrs Farnham was getting some help. I'm Mary.' She held out her hand for Em to shake.

'Hi Mary, I'm Em.'

'How are you finding working for Mrs F?'

'She's been lovely to me.'

Which was true. Nancy had been excellent at explaining what needed doing. Everything ran like clockwork already, so Em followed the checklists, and the first five sets of guests on her watch were now happily settled in. And Em's flat over the garages, though small, was nicely furnished and comfortable.

'I don't get on with her,' Mary said.

'Oh, why's that?' Em was curious. She could tell Mary wanted to talk. The cafe wasn't busy, presumably because the weather had scared the tourists away.

Mary sat down opposite Em and pulled a vape from her apron pocket. She looked like she was settling in for the rest of the morning. Through a cloud of lavender-scented smoke, she proceeded to supply Em with the details.

'I used to clean for Mrs F years ago when her husband was still alive. Let's say it was a fraught and short-lived relationship. Turns out, if you accidentally drop an irreplaceable heirloom soup tureen, your services are no longer wanted.'

'Oh, dear.' Em didn't know what else to say. She made a mental note to keep away from the dinner service.

'Though running over the dog didn't help,' Mary added.

Em didn't like the way this was going. 'I didn't know Nancy had dogs.'

'She used to. Basil was a big dopey golden retriever. Stupid bugger walked behind my car while I was reversing. We rushed him to the vets. He survived, but he lost a leg, poor thing. I swear Mrs F used to deliberately walk him in front of here afterwards to make me feel guilty.'

Em didn't want to dwell on the dog situation. She hated anything that involved animals in distress. Time to change the subject. 'What was Nancy's husband like?' There was a wedding photo on the grand piano but Nancy hadn't mentioned him at all.

'Xander? He was a handsome man. Something big in banking in London. She only ever saw him at weekends and holidays. I did feel sorry for her.' Mary leaned in closer, looking around to check no one else was in hearing range. 'When he didn't come home one weekend, Mrs F went to London and found him dead in their flat, handcuffed to the bed and stark bollock naked, if you'll forgive my language. That part didn't make it into his Times obituary. Massive heart attack, according to the coroner. He was only 62.' She leaned back in her seat and took a long drag on the vape. 'At least he died doing something he loved.'

Em was relieved she hadn't asked Nancy about the late Mr Farnham.

'Mrs F has been alone in that big house for the last 15 years. Seems happy enough, though.' Mary put the vape back in her pocket. 'Anything you want to know, just ask. I've lived in Dashford all my life. I know pretty much everything that goes on. So what brings you here?'

Em decided not to explain fully. She suspected anything she said would soon be all around the village.

'I needed a change of scenery.'

'Lover trouble then?'

'What makes you say that?'

'You've got a Midlands accent. No one moves a couple of hundred miles just because they fancy a change of scenery. At your age, it's got to be love. Either you're following someone or getting away from someone. I'm guessing, judging by the way you automatically asked for two hot chocolates and then changed your order to one, it's getting away from someone. Am I right?'

Em laughed. She could see how Mary knew everything that went on. 'You're wasted here. You should be in MI5.'

'How do you know I'm not?' Mary grinned. 'So, was he a bastard then?'

'Yep.' Not much point in lying about that. Mary probably kept thumbscrews behind the counter for use on customers who refused to give away their secrets.

PART TWO

SUMMER 2018

13

It was a gorgeous June day. Em was in the garden, checking whether the sheets on the washing line were dry. Nancy walked out of the kitchen door, clutching yet another mug of tea. She seemed to be fuelled purely by Earl Grey with lemon. Em hadn't seen her eat or drink anything else in the four weeks since she'd arrived. Nancy sat down at the table on the terrace and started flicking through the sketchbook Em had left there.

'Did you do all of these? Sorry, I shouldn't be so nosey, but they're excellent.' She laughed at the sketch of Mary, holding court on the bench outside the cafe, a mug in one hand and a vape in the other. 'You've captured Mary's character perfectly and in just a few lines - very impressive. How long have you been drawing?'

'Since I could hold a pencil. Drawing was my favourite hobby as a child.'

'I remember you saying you went to art college at the interview.' Nancy carried on turning the pages. There were lots of drawings and sketches to look through. Em had almost filled an entire book in the short time she'd been here.

'I specialised in portraits at university, but I'm concentrating on seascapes and landscapes now. I've started turning some of those sketches into fully-fledged paintings. I thought the gallery in the village might be interested in selling them. But people are my favourite subjects.'

Nancy looked at Em thoughtfully. 'What do you think about painting me? It seems incredibly vain, but my great-grandparents, grandparents, and parents all have their portraits on our staircase. I don't see why Nigel shouldn't have my eyes following him around the room when I've passed over. If you could flatter me with fewer laughter lines than I've got in real life, that would be a bonus.'

Em wasn't sure what to say. On the one hand, someone as full of character as Nancy would be incredible to paint. But how awkward would it be if she didn't like it?

Nancy must have read her mind. 'Don't worry - I'm not expecting to look like Marilyn Monroe. And I'm not expecting something akin to Cynthia's self-portrait either, ' she laughed.

It was an excellent opportunity to embrace her 'live your best life' attitude. She shouldn't turn it down.

'Yes, that would be amazing. We'd need a few sittings - just half an hour or so at a time. I'd want to take some photos too. But first of all, we need to decide on a setting and what you're going to wear.'

'Marvellous. Let's discuss it over another cup of tea,' Nancy said, heading back indoors. 'See you in five minutes.'

14

Friday was going to be an extra busy day as Em was having to cover for Mrs Rossiter, the cleaner, who had a hospital appointment. Nancy would have usually helped out, but she was having a long weekend away learning to rock climb with her friend Daphne, so today Em was covering the house cleaning duties as well as sorting out the guests' departures and arrivals.

May as well make her chores more entertaining. With her happy playlist on her phone belting out of her earphones and the drawing room's French doors wide open to let in the gentle morning breeze, she performed a dance routine with the cordless vac to her imagined audience of thousands in the garden. With no one to hear her, she sang at full volume, not caring that she was wildly out of tune. This job might not be a career move, but even doing the housework was much better than being stuck in the call centre. Breathing the fresh seaside air at Dashford Grange was a big improvement on the odour of stale farts that wafted through the office on Fridays, thanks to her former colleagues' love of Thursday curry nights at the pub next door.

Preparing for her grand finale, Em turned her back on the windows and raised the vacuum above her head, imagining it was a microphone stand. She felt a light tap on her shoulder.

Screaming, she swung round, the vacuum making contact with a six-foot, thirty-something male. He took a step back, rubbing his arm.

He didn't look much of a threat in his dark blue chinos, his white linen shirt and his perfectly polished brown brogues. He was saying something, but she couldn't hear him. She turned off the vacuum and removed her earphones, feeling her cheeks turn red.

'I'm so sorry. I didn't mean to startle you,' he said. 'No one answered the front door, so I … Well, I'm here now.' His voice was deep and calm with a public school accent, quite appealing if she was honest. He gave her a sheepish grin, which made him even more attractive. Her heart skipped a beat. Surely that only happened in romance novels? Why was this very conventional-looking man having this effect on her? And more importantly, who was he, and why did he have to walk into her life when she was making a complete idiot of herself?

'Do you speak English?' He looked concerned now.

Em realised she had been silently working out whether cerulean blue or cobalt blue paint would work best for capturing his striking blue eyes. 'Yes, I'm sorry - I, um … Who are you?'

'Jack. I'm a bit early. I hope that's ok. The traffic wasn't nearly as bad as I thought.' He held out his right hand. He had a reassuringly firm handshake. She felt her heart miss another beat as their palms touched. This was a whole new experience. Men did not have this effect on her. She knew she needed to respond, but no words would come out of her mouth.

'Professor Jack Carver,' he said slowly, giving Em the impression that he thought she might be intellectually challenged.

The penny dropped. One of this week's new holiday let guests. When she'd seen his name on the booking list yesterday, she'd pictured someone much older, with unkempt white hair, a bushy beard, and brown socks and sandals. Em gulped. She could hear Nancy's voice in her head. 'Always be charming to our guests - think of the TripAdvisor reviews.' This review was set to be a one-star corker unless she upped her game.

'Welcome to Dashford Grange,' she said, finally managing to speak. She gave Jack her best smile. 'I'm Emily. Em for short. I'm so sorry about the misunderstanding. I wasn't expecting you until after lunch, but your cottage is ready. Please take a seat while I get the keys.'

She tried to recover her composure. By the time she reached the drawing room door, she felt much calmer.

'I won't be long,' she said as she turned back to smile at him again, hoping it would help him forget the bruise that must be forming on his right bicep. He seemed happy enough now, relaxing on Nancy's velvet three-seater.

Feeling more in control, she walked into the hall, accidentally catching the vase of flowers on the table with the vacuum. Mercifully, the vase remained intact when it bounced on the floor, but the water was eager to escape all over the expensive rug underneath.

'Is everything ok?' Jack called after her.

'Yes, thank you. Nothing to worry about," she shouted as she dashed into the kitchen to grab a towel.

Perhaps Fridays in the call centre hadn't been so bad after all.

15

'Have you googled him?' Lucy had an eager expression on her face.

Em was lying on the sofa in her flat, trying to relax after the day's events while filling in Lucy on the latest news from Dashford. They'd started off exchanging a few WhatsApp messages, but as soon as Em mentioned her embarrassing encounter with the hot professor, Lucy had quickly suggested they switch to a video call.

'Why would I Google him?' Em was regretting mentioning the weird effect the professor had had on her. She had hoped Lucy would be the voice of common sense, telling her to ignore it; it was rubbish; it was too soon to start another relationship, especially with someone she was unlikely to have anything in common with. But instead, Lucy had activated full matchmaker mode, which rarely ended well.

'He gets your pulse racing. So we need to know if he's worth pursuing or not.'

'We??'

'I'm your chief emotional adviser! And I notice you only queried my involvement rather than the need to know more about him, so let's find out, shall we ...' Em could hear Lucy's fingers tapping away on her laptop keyboard.

'Professor .. Jack… Car … ver. There we go. Ooh, lots of juicy stuff.'

'What do you mean juicy?' Em was doing a lousy job of hiding her interest.

'Don't worry. I just mean that there's lots about him. Let's start with LinkedIn.'

'Won't he know you've looked? I thought they shared that with you on LinkedIn?'

'A. He doesn't know who I am yet, and B. If you view someone's LinkedIn profile from an incognito browser page, they can't see it's you because you're not logged in. How useful it is depends on what they share publicly …. ' Lucy's voice trailed off.

'You've done this before, haven't you?'

'Of course! I Google all the men I date. Don't you?'

Em didn't answer. She'd only had one serious boyfriend before Connor, and they'd known one another since sixth form, so there had been no need to research him. And Connor … she hadn't been that interested at the start, and then when she was in too deep, she'd thought he was an open book. How wrong she'd been!

'Assuming he started uni when he was 18, he's 36 years old.'

'A lot older than me,' Em said.

'Only seven years at most! That's not an outrageous difference when you're staring 30 in the face. And talking of faces, his is rather nice. He doesn't look 36.'

Lucy was right - Professor Carver looked about 32 at the most.

'Boyish good looks is how I'd describe it,' Lucy said. Em could hear her typing again.

'Oh,' Lucy's tone changed slightly. 'Professor of eighteenth and nineteenth-century British history - your favourite subject!' She pulled a face.

Em loathed history, though that was mostly thanks to the lecherous bastard who taught them in secondary school. He'd had a penchant for perching on the edge of Em's desk to get a closer view of her cleavage.

Lucy carried on. 'He's got a thing about ships judging by the books he's written. It looks like he's presented a few obscure documentaries on the History Channel. Let's go back to Google.' Lucy sounded like she was trying to change the subject to something more encouraging. 'More stuff about his academic work, how to contact him at uni… Ooh, well, you're not the only one that fancies him. The top related search is "Is Professor Jack Carver married"'

'Seriously?' Em felt a pang of jealousy. *Get a grip!*

'Yep, followed by "Professor Jack Carver wife".'

'There you go then - all the good ones are taken as they say.' It was a relief. Pulse-racing effects aside, a married 30-something history professor with a fan club was not what she needed in her life right now.

'I haven't clicked on it yet. We don't know if he is married.'

Em sighed, exasperated at Lucy's nosiness but also interested in knowing more. She could hear Lucy typing again.

'It's taken me to a society website. "The wedding of Lady Isabella de Vries to Doctor Jack Carver".'

'See - he's not on the market.' said Em with an "I told you so" air, though she was surprised at how strong the sinking feeling of disappointment in her stomach was.

'The article is five years old, Em. They might not be together anymore. Why's he on holiday on his own if they are?'

Later that night, Em lay in bed, trying to sleep, but the heavy rain drumming relentlessly on the Velux window above her bed was distracting. And then there were the questions that kept going around in her head.

Why is the professor on holiday on his own for six weeks if he is happily married?

Why does he turn me into a jabbering wreck just by looking at me?

Why does he make me have all the cliched romantic reactions when he's not my type at all?

Why am I worried about all this when I don't want another man in my life yet?

And what am I going to do if he puts in a complaint to Nancy about me attacking him with the cleaning equipment?

At least that last question was relevant.

Reading. That usually helped. She turned on the bedside lamp and picked up her book. *Persuasion* by Jane Austen. No, the trials and tribulations of Anne Elliot and Captain Wentworth would not help Em sleep tonight. She looked through other books in her 'to be read' pile at the side of the bed. There was a crime novel she'd picked up in the charity shop in Dashford last week. A curmudgeonly detective solving a gruesome murder should be a suitable distraction as long as the murder weapon didn't turn out to be a vacuum cleaner.

Ten minutes later, she put the book down. She was six pages in, but she couldn't have told anyone anything about the scene she'd just read, even if her life depended on it. The words were drifting across the page and not going into her brain. She was still thinking about bloody Professor Jack Carver.

Em looked at the clock. 1.05 am. This was ridiculous. There were three sets of guests leaving today and three new families replacing them. Another full-on day, and it would be a lot easier to cope with if she had a good night's sleep.

Beep. She looked at her phone. An email from Lucy, with a 'Read this' subject line. Usually, Lucy only contacted Em this late if she was blind drunk, but she'd been stone-cold sober on their FaceTime call earlier. She hadn't sounded as if she was in the mood for drowning her sorrows. And she usually texted rather than emailed. It could be one of those spam messages that pretended to come from someone you knew.

But Em was curious. If it was spam, as long as she didn't click on any links or open any attachments, it should be fine. Em risked opening the email.

There was an attachment called Jack-Carver-Dossier.doc. That filename was far too relevant to be spam. She opened it. Five A4 pages of screenshots from newspaper articles, photos, and links to academic papers, plus Jack's LinkedIn profile and even some posts from his private Facebook page. How on earth had Lucy managed to get those? Judging by the detail, it had everything that was on the internet about the professor. Lucy must've spent the last four hours compiling it.

There was no way Em could ignore it until the morning. She settled back on her pillows and started to read.

16

Despite only getting four hours' sleep, Em had managed to wake up in time to politely wave off last week's guests, clean their properties and even welcome two of the families who had arrived early for this week. And all without injuring any of them. So far, so good. Just one more set of guests to deal with, and then she would be finished for the day.

The rain had blown over by lunchtime, and now Em was hurrying across the lawn with a basket of wet bedlinen, hoping to get it all dry in the warm sunshine that was bathing North Devon that afternoon.

Suddenly she felt herself lurching forward uncontrollably. She crashed into the ground with a thud. Shaking, she pushed herself onto her knees, looking at her muddy hands and then the wet sheets strewn across the lawn and the path. She must have caught her foot on that loose paving slab that Nancy had asked the gardener to sort out.

She tried to stand up, but the pain in her right ankle was excruciating. Shit! The final set of guests would be arriving soon, and she hadn't finished making their bed.

She sat back down on the grass. What had she learnt at first aid training? If the casualty could move their limb, there were no broken bones. She tentatively attempted to rotate her right foot. It was moving in the correct direction but it hurt. A sprain, then. Fingers crossed, it wasn't a bad one. Perhaps once she'd bandaged it, she could hobble over to the holiday cottage to finish prepping it. She remembered seeing an old walking stick in the boot room off the kitchen. She could use that to support herself. Yes, that would work.

But the first challenge was to get back indoors to get the first aid box. She looked at the steps up to the top terrace. Ten in total and no handrail to hold on to. No choice, then. Glad she was wearing her jeans, Em crawled to the steps and started her ascent on her hands and knees.

She was nearly at the top when a pair of highly polished brogues appeared in her line of sight. Her heart sank.

'Are you ok?' Jack knelt down. The concern in his voice made it sound even more appealing.

'Yes, thanks. I do this to atone for my sins.' *Why did you say that?*

Jack raised an eyebrow. 'Seems harsh. How many other people did you hit yesterday?'

His wry smile temporarily took her mind off the pain, if not the embarrassment of looking like a dork again.

'Where does it hurt?' he asked.

'Just here.' Em indicated the outside of her ankle. Much as she wished he wasn't here to witness her embarrassment, she was glad there was someone to help.

He walked down a couple of steps and gently helped Em to her feet. She couldn't avoid leaning into him, enjoying the smell of his aftershave and the touch of his hand on her waist. A warm glow spread around her body. Connor had never had such a strong effect on her. *Get a grip, woman.*

'Where are we aiming for?' Jack asked.

'That door there, please,' she said, expecting him to help her limp to the kitchen. But he surprised her by scooping her up and carrying her indoors.

Wow! Enjoy this while it lasts because you're not doing anything about it.

Fifteen minutes later, Em was sitting on a sofa in the drawing room with a neatly bandaged ankle resting on a cushion on one of Nancy's side tables. Jack had made a very able nurse, making her comfortable and finding a bag of frozen peas and some paracetamol to ease the pain. He'd even retrieved the sheets from the garden. But now, all she could think about was her job.

'Are you sure you don't want me to take you to hospital?' Jack looked concerned.

'Honestly, I'll be fine. The pain's easing already. I must finish getting Rose Cottage ready.' She tried to edge herself off the sofa, grabbing the walking stick that he'd thoughtfully put next to her.

'You need to rest.'

'But the new guests will be here soon. '

He gently took the stick off her and moved it out of reach. 'You can have it back if you promise only to use it in an emergency.'

'This is an emergency! Mrs Farnham will be sacking me if I screw up.'

'Somehow, I don't think she will. What needs to be done?'

Em wished she had his confidence. 'The duvet cover needs putting on in the main bedroom, and fresh towels need to go in the en suite. They are all on the kitchen table in the cottage. It won't take me long.'

'It won't take you any time at all because I'll do it.'

'I can't ask you to do that. And I've got to welcome them.' What would Nancy say if she knew Em was getting a guest to do her job?

'I can do that too. I know exactly how you do it.' That twinkle in his eyes again. Em felt her face going red, remembering yesterday's disaster. He left the room before she could object further.

'Are these the keys?' Jack stuck his head back around the door and waved them at her. She nodded. 'I'll bring you some tea when I've finished.'

And this is why he's happily married. She heard the front door close before she had a chance to thank him.

Jack was as good as his word. Half an hour later, he returned with the news that the final guests had arrived while he was putting the finishing touches to their cottage.

'I made sure they knew where everything was. They're a lovely couple. I don't think they'll be much bother.'

'Thank you - I really appreciate it.'

'Tea?'

'Yes, please.' He disappeared into the kitchen again. At least she could relax now.

He returned a few minutes later carrying a silver tray containing a teapot, mugs, a milk jug, a sugar bowl with cubes and tongs, and some milk chocolate digestives on a plate. He seemed to have a natural ability to find things. The upper classes must have a standard kitchen layout.

'I wasn't sure how you took your tea,' he said, setting the tray on the coffee table.

'This is like being at the Ritz.'

'Not quite,' he laughed. 'I drew the line at making cucumber sandwiches.'

Em had never had tea at the Ritz, but she suspected Jack had. He poured tea for her, making sure it was exactly how she liked it. Then he did the same for himself, relaxing back on the sofa opposite. If it weren't for the pain in her ankle, she would have thought she was having a dream about the perfect man waiting on her.

'So, what brings you to Dashford for the whole summer?'

Detailed as Lucy's research had been, it hadn't revealed the reason for Jack's extended stay. 'Most of our guests stay for two weeks at most.'

Jack looked thoughtful. 'I'm finishing the book I'm writing. Too many distractions in town.'

'London,' he added, noticing Em's puzzled expression. 'What about you?'

Should she tell the whole story or trot out the standard answer she'd given to everyone else apart from Mary and Nancy? Best to stick to the standard answer for now. 'I needed a change of scenery and a job that gave me time to paint.'

'What did you do before?'

She told him about the call centre and how she realised she wasn't getting anywhere near her plan to become a professional artist. She kept the story as upbeat as possible. She didn't want him to think she was a whinger.

Em was wondering what to ask him about his life without giving away how much she already knew when his phone beeped. He looked at it and sighed. 'I'm really sorry. I need to follow up on this. Will you be alright if I leave you here?'

'Yes, I'll be fine.'

'Are you sure? Do you want my mobile number in case you need anything?'

'Thanks, that would be a good idea.' He was so considerate. They exchanged texts.

'I'll put all this back in the kitchen.' He picked up the tray. 'Don't hesitate to call me if you need anything. See you soon.'

17

'Hello, you.' Jack's cheery voice echoed across the courtyard.

Em looked up from her novel and smiled. 'Hello.'

It was Monday lunchtime. After spending the whole of yesterday resting her ankle in her flat, Em had come outside to read in the shade to stop herself from going stir-crazy.

'How's the ankle?' Jack walked over to the bench where she was sitting. He was wearing pale blue jeans coupled with a battered pair of walking boots instead of his chinos and brogues.

'Getting better, thanks. I can manage without the stick now, but the marathon training will have to wait.'

'You're planning on running a marathon?' He looked impressed.

'No, I was joking. 5k is my limit. I used to enjoy running back home, but it's too hilly around here for my tastes. Are you off out?'

'I'm going to walk down to the beach. I should be working on my book, but it's such a lovely day it seems a shame to waste it stuck at my desk.'

'I can understand that. I was desperate to get some fresh air.'

'It'll be even fresher by the sea. Do you want to join me?'

Em hadn't risked driving yet with her dodgy ankle, even though it felt much better. It had only been two days since her fall, but she was already missing her daily walk along the beach. Even if she could only manage a short distance, it would be good to get down there again, but there was no way she could walk the mile and a half into Dashford and back again. 'Thanks, but I don't think my ankle is up to walking that far.'

'We can take my car?'

An opportunity to get to know Jack better or re-reading *Persuasion*? Lucy would say it was a no-brainer. 'If you're sure that's ok. I'll go and change my shoes.'

Jack's driving was a lot calmer than Nancy's. Em relaxed in the passenger seat and concentrated on enjoying the view to take her mind off how close together they were as they drove in companionable silence down the narrow lanes towards Dashford.

She noticed Jack's left hand on the steering wheel - no wedding ring. Not that that meant anything. *And it's irrelevant*, her inner voice nagged her. She wondered how it would feel to stroke his leg like she used to stroke Connor's when he was driving. *What are you thinking? Stop torturing yourself.*

'Sorry I've spoilt your walking plans,' she said as Jack pulled into the last space in the seafront car park.

'It's good to have some company. I wouldn't have offered otherwise.' That smile. 'I've done that walk so many times. Missing it once doesn't matter.'

'You've been here before then?' Em asked as they got out of the car.

'Yes, didn't Nancy tell you? She is best friends with my mother. We often spent the summer holidays here when I was a child. We used to stop in the main house then. Pa would come and visit at weekends. Happy days.' He seemed wistful.

That explained his familiarity with the kitchen layout on Saturday. 'Happier than now?' Em couldn't help being curious about his current situation.

'Yes.' He looked as if he was about to say something else but changed his mind. 'Shall we head down to the beach?'

The tide was out, so the surface was mostly compacted, damp sand. It should be more comfortable to walk on than the hard concrete esplanade. Her walking boot should support her ankle.

'Will you manage the steps?' he asked.

'I think so. Let's see.'

She used the handrail to take most of the weight on her right-hand side. When she wobbled slightly, Jack put his hand on the small of her back to steady her. It felt very reassuring. There were some advantages to having an injury.

'Have you seen the old wreck?' Jack asked as a pensioner glided past on a mobility scooter on the promenade above them.

Em looked puzzled. She didn't think Jack was the sort who would be offensive.

Jack laughed. 'The shipwreck!'

He pointed towards what looked like a cave with a few pieces of wood sticking up through the sand in front of it. 'It's only visible at low tide.'

Em hadn't noticed it before. They set off together across the beach, Jack letting Em set the pace.

'There's not much of it left now,' he said as they neared the wreck. 'Much less than when I used to play on it as a boy. It's amazing it's lasted all this time.'

The old timber had some interesting textures. The reflections in the small pools of seawater left behind by the tide caught her eye too. Em got her phone out to take some photos. 'These will look good on the house's Instagram page.'

Nancy had given her access to the Dashford Grange social media accounts a few weeks ago, saying she'd grown tired of keeping them up to date. 'But it does bring in business, so if you could take over, that would be helpful.' Em was happy to oblige.

She walked around the remains. 'How long has it been here?'

'Over 150 years. The Countess Genevieve. She set sail from Canada, heading for Bristol. Imagine battling across the wild winter seas of the Atlantic only to get blown off course so close to home. The local lifeboatmen managed to rescue all the crew. It's what got me interested in old ships.'

He moved to the front of the wreck. 'Nancy's son used to pretend to be a pirate, and I'd be the captain bravely fending him off with my wooden sword.' Jack stood in front of what little was left of the bow, re-enacting the scene with all the enthusiasm of a nine-year-old.

Em laughed. 'Nigel?'

'Good god, no. Nigel wanted nothing to do with us. He must have been 18 years old at the time, getting ready to go to Oxford. No, it was Mark.'

'I didn't realise Nancy had another son.' Nancy had never mentioned any child other than Nigel.

'I don't think they speak much now.' His expression clouded over, the joy of his childhood memory gone. 'The tide's coming in. We better go back.' He set off, head down, deep in thought, his long legs striding out. Em would've struggled to keep up even if she hadn't got a bad ankle. She hobbled after him.

It took him a minute to realise she wasn't beside him. 'I'm so sorry! I completely forgot about your injury,' he shouted, running back to her.

He had that thoughtful look again and a slight redness around his eyes. 'Is everything ok?' she asked.

'Yes, I'm fine now.' He looked flustered. 'Are you ok? It looks like your limp is getting worse.' Jack, the gentleman, was back.

Em had overdone it, but she didn't want to appear needy again. She could manage. 'I'll be alright. I don't need you to carry me again.' *Why did you say that?*

'That's a shame.' *What? You don't need him making a play for you. You're enjoying being single, remember?*

But he looked more amused than anything. 'Lean on me instead.'

They headed slowly back towards the promenade, their arms around one another. It felt so natural - too natural. *You mustn't get used to this.*

'Are you sure this is alright?' Em looked up at him, not wanting him to stop but concerned about how it might look.

'Yes, why wouldn't it be?' He gave her shoulder a gentle squeeze.

Obviously, he wasn't worried about being seen in public looking like he was hugging another woman. Perhaps he was divorced.

'Do you know what I could do with?' he said as they got back to the steps. 'Proper fish and chips. All this fresh sea air has given me an appetite.'

Their walk had given Em an appetite, too, but not the sort that Jack was thinking of. She sat down on a bench, blushing at the thought. It was so confusing. Why had he come into her life now when she was avoiding men? 'Nancy recommends the one by the church to all the guests,' she said.

'No, the Dolphin Fish Bar is better - it used to be anyway.' He looked at his watch. 'Probably shutting soon, though.' He sounded disappointed.

'Why don't I sit here, and you go? We won't get there in time otherwise.'

'Excellent plan - text me your order.'

She watched him running eagerly up the hill.

Em sat gazing out over the waves thinking about Jack. Her phone buzzed. A text from Lucy.

HAVE DATE WITH THE HUNK

This momentous news warranted a phone conversation. Lucy had been flirting with 'The Hunk', who frequented the same sandwich shop as she did, for several weeks, but he'd resisted her charms until now. Em called Lucy's number.

'What clinched it?' Em asked.

'My sandwich order. Apparently, a woman who likes "smoked salmon and cream cheese on rye, no spread" is date material.'

'That's where I've been going wrong all these years - granary's obviously not a turn-on.'

'It will be those seeds getting stuck in your teeth. No man wants to see that.'

'So where's he taking you?'

'Ice skating.'

'You hate ice skating. Last time we tried it, you wouldn't let go of the bloody penguin support thing, even when that mother demanded it for her poor four-year-old.'

'He's going to teach me. He used to be a semi-professional ice hockey player. How much fun will it be falling into the arms of a 6ft 2 blonde Canadian? And if I get cold and shivery, he'll have to hug me close to his broad, muscular torso. Hmmm.'

'So long as you don't end up in the sin bin,' Em laughed. 'When are you going?'

'Friday night.' That meant Em would have to cope with nearly three whole days of texts from Lucy mulling over the pros and cons of what to wear, whether she should drink or not, and whether she should kiss him on the first date. Despite being a confident extrovert, Lucy was a chronic overthinker when it came to first dates.

'There you go,' Jack sat beside Em and handed her a polystyrene take-out box. The smell of the warm fish and chips made her stomach rumble.

'Who's that?' Lucy whispered down the phone.

'Jack. He's just bought me lunch. Gotta go.' Em thought she heard a 'What??' as she mischievously clicked the end call button.

18

'I nearly had a stroke today with all the stress worrying about Friday's date and wondering what you've been getting up to with Jack.' Lucy had texted Em several times after their phone call earlier, and now Em had finally given in and phoned her back.

'We went for a walk.'

'How did you manage that with your dodgy ankle?'

'He drove me down into Dashford, and we had a short walk on the beach.'

'So it wasn't just a walk. You went for a drive as well. Sounds like a date to me.'

'A date is when you spend time flirting with someone, working out whether you want to form a more meaningful and physical relationship with them.'

'Is that the official dictionary definition?'

'No, it's the Emily Gillespie definition. And by my rules, it wasn't a date.'

'You went out for a meal as well.'

'I'd hardly call eating fish and chips on a bench while fending off a hungry seagull going out for a meal.'

'Well?'

'Well, what?'

'Is he still married?'

'I've no idea.'

'You must've spent at least a couple of hours alone with him, and you still don't know his marital status. You're hopeless without me.'

Em laughed. 'I can't ask him outright, can I? He'll either think I've got the hots for him or realise that I've googled him, which also means I'm interested in him.'

'You are interested in him!'

'Not in that way. I'm avoiding men for a while, remember? Especially attractive ones - they're just trouble.'

'How long's a while? I think you're starting to cave in.'

Perhaps Em was. Spending a few hours with Jack had been enjoyable. No working out what his motives were, or dodging overly familiar wandering hands like on her first date with Connor. Apart from that brief moment when he walked away from the shipwreck, Jack seemed remarkably straightforward, just wanting to enjoy the moment. She wouldn't object to a few more afternoons like that. He was good company.

19

'What do you think of my godson?'

The warm early evening light streamed through the drawing room window. Nancy was back from her rock climbing course. She was sitting in the wing-backed chair, looking out over the garden while Em worked on her portrait. It was nearly finished, but Em wanted to make a few minor adjustments before she allowed Nancy to see it.

'Jack? He's lovely.'

'I gather you've done a good job of looking after him while I was away.'

'He's been looking after me.'

'He's a good boy. Don't tell him, but he is my favourite godchild.' Nancy made it sound like Jack was seven. She adjusted the cushions to make herself more comfortable. 'I'm glad I was able to help him.'

'Help him?'

'Yes, by giving him somewhere to hide away from that dreadful wife of his.'

Em paused her painting. So Jack was married then. But 'hide' and 'dreadful' weren't words you'd expect someone to use when talking about a happy marriage.

'Sounds like you don't like her.'

'I did at the start - we all did. Isabella was perfectly charming. She appeared to adore him, and he was besotted with her.'

Em squeezed some more white paint onto her palette. 'So what happened?' she asked, trying her best to appear nonchalant.

'My son Mark happened. I'm ashamed to say he fell for Isabella's charms, foolish boy. Poor Jack caught them in bed together.'

Shit! That explained Jack's mood after talking about Mark at the shipwreck yesterday. How awful for him.

Double shit - the shock had caused Em to put completely the wrong colour on Nancy's cheek. Wiping it off would make it worse. She'd have to wait for it to dry then paint over it.

'So he left her?' *Don't sound too happy at the prospect.*

'No. She persuaded Jack it was all his fault. He'd been busy writing a book, and he wasn't devoting enough time to her, so she had no choice but to seek solace in the arms of his best friend. Feeble excuse - what's wrong with reading or yoga? That's how a normal person would have kept themselves entertained.'

Nancy leaned forward towards Em. 'If I'm being uncharitable - and I usually am where Isabella is concerned these days - I'd say she used Mark deliberately. She seems jealous of anyone who takes Jack's attention away from her.'

Just like Em's mother was with her father. She wouldn't wish someone like that on Jack.

'How's Mark?'

'I don't know. We had a massive argument about it. I haven't spoken to him for nearly two years, sadly. Neither has Jack, as far as I know. Mark left his legal practice and moved to Spain. Judging by his Instagram feed, he's hiring out jet skis during the day and bartending in the evening - a waste of a good education. So there you are. She's hurt two of the most important men in my life, and they've both lost their best friend. The only good thing is Jack's finally seen the light. He's trying to divorce her. '

'Trying?' Surely divorce wasn't that difficult these days.

'She's contesting it. Claims to still be in love with him. Desperate to have him back and similar rubbish.'

'Why do you think it's rubbish?'

'Because of other things she's done. She doesn't care about his feelings at all.' Em was intrigued but she felt she'd shown too much interest in Isabella already.

'So that's why Jack's here then - avoiding Isabella?'

'Yes. His mother, Olivia, thought it would be good for him to get out of London to reduce the chance of Isabella persuading him to take her back again. So I offered Jack one of the cottages for the summer. Olivia's very worried about him. He's not his usual self, unsurprisingly.'

'Poor Jack.'

'Don't mention I've told you all this. I'm not meant to know some of it, but Olivia and I share everything.'

Oh no, more information that Em wasn't supposed to know. Talking to Jack was a minefield already thanks to Lucy's detective work, but now it would be even harder. Em needed to find a way to get him to spill the beans himself.

Nancy interrupted her thoughts. 'I'm glad you've been spending time with him. It's not good for him to be completely on his own. Let me know if there's anything I should worry about.'

'Yes, of course.' Em said distractedly.

'Is it done then?' Nancy waved at the portrait as Em had clearly stopped painting. 'I'm dying to see it.'

Em looked at the white splodge on the canvas where the corner of Nancy's mouth should be. It wasn't dry enough to paint over yet. 'I just want to make a few more tweaks. Then we can have the big reveal tomorrow.'

20

'Hello, you.' Jack had arrived at Em's front door with a mystery basket.

They'd bumped into one another in the courtyard earlier and established that they were both planning to watch the men's Wimbledon semi-final that afternoon. Mindful of what Nancy had said about keeping Jack company, Em had decided to invite him over. 'The TV in my flat is bigger than the one in your cottage,' she had said.

And now here he was. 'Do you like Pimms?' he asked as he walked into her hall.

'Yes, I love it, but I don't think I've got all the ingredients,' Em said.

'Don't worry - I've brought everything we need,' he said, indicating the basket. 'Point me in the direction of your kitchen, and I'll make us a jugful.'

He unpacked a large bottle of Pimms, along with lemonade, oranges, strawberries, half a cucumber and a bunch of mint. He'd even got a bag of ice cubes.

'You can come again!' Em smiled, enjoying the novelty of being waited on. Connor wouldn't have had a clue where to start. His idea of making her a drink was opening a bottle of Diet Coke.

All they were lacking was a jug. Jack didn't seem too bothered. 'We'll use this saucepan instead.'

'How's the book going?' she asked while he was slicing ingredients.

'Very well. I couldn't sleep properly last night, so I got up and did some more editing. I'm ahead of schedule for the first time. How's Nancy's portrait?'

'Finished! I was up early, too, doing the finishing touches. I'm showing it to Nancy when she gets back from water skiing later.'

'She still water skis?'

'Oh yes. When I looked shocked at where she was going, she informed me the world's oldest water skier is 94. She reckons she's got a good few years in her yet.'

Jack laughed. 'Can I have a peek at the painting?'

'Yes, it's at the back of the living room.' Em hoped he liked it. She was still veering between being pleased with it and finding new flaws.

Jack dropped the last piece of cucumber in the saucepan and went into the living room. Em busied herself slicing strawberries, not wanting to see his reaction. She realised she was holding her breath.

'That's amazing. The likeness is excellent, and you've captured that mischievous twinkle in her eye. There's a tenderness to it as well.'

It sounded like genuine praise. What a relief. 'Thank you. I hope Nancy likes it.'

'She'll love it. You should take commissions professionally.'

'I need a bit more practice. This is the first portrait I've done since art college.'

'You can't tell. I don't think you need more practice at all. Who will you paint next?'

Em emerged from the kitchen with two glasses of Pimms.

'I don't know.' She looked at Jack's profile as he carried on admiring the painting. She imagined drawing his perfect nose, long eyelashes and bright blue eyes. Capturing the waves in his hair would be trickier though she'd enjoy the challenge. But the last time she'd painted someone she was attracted to - a hot Argentinian engineering post-grad she'd met in the Students Union bar in London - it had resulted in a passionate three-week fling.

'Penny for your thoughts?' Jack was looking at her now.

Em came back into the present. 'They'll cost a lot more than that.'

He looked intrigued, but a convenient round of applause came from the television, distracting him from asking why. 'Time to take our seats,' he said.

Two hours into the match and Em and Jack had finished their third large glass of Pimms.

Em swayed slightly as she returned from a quick trip to the bathroom. 'I think we need to slow down. It's the first time I've had any alcohol since I've been here.'

'Have you been to Wimbledon?' Jack asked as she settled back down on the sofa.

'Yes, several times. We usually camp out for tickets on the day.'

'You and Connor?'

'No, me and my best friend, Lucy' *Hang on. Connor?* 'How do you know about Connor? I don't think I've mentioned him.'

It was Jack's turn to blush. 'I've been rumbled. Nancy told me what happened with you and your ex.'

'Did you ever go to Wimbledon with Isabella?'

He laughed. 'Don't tell me. Nancy told you all about me and my soon-to-be ex.'

'Yep.'

'Did she ask you to look after me too?'

'Why? Are you looking after me then?'

'Yes,' he said. 'Nancy said she was worried you'd be lonely while she was away, so she asked me to keep an eye on you when I arrived. I think someone's up to her old tricks. She enjoys a bit of matchmaking.'

Em didn't know what to say to that. Part of her was disappointed that his attentiveness had been at Nancy's instigation. But then it had all felt a little bit too good to be true. And her sensible side was relieved that he didn't have feelings for her. No risk of Em losing her resolve to stay single and then hurting him.

Jack must have sensed her confusion. 'I enjoy your company. I'd be spending time with you regardless of what Nancy asked me to do. I wouldn't be sitting here on your sofa now if I didn't. Can we still be friends?'

'Of course.'

'Thank you,' He leaned over and hugged her. Oh god, did he have to be so bloody nice?

'Thirty, love,' shouted the umpire.

The tennis match had gone on for well over six hours. They'd run out of Pimms a couple of hours ago, so Jack had popped over to his cottage to fetch a bottle of wine.

Em's phone beeped with an appointment reminder. 'I'm supposed to be showing Nancy her portrait.'

Jack pulled a face. 'We can't stop watching this now. The match could finish at any minute. Nancy's a big tennis fan. She's bound to be watching it too.'

Em hoped he was right. 'I'll text her to say we'll be over when the match finishes.'

Fifteen minutes later, the crowd cheered as the South African player hit the winning shot.

'Finally! Time for the big reveal.' Em stood up and peeled off her t-shirt, revealing her scrappy top underneath.

Jack lifted his eyebrows.

'The portrait.' Em slurred. 'I'm going to put a fresh top on.'

'Ah,' he said. 'I'd forgotten about that.'

Em headed for the bedroom, bumped into the sofa, lurched into the wall and stubbed her toe on the door. 'Shit! I'm not sure I'll make it to Nancy's.'

'We only have to walk across the courtyard. We're not fleeing from Dunkirk.'

'I know, but I shouldn't have had that last glass of wine.'

'You don't think the other glasses of wine and Pimms might have something to do with your current state as well?' Jack grinned. His words were slurred but not as bad as Em's.

'Smart arse. You're the one who came round here, plying me with alcohol.'

'I'm sorry. Let me carry everything across to the house for you. I'm not entirely sober but I'm more steady than you.'

Em checked her phone - a text from Nancy.

'Nancy says she's gone into the kitchen, so we can come over now.'

21

Ten minutes later, Jack had carried the canvas safely into the main house, with Em following, using the easel to support her. She set up the easel in front of Nancy's favourite chair, and Jack propped the canvas onto it, covering it with a sheet.

'Can I come in yet?' Nancy called from the hall.

'Yes.' Em replied, turning to Jack, who was standing on the other side of the easel. She held up both her hands with her fingers crossed.

Nancy walked in and sat down. 'Ready when you are.'

'Ta-dah!' Em flamboyantly pulled the sheet off the canvas, which wobbled dangerously for a second until Jack put his hand out to catch it. Nancy looked amused but didn't comment - she was transfixed by the portrait.

There was silence. Em chewed her lip. *She hates it.*

'Oh, my word - that's better than I could have ever thought. You've made me look at least ten years younger.' Nancy picked up her reading glasses from the side table and walked over to the painting to inspect it more closely. 'Such energy. The way you've captured the light is exquisite. How have you managed to do all that in so few brush strokes? I'm thrilled. Thank you so much. You're so talented, ' Nancy squashed Em into a big hug.

'Told you,' Jack mouthed at her behind Nancy's shoulder.

'I'd normally suggest we open a bottle of champagne to celebrate,' Nancy said, 'but perhaps sparkling water might be better today.'

'I thought she hadn't noticed,' Jack whispered to Em while Nancy was in the kitchen. 'Well done, you.'

Em liked the way they were interacting now. This afternoon's conversation has made it so much easier to be in his company.

Nancy returned with a tray and glasses of water with ice and lemon.

'I think we should have another unveiling once it's framed,' she said. 'I'll invite all my friends, and hopefully, we can drum up some business for you. It will be at the framer's for a couple of weeks at least, so we've got plenty of time to organise it all.'

Em felt nervous again. 'That's so lovely of you, but I'm not sure I feel ready yet. I want to do at least one more practice piece before I start charging.'

'You're more than good enough already. But if you insist, we'll have to find a volunteer. Now let's see. Who do we know who's got time to do several sittings for you in the next few weeks?' Nancy stared at Jack.

'I'm supposed to be finishing my book.'

Nancy put her hands on her hips. 'You told me you were ahead of schedule, and it won't take that much of your time. If I can squeeze it into my busy life, I'm sure you'll be able to.'

'You don't have to let me paint your portrait if you don't want to,' Em said to Jack as they walked out into the courtyard. 'Nancy did railroad you into agreeing.'

'She will never let me hear the end of it if I don't,' he laughed. 'Anyway, it will be interesting to find out how you really see me. When do you want to start?'

'We need to decide what you're going to wear, what the backdrop will be, what size you want.' Em was struggling to remember everything, thanks to the alcohol. 'I need to draw up a checklist if I'm going to take on paying customers.'

'Tomorrow? We can brainstorm the list together if you want.'

'It's Saturday ... only two changeovers this week, so I should be free after 5 pm - if they both turn up on time!'

He thought for a moment. 'I won't risk booking a restaurant. How about I cook dinner? I am supposed to be looking after you after all.' He grinned.

'That doesn't sound fair. You sorted out the drinks for today. I'll cook for you.'

'But you'll have been busy all day sorting out the guests.'

'No, I insist. I'll do something simple.' It was all she could do anyway, but Jack didn't need to know that yet. 'Anything you won't or can't eat?'

'No, I'm flexible,' Jack said as Em heard her phone vibrate with a new text.

'Oh shit!'

'What's wrong?'

'My friend Lucy went on a first date this evening, and I forgot to check if she was ok.' Em showed him the text.

```
Been kidnapped by white slavers thanks for
asking!!
```

'Looks like the slavers have let her keep her phone,' Jack said.

'I better check she's alright.'

```
How did it go?
```

Three dots appeared. They both waited for the answer to

appear.

    `It's still going. Can't text more now - got my`
`hands full`

'She sounds fine.' Jack laughed. 'Night, Em.'
He hugged her. A warm glow spread through Em's body. New touchy-feely, friend-only Jack was more appealing than ever, unfortunately.

22

'O.M.G! We finally find out he's available, and he friend zones you.' It was Saturday afternoon, and Lucy had torn herself away from the lovely Lars, as The Hunk was now known, long enough to FaceTime Em.

'I don't mind. It's a relief. I'd be suspicious he was on the rebound under the circumstances.'

Lucy raised her eyebrows as if she didn't believe her, which was fair. Em didn't entirely believe it herself. Disappointed would be a more accurate description. The more time she spent with Jack, the more time she wanted to spend with him. Perhaps she was on the rebound. He was everything Connor wasn't - domesticated, considerate, attentive. But she'd need at least an hour's heart-to-heart with Lucy to work through all her conflicting emotions, and she hadn't got time for that now.

'My primary concern is that in my drunken optimism, I offered to cook for him tonight.'

'You did what?' Lucy laughed. 'Well, that will kill any hope of romance. Can't you get takeout?'

'Thanks for the vote of confidence!' Em said. 'And no, I checked. There are no takeaways within 20 miles unless you include the chippies in Dashford. I'm keeping it simple. I bought two steaks when I went to the supermarket this morning, some triple-cooked chips that you stick in the oven and a bag of salad. Even I can't mess that up.'

'Best of luck to Jack!'

'Charming! Anyway, enough about me. It sounds like your love life is way more exciting than mine. How many times did you fall into Lars' arms?'

'On the ice rink or afterwards?'

'Both.'

'Let's just say we didn't stay at the ice rink long. And he prefers coffee and toast for breakfast.' Lucy looked dreamy.

'I thought you'd decided you weren't even going to kiss him on the first date.'

'A girl can change her mind. We needed to do something to warm up after that freezing time on the ice.'

'It was 23 degrees outside yesterday!'

'I know - we had to strip off.' More distant looks.

Em heard Lucy's doorbell ring. 'Got to go. Lars is cooking dinner.'

'It's only 3 o'clock in the afternoon. What's he planning on serving - a 12-course banquet?'

'We need to have a detailed discussion about the menu first.'

'Of course you do - enjoy!' Em closed the call, glad that at least one of them had found romance.

'Is everything ok?'

Jack looked concerned by the sound of the smoke alarm going off as Em welcomed him into the hallway of her flat.

'Yes, don't worry! Everything's in hand. I always use smoke alarm to tell me when dinner's ready,' she said, desperately trying to make light of the situation as she raced back into the living room to wave a tea towel at the alarm on the ceiling.

"I'm just going to put this in the fridge," Jack said, holding up the bottle of wine he'd brought with him. 'I think it might be the oven that's the source of the problem,' he called from the kitchen.

'I'm grilling our steaks.' She said by way of explanation. 'It's one of those dual grill/oven things.'

'Were you going for the flame-grilled effect because it looks like the fat has caught fire?' asked Jack.

Em ran into the kitchen. Thin trails of smoke were escaping around the sides of the oven door. 'Oh shit!'

'I'll take that as a no, then,' he said, turning the oven off at the wall.

'I'm not used to using the grill yet.' He must think she was an idiot.

'Do you mind me asking why the chips are in that frying pan?'

'They're oven chips, but then I realised that I needed to use the oven as a grill, so I cooked them for half the time in the oven, then I was finishing heating them through on the hob while I grilled the steaks when the smoke alarm went off . Perhaps I should've cooked the steaks on the hob instead.'

'Perhaps,' he agreed. 'What else have we got to eat?'

'Salad?'

'And is that in the microwave?' He was doing that fake serious thing again. Or she hoped he was. Time to be cheeky back.

Em flicked his backside with the tea towel. 'Don't mock the afflicted. I find cooking very stressful.'

They both laughed. At least he was taking his first experience of her culinary disasters in good spirits.

Jack looked at his watch. 'Shall we wait until we're sure the flames are out and then walk up to the Kingfisher? It's a lovely evening. We can probably eat in the beer garden.'

'I'm really sorry!'

'It's fine. My turn to cook next time.'

Em was just glad he thought there would be a next time.

23

The sun was setting, and the pub garden was starting to empty by the time they arrived.

'Inside or out?' Jack asked.

'It's still so hot. I'd prefer to be in the fresh air. I'll grab a table.' Em found a picnic table with a sea view while Jack went inside to order drinks and get a menu. She felt the tension in her shoulders fade as she watched the sun sink towards the horizon.

A deep voice snapped her back to reality. 'What's a pretty girl like you doing on your own on a Saturday night?' Or that's what she thought he'd said - it was impossible to be 100% sure as the words were very slurred.

A sunburnt man in his mid-twenties sat down next to Em, clutching the remains of a pint of beer. She guessed it was far from his first pint of the day. There was a cockiness about him that reminded her of Connor but with a South London accent.

'I'm waiting for my friend to come back from the bar.' Em said. *Pity you didn't use that line on Connor all those years ago.*

'I've heard that before,' he edged nearer to her, blatantly looking down her top. Em believed him. Even sober, he wouldn't have scored highly on the desirability scale.

'Please leave me alone.' She turned away, picking up her

phone, trying to ignore him, but he moved closer until their thighs touched. The feel of his hot, sweaty flesh made her cringe. The overwhelming smell of stale beer wasn't appealing either. Em slid away from him to the end of the bench.

'I asked you to go away,' she said loudly so the rest of the people in the garden could hear.

'Come on, Si. Leave her alone.' Another man approached him, presumably a friend. But Si defiantly sat there staring at her.

'I don't give up that easy, sweetheart. What will it take to get you to come home with me?'

'She's not coming home with you.' Jack was back. He put their drinks down on the table.

Si stood up and squared up to him. 'And who the fuck are you?'

'The man she is coming home with.' Jack didn't seem intimidated by Si being about 4 inches taller and twice his width.

'Oh yeah.' Si lurched drunkenly at Jack, looking like he was about to punch him. But he soon found himself sprawling on the floor after Jack made some martial art style moves that caught him on his outstretched arm and knocked him off balance.

There was an appreciative 'ooh' from the rest of the pubgoers. Two of the onlookers grabbed their phones, ready to video any further action.

Si's friend picked him up off the ground. 'Come on, mate. Let's get out of here.' Si seemed keen to comply.

'How was I to know she was going out with Stan Fucking Lee?' Em heard Si say as they weaved their way towards the car park.

Lucy's research hadn't revealed anything about Jack having self-defence skills. Em looked at him, gobsmacked.

Jack grinned at her. 'Appalling, isn't it - confusing Stan Lee with Bruce Lee.'

'It wasn't that that surprised me.'

'I don't have my head stuck in books all day,' he said, sitting beside her. 'I do Taekwondo in my spare time. I thought it might come in useful living in London. I never thought I'd need it in rural Devon.'

Em and Jack were walking back up the lane after a dinner of perfectly cooked steak and chips and a helpful discussion about his portrait. Jack was slightly ahead, lighting the way with the torch on his phone.

Em was thoughtful, looking at his profile backlit by the narrow torch beam. *Why does he put up with you?*

Jack turned to look at her. 'You're quiet. Is anything wrong?'

'I was just thinking that you must be fed up of rescuing me.'

'No!' Jack seemed genuinely surprised. 'I'm happy to be useful. That's what friends are for. It's not as if you play the damsel in distress card. You're always independently trying to resolve whatever crisis is happening. You never ask for help.'

'Thanks, but it seems a bit of a one-way friendship.'

'I don't think so. I've told you I enjoy your company. I like the way you see the world. You make me laugh. It takes my mind off my messy divorce.'

If it hadn't been for the Si incident, Em would have asked more about the divorce, but right now, she wasn't interested in anything or anyone. 'Sorry I'm not making you laugh now. I'm just feeling really down. I think it was that bastard at the pub, reminding me what it's like being out in the big, bad world. I've been in a protective bubble since I moved here. But I will have to leave that bubble at some point.'

Jack looked thoughtful. They carried on walking side by side down the drive to Dashford Grange.

When they got to the courtyard, Jack broke the silence. 'Do you want to talk about it? I could put the kettle on.'

'I think I've taken up enough of your time this evening.' Em could feel herself tearing up. *Don't bloody cry now!* She ran up the steps to her front door so he wouldn't see.

'If you're sure. You know where I am if you need me,' he called after her.

Oh, Jack, I do need you. *Shut up, woman. It's the wine talking.* 'Thanks. Night, Jack.'

'Night, Em.'

24

A text from Jack.

```
Are you awake yet?
```

Em looked at the time on her phone. 8.45 am. Bit early for a Sunday. She usually slept in after the exertions of the guest changeovers on Friday and Saturday, and she'd been hoping to do that today, especially after last night's stressful events.

```
Just about
```

Three dots appeared immediately

```
How do you feel about going on a pirate hunt?
```

What was he on about? Was she still asleep? Em responded with a puzzled face emoji.

The three dots appeared again. They stayed there for a while. It must be a long reply.

You'd be helping me if you did. It involves
heading to the south Devon coast via Dartmoor,
doing some ankle-friendly walking, and taking a
few photos. Then we'll have Sunday lunch somewhere
if you're up for it?

Em got out of bed and opened the curtains. Gorgeous
sunshine and a clear blue sky. Jack's proposition was more
interesting than doing housework indoors, even if she'd have
to forego her lie-in.

OK then

That didn't sound very enthusiastic. She sent Jack a follow-up
message:

Sounds fun

Jack replied:

Excellent. See you in 30 minutes in the
courtyard. Bring a water bottle and walking boots.
I'll sort out the rest.

'So you're going to be more Captain Jack than Professor Jack?'
    Jack smiled. 'Yes, I suppose so.'
    Today's trip had turned out to be additional research for
Jack's new book. Em had assumed it was another academic
text on 19th-century shipping, but it was on a more
mainstream topic. 'My agent suggested we do something

commercial. So we pitched British Pirates to a few television production companies. I spent this spring recording a 2-part documentary, and now I'm finishing editing the book, so it's ready to come out when the programme airs next spring.'

She looked at him curiously as he drove across Dartmoor, heading for their first stop, Littleham.

'Stop trying to picture me with black eyeshadow and long hair,' Jack said.

Was she that easy to read? 'A head scarf might suit you. And if you ever want to borrow my eyeliner, just ask.'

'Good to see that you're your usual happy self again.' He smiled.

'Sorry about last night.'

'No need to apologise. I'm glad you can be yourself with me.' He kept his eyes on the road.

'Thanks for coming to my defence. I don't think I said thank you properly last night.'

'That's ok. But I was worried that the woman with her phone out had recognised me.'

Em unlocked her phone. 'You're not trending on Twitter. I think you've got away with it.'

She turned her attention back to the roadmap on her lap. Jack had warned her that the data signal was patchy on the moor, so navigating the traditional way would be better than relying on the satnav.

She found Littleham slap bang in the middle of Dartmoor. ' If you're researching pirates, why are we going somewhere as far away from the sea as you can get in Devon?'

'Because that's where the other Em in my life at the moment was born.'

'Another Em?'

'This one's an Emma, and she's been dead for nearly 300 years, so no need to get jealous. There are some notes on her in the back of the map book.'

Em found a sheet of A4 lined paper filled with beautiful handwriting tucked between the final page and the book cover.

'Did you write this?'

'Yes.' He said with a hint of 'who else would've written it' in his tone.

'It's very neat. I didn't think anyone wrote by hand now.'

'Sometimes it's quicker than typing on the laptop, and I get fed up with staring at a screen all day.'

She read the first paragraph:

Emma Starling, 1688 to 1735, born in Littleham, Dartmoor. Killed by the British Navy in the Caribbean on board the Black Dragon.

'You've spoilt the ending,' Em said.

'I might write it differently in the book. Thank you for the tip.' Jack laughed.

'I thought women weren't allowed on ships. Something about them being bad luck or a distraction for the male crew members?'

'Where did you learn that?' Jack sounded surprised.

Em was going to have to fess up now. Lucy's dossier had mentioned that one of Jack's TV series was on Netflix. Em hadn't been able to resist checking it out. She'd enjoyed watching him on screen. He was a very engaging presenter. 'I may have watched a documentary by a certain Professor Carver.'

'Did you? You didn't mention it.'

'I didn't want to make you big-headed.'

'It's true that having a woman on board ship was generally frowned upon, but there were some women who did go to sea. If you'd watched the next episode, you'd have learnt that.'

'I was saving that excitement for another day.'

Jack grinned. 'They either disguised themselves as men or,

like Emma, paid their crew generously, which had the remarkable effect of dispelling any superstitions.'

They turned down a track marked 'Private' which went uphill for about half a mile. As they reached the top of the hill, a ruined house came into view in a valley all on its own. Jack parked the car on the side of the track, away from the building.

'What a shame it's been abandoned. It's beautiful here.' Em got out of the car and looked around. There were no other signs of habitation in sight.

'I thought you'd like it. I was here in the spring, but it was raining the whole time. I want to get some sunny photos for the book.'

They put on their walking boots, Jack grabbed his rucksack from the car, and they headed towards the house.

'How long has it been ruined?' Em asked.

'It's been abandoned several times in its history. The first time was when Emma was widowed. That's why she became a pirate. Her husband was killed in a fight about gambling debts. He left her penniless. She didn't have many options for earning a living in the 18th century.'

'A better choice than selling your body, I suppose. Are you alright there?'

Jack was messing with the fancy camera he'd pulled from his rucksack. She looked over his shoulder.

'I want more detail in the brickwork, but it's coming out as a solid black shadow,' he complained.

'You need to use exposure compensation.'

'I have no idea what that means.'

'Can I try?'

Jack passed the camera to her. It was the same make as the one she'd used at college. It should be easy to get the setup right for what Jack wanted. She twisted a couple of dials, then took a photo. Right first time. She showed him the result.

Jack looked impressed. 'That's exactly the effect I was aiming for.'

'Don't sound so surprised. I studied photography as part of my art degree. I think one from that angle would work well,' she said, pointing to the opposite side of the building.

'Over to you, Annie Leibovitz.' Jack smiled as he sat on an exposed rock while Em took several more photos. She even managed to sneak a couple of candid shots of him relaxing with the house in the background.

Em looked at the tree on the top of the hill. If she could get in a position so that it framed the house, it would make a stunning image. 'I'm just going up here,' she said, heading uphill.

'Ok,' he shouted back.

Em walked up the slope and over the brow of the hill. She lay down in a hollow just over the crest. The sun was in exactly the right place to emphasise the textures of the ruined walls, and the tree was in the ideal location. Click. She looked at the result on the back of the camera. Perfect.

She rolled onto her back to get up and came face to face with a large sheep with curly horns, glaring aggressively at her. Sheep weren't aggressive, were they? Judging by a large amount of flesh dangling between its rear legs, it was a ram. It started pawing the ground. Surely only bulls did that? *Stay calm. Wave your hand, and it will go away.*

It didn't. Instead, the ram took a step closer, staring even harder at Em if that was possible. Why did she have to encounter a stroppy herbivore today? She looked around. There weren't any loose branches or rocks she could throw to distract it. She would have to ask for help to get out of this situation.

'Jack!' Em shouted. The noise didn't faze the ram.

'Yes,' she heard him reply in the distance.

'You know you said I didn't do the damsel in distress

thing.'

'Yes?'

His voice was getting nearer, thank god.

'I am now. Help!'

'I'm coming. What's wrong?'

'An animal has cornered me. It must have sneaked up on me while I was concentrating on taking a photo.'

'What the hell ....? ' Jack crested the hill, out of breath from running and stopped dead in his tracks.

'Seriously? It's just a sheep. I thought you were about to be mauled by the Beast of Dartmoor.'

'There's a beast here?'

'Most likely not. Don't worry about that now. '

Em tried to edge back up the slope of the hollow without turning her back on it.

Jack started waving his arms and walking towards the ram. It looked at him impassively for a second or two, then decided they weren't worth the effort. As it ambled off towards the next hill, Em breathed a sigh of relief. *Get a grip, woman. Jack's going to think you're flaky.*

'It's gone now. Come here.' He helped her upright. 'You're shaking.'

'Sorry, it surprised me, that's all. '

He pulled her into a hug, stroking her back. She buried her head in his chest, the few chest hairs sticking over the top of his shirt tickling her forehead. She felt safe now and ever so slightly turned on.

'You're still breathing fast,' he said.

'It takes me a while to get back to normal when I've had a shock.' *Especially with you in close proximity*. She started to pull away from him. 'I'll be fine now.'

Their eyes met. She felt a desperate urge to kiss him. *Stop it - friends only, remember!*

'Shall we head for the coast? No sheep there,' he smiled

reassuringly.

25

Em ordered roast beef for her pub lunch.

'You're not tempted by the lamb, then?' Jack asked with a mischievous look.

'I wouldn't worry about that demonic ram ending up on the butcher's slab, but I prefer beef.' She changed the subject. 'Nancy said your mother's visiting us for a few days next week.' Nancy had been excited about the prospect of her best friend coming to stay.

'Yes, that will seem odd. It's been years since we were both here together.'

'Do you get on with your mum?'

'Yes, she's brilliant. Always on the go. She got bored when she retired, so she's taken up loads of new hobbies and good causes. I barely see her. She was a great mother when my sister and I were growing up. She still is.'

Em was slightly nervous at the prospect of meeting Olivia. *She's not going to be your mother-in-law, so why do you care?*

'Do you see much of your sister?' Jack hadn't mentioned having a sibling before.

'Not now. She lives in Edinburgh with her husband and children. I've not had a chance to see her for a long time. But we were really close when we were teenagers. We supported one another when my father left us.'

'I didn't realise.' Nancy had only ever mentioned Olivia and nothing about Jack's dad, so Em had assumed he'd passed away.

Jack went quiet for a moment. 'He had an affair when I was 12. I have a feeling it wasn't the first time, either. My mother kicked him out.'

'That must've been difficult.'

'It was, and it wasn't. He used to be a barrister. He worked long hours. We never saw him in the week. He left for work before we got up every morning, and he came home after we'd gone to bed. Then he was out on the golf course at weekends. So I wasn't that close to him. My mother was upset, obviously. That was the hardest part. Seeing her cry and not being able to do anything about it. Though she hid it well most of the time.' He looked so sad for a moment that Em thought he was going to cry. 'My father lives in France now with the woman he ran off with. He bought himself a rundown chateau to do up. The last time I saw him was at my wedding. What about your parents?'

Em wasn't sure what to say. 'My dad's a swinger, and my mum was a controlling narcissistic bitch' would be an accurate description, but she felt she needed to know Jack better before she revealed all the skeletons in the family cupboard.

She settled on, 'They stayed together until my mum passed away two years ago.'

'I'm so sorry. I didn't realise you'd lost your mother. Was it sudden?'

Normally Em brushed the subject away. But she wanted Jack to understand what it had been like.

'She had a stroke out of the blue. I suppose they usually are.' It was hard finding the right words. 'I was working in London at the time. I'd been there since uni. But it was unfair to expect Dad to cope with her alone. I'm an only child. She refused to have a carer. She was a difficult woman at the best of times, so I moved back to Birmingham to help him. And then a year later, she had another stroke, and that was that.' She stopped herself from admitting that that final stroke had been a relief, that she'd cried at her mother's bedside in the hospital, but they were tears of relief, not grief. Anyone who hadn't been subjected to years of mental abuse had difficulty understanding that.

'How did you feel about moving back home?'

'It was a struggle. She expected us to wait on her hand and foot. She wasn't grateful for any help at all. Not that I was expecting much gratitude. But it's difficult caring for someone who doesn't appreciate what you're doing and who has no concern for your well-being, particularly when they're your mother.'

'Not all mothers are loving and caring.'

What a relief that he understood that. Not everyone did. 'I thought it was something I was doing wrong. That I wasn't loveable.' *Don't cry.* She took a deep breath and looked away.

'Did she appear to be the perfect mother to everyone else?'

Jack really did get it.

'Oh yes, she put on a great act when we were with other people. Not my dad. But anyone else - family and friends. Not that she had many friends - not that stuck around anyway.'

Jack looked thoughtful. 'How was she with your dad?'

Something about his demeanour made her want to open up. 'Dismissive. Bullying. Controlling. Same as she was with me.'

'But he stayed with her?'

'Yes. He thought she would get better, back to the person he fell in love with. But she didn't. So many years wasted.'

Jack looked like he was debating what to say next.

Eventually, he broke the silence, 'Your mother sounds a lot like Isabella. She changed from being a loving girlfriend to someone else entirely on our honeymoon.'

'What happened?'

He started drumming the table nervously with his fingers. 'She flirted with one of the waiters at our hotel - more than flirted. I went for a swim one afternoon while she took a nap. I realised I'd forgotten my towel, and when I went back to our room to get it, they were kissing passionately. If I'd arrived a few minutes later, who knows what they'd have been doing.'

'On your honeymoon? Seriously?' Poor Jack.

'Yes. I haven't shared that with anyone else before.'

'Because she told you it was all your fault?'

It was Jack's turn to look relieved that he was being understood. 'Yes. I'd been coming on to the woman on the Reception desk, apparently. But I hadn't.'

'I believe you.'

'Thank you.'

Em was going to ask more, but the waitress arrived with their food.

'Enough about me. How did you end up in the call centre?' Jack asked when they were alone again.

'I wasn't prepared to give up my independence entirely. I hadn't been able to save any money in London, and I needed to have some escape from the house. So I looked for a part-time job. I wanted to carry on being a graphic designer - that's what I'd been doing since I left art school, and I loved it - but there was nothing available. So the call centre was a stopgap. One that turned into a three-year-long stopgap.' Oh no. That crying sensation again. She turned to look out the window so Jack wouldn't see.

'This was meant to be a trip out to cheer you up, and so far, a sheep has terrorised you, I've bored you with the sorry tale of my marriage, and I've made you revisit a traumatic time in your life. I'm sorry. I should stick to ships.'

Em laughed. 'Perhaps we should change the subject completely.'

26

Ominous black clouds had rolled in from the sea while Jack and Em were finishing their lunch, and now huge raindrops were starting to hit the promenade where they were standing.

'I'm sorry. I left my umbrella in the car,' said Jack. The car park was five minutes walk away.

Em looked at the building across the road. 'We could have a look at the aquarium?'

'Good idea. I haven't been in there since I was a child.'

They ran inside as the downpour started. There wasn't a queue.

Jack walked up to the counter. 'Two adults, please.'

'Any concessions?' The woman at the till was slowly chewing gum, looking bored.

'Are you over 60, dear?' Jack asked Em.

'No, I've just had a hard week.'

'No, then.' He turned back to the woman, who gave him a look as if she would love to say "You think you're so bloody funny, but I've heard it all before".

'What do I owe you?' Em asked as Jack handed her a ticket.

'Nothing. You pay for drinks afterwards if you like.'

It was only a small aquarium. They looked at some seahorses bobbing around. And then a big tube containing jellyfish. There was a lobster that barely moved. Then they rounded a corner into another room and saw an octopus.

'Awww!' said Em. 'I always feel sorry for octopuses in captivity.'

'This one looks like it's got a big tank.'

'I know, but they're supposed to be incredibly intelligent. It can't be much fun having people stare at you all day.'

'Would you prefer we turned our backs on it then?' Jack suggested.

'No. It would be even ruder to ignore the poor thing. I wonder if this one waves?'

'Waves?'

'Yes, there's one in a zoo somewhere that waves at her keeper. I can't remember where she is, though.' Em tentatively waved at the octopus. It just stared back at her impassively.

'He thinks you're mad.'

'How do you know it's a he?'

'It's those patches on its head. Only male octopuses have those,' said Jack, very seriously.

'Blimey, you know so much.'

He chuckled.

'It says it on the sign, doesn't it?' Em laughed. 'I am so gullible!'

'Sorry, I couldn't resist.'

'Lucy and I have this phrase we use "Be more octopus".'

'Why?'

Em explained about the rock-throwing octopus.

'So you and Lucy preferred to throw rocks at annoying boys?'

'Only metaphorically,' she laughed. 'We didn't want to get detention.'

'What did you do instead?'

'We used a few sharp elbows or knees to the groin area. It

worked in the end. They soon moved on to pestering this poor girl called Amanda instead. But, I suspect that was because she grew tits before everyone else.'

'We never did that sort of thing at my school.'

'I suppose you were much better behaved at private school?'

'No, there was no one of the opposite sex to gawp at. Which is why girls were a mystery to me. Still are a lot of the time. I spent my formative years admiring them from afar on the bus. They were terrifying, the way they constantly flicked their hair and never stopped talking.'

'You're not terrified of us now, are you?'

'Some of you. Perhaps not you, though, except when you've got a vacuum cleaner in your hand.' That cheeky grin again.

'You're never going to let me forget that, are you?' Em could feel herself blushing.

'You've traumatised me. I will never be able to hoover again,' said Jack, dramatically. 'And I like to remind you every now and again because blushing suits you.'

Is he flirting with you?

She didn't get a chance to find out. A crowd of cub scouts charged into the room, bustling past them to get to the octopus, which decided that now would be a good time to squeeze behind a rock.

'Shall we head outside again?' Jack shouted so Em could hear him over the noise.

She nodded.

27

There was a silver Mercedes' soft top in front of the main house when Em and Jack got back from their day trip.

'Nancy didn't say she was having visitors today. '

'That's my mother's car.' Jack smiled.

'I thought she wasn't coming until Tuesday?' said Em.

'So did I. But she is very spontaneous. It looks like she changed her plans. Let's go and say hello.'

As they walked into the main house, Em could hear women's voices laughing and talking in the kitchen. She recognised Nancy's. The other higher voice must be Olivia.

'Jack!' A glamorous-looking woman with white hair in a classic Marilyn Monroe style and a fifties circle skirt dress to match got down from a stool by the island and opened her arms wide. She must be Nancy's age, but she seemed much younger.

'Mother!' Jack went in for a hug.

Olivia stood back and looked her son up and down. 'You've got some colour in your cheeks again.' She looked delighted. 'And you've put on weight.'

'Not too much, I hope.'

'No. You look just right. Your clothes fit you properly again. You'd lost so much weight you looked like a skeleton. I knew you weren't eating properly.'

Em looked at Jack. Olivia was right. Em hadn't noticed the change, but he had filled out slightly since that first day.

'You make it sound like I was at death's door.'

'Oh, darling. I'm so pleased.'

'The Devon air must suit you, Jack.' Nancy had stopped cooking. 'And the company.' She looked pointedly at Em.

'Mother, this is Emily. Em's an artist, and she helps Nancy with the holiday lets when she's not painting. '

That was a lovely way to introduce you. Even Em's inner voice sounded positive today.

Oliva turned her dazzling smile on Em.

'I'm so pleased to meet you at last. Nancy has been singing your praises ever since you arrived here.'

It was Em's turn for a hug. Olivia squashed her against her ample chest, nearly suffocating her in a cloud of Chanel No 5, then stood back to look her up and down too.

'You look lovely as well.'

Em wasn't sure her jeans and strappy top were that lovely, especially after a day on the road, but at least Jack's mother seemed to like her.

'Will you join us for dinner? Nancy's making her amazing paella. There's enough for everyone, isn't there, Nancy?'

'Of course. You must eat with us. You can tell us all about what you and Jack have been doing today. ' Nancy seemed equally as enthusiastic about Em joining them.

'We did have a big Sunday lunch earlier,' Jack said, looking at Em. It looked like he was trying to read her body language to decide how to respond to the invite, or perhaps he hoped she'd say no.

'But we could just have a small portion of paella for dinner?' Em looked at Jack.

He smiled. 'Yes, let's do that.'

She'd given the correct answer, then.

'Have I got time to freshen up, Nancy?' Em asked.

'Yes, dinner will be ready in 20 minutes.'

Em arrived back in the house just as Nancy was serving the paella.

'I was about to send Jack to get you,' Nancy said.

'Sorry - I lost track of time.' That wasn't entirely true. After a quick shower, she'd spent the little time she had left trying on different outfits.

She settled on a floral sundress which she hadn't worn for ages. It seemed more appropriate for a meal in Nancy's grand dining room than jeans and a T-shirt.

Jack noticed the dress. 'That's pretty. I haven't seen you in a dress before. It suits you.'

'Thanks. I fancied a change from jeans.'

'So, tell me all about your art,' Olivia said. 'Nancy sent me a photo of her portrait. It's excellent.'

'Thank you. I've got several pieces I'm working on currently. A couple of landscapes that I'm hoping the gallery in the village will be interested in. And then there's Jack's portrait, of course. We haven't completely settled on the background for that, have we?' she said, trying to bring Jack into the conversation, so it was less of an interrogation.

'I assumed it would be in your office, darling,' Olivia said, not giving Jack a chance to answer. 'Though perhaps that's not such a good idea at the moment with you know who around.'

'Em knows about Isabella.' Jack shifted uncomfortably in his chair.

Olivia hesitated for a moment. 'She came to see me the other day. I'll talk to you about it later.'

Jack looked even more worried now. 'You can tell me in front of Nancy and Em.'

'If you're sure.' Olivia didn't look entirely convinced. 'She begged me to tell you she wants to get back together. She told me how sorry she was about what had happened. That it was a misunderstanding.' Olivia kept glancing at Em to see how she was reacting. Em concentrated on her meal, feeling very awkward. 'I told her I didn't trust her, and neither did you now. I asked her to leave you alone. I hope that was ok.'

'Yes, thank you. I've got to go back to London for a few days next week. I'm hoping she won't pounce on me.' Em pricked up her ears at that. He hadn't mentioned a London trip to her. But then why would he?

'Is she expecting you?' Olivia looked concerned.

'It's a summer school. I've got to deliver a couple of lectures, that's all. It's not a public event, so she shouldn't know anything about it.'

'You can stop in my London flat,' Nancy offered. 'She's never been there, so hopefully she won't find you, in case she's got someone watching your flat or your mother's house. I wouldn't be surprised if she has.'

Em didn't know Nancy had a London home as well. Surely she hadn't kept the one where she'd found her husband dead in bed? Em kept her head down, thinking her thoughts must be written all over her face.

'When are your lectures?' Nancy asked Jack.

'Monday afternoon and Tuesday all day. I'll come back on Tuesday evening or possibly Wednesday morning.'

'Excellent. Why don't you take Em? She could take some photos of you in your office. That might help you decide on your portrait background. And you were talking about seeing some exhibitions, weren't you, Em.'

Em had mentioned going to the Summer Exhibition at the Royal Academy, but that was weeks ago. Nancy remembered everything. But the bigger issue was spending a large chunk of two days with Jack. She was getting more attracted to him than ever. She wasn't sure she could trust herself alone with him. She imagined what Lucy would say when she told her. Something along the lines of 'Get in there and take your best lingerie'. 'I'm sure Jack will want to be on his own, and I've work to do here as well.'

'Nonsense. I'm sure he'd love to have you there. It's a big flat with three bedrooms, so he can still have peace and quiet to work on his book. And you needn't worry about the work here. No one's booked the extra maid service that week, and I can keep on top of the admin while you're away. So that's decided then. More wine, anybody?'

'It would be lovely if you came with me. But only if you want to,' Jack said, looking at Em kindly.

Should she say yes? She was supposed to be making a fresh start and having new experiences, after all. 'I haven't been to London since I moved back to Birmingham four years ago.'

Olivia looked horrified. 'You poor girl. Then you absolutely must go. I can't imagine being away from town for that long. I love it here, but I don't know how Nancy spends so long in such a sleepy location. I would die being in Dashford for any length of time. I need London's energy and vibrancy to keep me alive.'

'Not everyone thinks that way, Mother. Some of us enjoy the tranquillity.'

Olivia laughed. 'You take after your father. He is a country bumpkin at heart. That's why he's ended up in the middle of nowhere with that red-faced milkmaid of a woman.'

'My stepmother's family owns half of Oxfordshire,' Jack said to Em, smiling. 'I don't think she's spent too many early mornings in a milking parlour, just in case my mother gave you a different impression.'

Olivia looked disapproving and changed the subject, 'So what are we doing to keep us occupied tomorrow, Nancy dear?'

Having turned down dessert, Em and Jack left Nancy and Olivia deciding between wild swimming or driving to Penzance for a helicopter ride to the Isles of Scilly. 'They'll never settle for a nice cup of tea and a scone at a country house, will they?' Em looked amused as she and Jack walked across the courtyard in the twilight.

'Only if it involved learning to sword fight or abseiling down a castle wall.' He laughed.

'I hope I'm like them when I retire.'

Jack smiled. 'I hope you're a bit calmer than that. I don't think I could cope otherwise.'

An interesting thing to say. He must've realised how it sounded because he was definitely slightly redder in the face than he had been a few seconds earlier.

'Blushing suits you too, Jack.' Em said as she waved him good night.

'There you go then. He's thinking about the two of you growing old together.' Lucy could barely hide her excitement when Em updated her via FaceTime later.

'Thinking about it and doing something to make it happen are two entirely different things.'

'You're not feigning disinterest any more, I notice.'

'No, I admit I'm attracted to him. And the more time I spend with him, the more I realise he might be my ideal man. I've never felt that before.'

'There must be something wrong with him?'

'Oh great. The minute I say I'm interested, you start looking for reasons to slag him off.'

'No, it's just he can't be perfect. No one is.'

'My only issue is his reluctance to do anything about it.'

'I can understand him being reluctant to make a move in Devon when Nancy is pushing him in your direction. But we'll see how long he can resist you when it's just the two of you in London. Have you got any decent lingerie?'

'I knew you were going to say that. I'm not going to throw myself at him. I'm just going to enjoy the trip, and if anything comes of it, so be it. Technically, he is still married, remember.'

'But he's trying not to be! And it's not as if he's playing the "my wife doesn't understand me" card while the wronged wife sits oblivious at home. Olivia and Nancy both think she's a nasty piece of work as well. Anyway, how's his portrait coming along? Based on your previous experience painting a fit man, you might not have to wait until the London trip to get some action.'

Em didn't want to think about that. 'Let's stop talking about Jack. How's the slagging off the stag weekend planning going?

'It's all in hand. Nothing for you to worry about. Only two weeks to go!'

28

'We need to decide what you're going to wear.' Em was standing in Jack's living room, clutching her sketchbook and pencil case to her chest in readiness for the first sitting for his portrait. She was ever so slightly on edge at the prospect of drawing him, knowing it would feel more intimate than casually spending time together.

'I thought what I've got on now.' Jack stood opposite her in the chinos he'd worn when they first met. But today, he'd teamed them with a dark blue cotton shirt. 'It's what I usually wear. Is it smart enough?'

Em hesitated.

'Or do you think I should put a suit on?'

'I've never seen you in a suit.' Em wasn't sure she'd like to draw him in formal wear. He wouldn't look like her Jack. *Your Jack! For god's sake, he isn't anywhere near being your Jack.*

'I only wear suits to weddings or funerals or the occasional work event. Or there's my academic gown? Impractical thing. I'd need to wear a suit with that. I'll have to pick them up from home when we're in London.'

'Stick with what you're wearing. Except I prefer your light blue shirt. It brings out the colour of your eyes better.'

'Does it make that much difference?'

'Yes, it does. The colours you wear reflect off your skin. They can make a massive difference to how you look, particularly what you wear close to your face.'

He seems reluctant to get changed. 'I think that shirt needs ironing.'

'It doesn't matter. I'm just going to do some rough sketches. I won't draw the creases.'

'I bow to your greater knowledge,' he said, bounding upstairs.

Em looked around the living room working out where she was going to ask him to sit. There were a few personal touches that he'd added, presumably to make the cottage feel more like home. A model of the Countess Genevieve sat on the windowsill above his desk. And there were several piles of books: one by the side of his desk and a couple more next to the coffee table. They were all leather-bound hardbacks, several of them with gilt edges. They looked Victorian or older. Post-it notes stuck out from the edges of most of them. He must be referring to them for his writing.

Jack reappeared in Em's favourite shirt. 'Better?'

'Much.' Em felt mesmerised by his bright blue eyes. *Say something, or he's going to think you're weird again.*

'Are you ok with sitting on that dining chair if we put it by the window?'

'Yes. I'll move it.' He picked up the heavy wooden chair and carried it easily across the room. 'Here?'

'Perfect.'

'I suppose I'll need to keep still?' he said as he sat down.

'Not this time. I'm just doing some exploratory sketches today.' Em picked up her drawing pad and made herself comfortable on the sofa. 'I'll ask you to keep changing your position every few minutes so that I can work out the best pose.'

'This is my best side,' Jack moved slightly on the chair.

She looked up to see if he was joking or not. Most people did have a best side, but they had no idea what it was. Had Jack been studying himself in the mirror? He hadn't struck her as vain.

He must've sensed she thought it was an unusual thing to say. 'So I've been told,' he said.

'Who told you?' Em was curious now.

'One of the crew when we were filming the great ships documentary. I've no idea whether that's true or not. I hate watching myself on screen.'

Not vain, then, thank God. 'Let's see, shall we.' Em started to draw.

After a minute or two, Jack started tapping his knee with his fingers. He seemed nervous. Perhaps he'd picked up on her feelings. Though now she had her pencil in her hand, she'd started to relax. Maybe he was just bored.

'Are you alright, Jack?'

'Yes. I guess I feel on edge with you studying me in detail.'

Em hadn't expected that at all. He normally exuded a quiet confidence.

She tried reassuring him. 'If I appear to be staring, I'm only looking for light and shadow. You're just a series of lines and shapes to me when I'm in the zone.'

'I'm not sure how to take that. It feels like you're looking into my soul.' He laughed nervously.

What was he worried about her seeing? How did he want her to see him? Better not ask that. It could all get intense very quickly. She remembered the hot Argentinian. Moving Jack into a pose where he wasn't looking directly at her might help. 'Can you swing around about 45 degrees to your left? Focus on that painting on the wall.'

Jack followed Em's instructions, but he was soon drumming his fingers again.

What could she talk to him about that would distract him

in a good way? 'How did you become a television presenter?' she asked.

'A production company asked my old professor to write and present a documentary, but he didn't have time. He suggested me instead. I wasn't particularly interested, but I'd just finished my PhD, and I needed the money, so I agreed to do a test shoot. Apparently, I came over rather well. And the rest is history.' He grinned at her.

Em groaned. 'If anyone ever suggests you do standup comedy, say no.'

At least he'd relaxed now. But not for long. He started to look pensive.

'Are you uncomfortable?' Em asked. 'You can move again if you want.'

'It's not that. I was thinking that if I'd said no, I would never have met Isabella. Funny how one quick decision can have a massive impact on one's life.'

'How did you meet Isabella?' It wasn't a question that would make him relax, but Em had been looking for an opportunity to find out.

'At the television production company offices. They were throwing a party - their tenth year in business or something similar. Isabella was a guest too. She was going out with one of their directors. She made a beeline for me. She told me how she loved watching my documentaries. She asked if I'd give her a personal tour of the Maritime Museum. So we exchanged numbers, and a couple of days later, that's what I did. '

'Is she interested in ships?'

'No. Not at all. But I didn't know that then. She fooled me into thinking she was. She hung on my every word. I was flattered. I fell for her. We exchanged lots of texts. Went out for a meal. The following weekend she turned up on my doorstep saying she'd left her boyfriend and asking if I could

I give her a bed for the night. We were rarely apart after that.'

He was still looking thoughtful.

'Can you move again, please?' Em asked.

Jack turned. He was looking directly at Em now. 'Is this ok?'

'Yes,' she said.

She started drawing him on a new sheet of paper. His look was soft, almost appreciative. Em found it incredibly sexy. She began to feel uncomfortable in an 'I want to walk over to you and tear all your clothes off right now' sort of way. More memories of the hot Argentinian came flooding back. Jack looked away for a moment.

'Tell me how you met Connor,' he said.

Talking about Connor was the last thing Em wanted to do, but at least it would break the sexual tension. Had Jack done that deliberately?

'It was at a work colleague's wedding in Birmingham. I almost didn't go. I knew I'd be the only one without a partner there. But it was either that or sitting at home with my parents, so I dragged myself out. And I had a good time until the end of the evening.' She realised she'd stopped drawing. Jack was watching her closely again.

'The slow music came on, and everyone coupled up except me. I was sitting on my own at a table. And then, a drunk Connor appeared and asked me to dance.'

She hesitated. She'd made it sound more romantic than it actually was. 'Well, what he actually said was, 'Don't sit there on your own looking miserable. You may as well be miserable with me.' Quite prophetic, as it turned out. I found out later his girlfriend had walked out on him about ten minutes earlier. She'd caught him by the toilets touching up one of the bridesmaids. There's a lovely moment on the wedding video where you can see her in the background slapping him across the face. Anyway, I took him up on his chivalrous offer. And you know the rest.'

'You deserve better than that.' Jack was still looking at her intently.

'Thank you,' she said. 'You're right. One quick decision can have a massive impact on your life.' She sighed. 'I think I've done all I need to for now. Shall we call it a day?'

29

That afternoon a text distracted Em from the landscape she was painting in her living room. It was from Jack.

    I'm cooking chilli tonight. Do you want to
join me for dinner? 6.30?

A microwave ready meal on her own or Jack's home cooking with Jack for company? Normally, it would be no contest, but after the morning's intense portrait session, was going around to Jack's again a good idea? Probably not, but sod it.

    Yes, please. I'll bring wine.

Jack replied immediately:

    Excellent. There's a new detective series
starting on Netflix today if you want to watch it
afterwards?

Em sent a thumbs-up. She laughed and texted Lucy.

Having a Netflix and Chilli session with Jack
tonight.

Em wasn't surprised to see Lucy reply straightaway:

Is that a typo?

Em:

Sadly not.

But it was still something to look forward to. Em relaxed back into her painting session.

Two hours later, she packed up her paints, took a shower to freshen up, put on her favourite perfume and headed over to Jack's.

'You're early,' he said as he opened the door.

'You said 6.30.'

'Did I? I meant 7.30. I'm sorry.'

'I can go back home. It's not as if it's a long journey.'

'No, please stay. As long as you don't mind the mess. I haven't finished tidying up yet.' He ushered her inside.

The living room didn't look that bad. A few books were open on the desk, several used mugs were on the coffee table, and the ironing board was in the centre of the room.

Jack must've seen her looking. 'I thought I better iron that blue shirt you liked ready for tomorrow's portrait session. I'll only be a couple of minutes.'

'You don't have to iron it on my account. I told you, I'm fine with the creases. I hate ironing.'

'I've never understood why anyone hates ironing. It's satisfying. You start with a crumpled shirt, and two minutes later, you've transformed it into a smart, smooth one.'

She hadn't got Jack down as an ironing enthusiast. Was

that even an attractive quality? As far as Em was concerned, there were better ways to spend your time. 'Two minutes? More like ten minutes, and by then, I've got rid of the original creases but added several more.'

'How on earth does it take ten minutes?'

'If I'm having a bad day, it can take 15,' Em laughed. 'You think it only takes you two minutes, but I bet it's a lot longer.'

'Is that a challenge?' he grinned at her and folded his arms.

'Do you want me to time you?'

'Ok then,' he said defiantly. He walked over to the ironing board and grabbed the shirt. 'Tell me when to start.'

Em got the stopwatch on her phone, not quite believing they were doing this. She imagined what Lucy would say, and it wasn't complimentary. 'Ready, steady, go.'

Jack sprang into action, starting with the underside of the collar. He soon moved on to the cuffs and sleeves, wielding the iron expertly across the fabric. 'How am I doing?' he asked as he ironed the back.

'One minute, 10 seconds so far.'

He worked on the shoulders next, then quickly moved on to the fronts. She had to admit, he seemed to have got the whole process down to a fine art.

'Ta-dah,' he said, putting the finished shirt on a hanger.

Em tutted and shook her head. 'Two minutes, four seconds.'

'What are four seconds between friends? At least it was nowhere near as long as ten minutes.'

'I'll let you off the extra four seconds if you've got all the creases out.' Em got up to inspect the finished shirt.

It was annoyingly perfect.

'Your turn,' he said, handing her another shirt from the wash basket.

'Is this just a ploy to get me to iron the rest of your shirts?'

'Why would I do that if I can do them five times faster?' he laughed. 'I'm just intrigued how it takes you so long to iron one shirt.'

He perched on the arm of the sofa to get a good view of the ironing board and got the stopwatch on his phone ready. '3, 2, 1, go.'

Em usually started with the shoulders, but, remembering Jack's technique, she tried the collar first. It was only slightly wrinkled, so this should be easy. Em ran the iron across it. Three new creases appeared around the stitching at the end of the collar. Jack winced. She moved the iron back over the collar, removing the new creases but introducing two more at the other end. She quickly flipped the shirt over so he wouldn't see them.

Em moved on to the sleeves, smoothing one onto the board with her hands. She ran the iron over it and turned it over. She'd created a massive crease on the back of the sleeve.

Jack turned the stopwatch off.

'I haven't finished yet,' Em objected.

'I can see how it takes 10 minutes now. It's painful to watch. Do you want me to teach you how to do it quicker?'

'Go on then.'

'Let's start with the collar where you added the extra creases.'

So he had noticed.

'Don't iron the whole collar in one movement. Start from the tip and gently stroke down.'

Was the double entendre deliberate? Or was it just her mind going to places it shouldn't? Em tried to follow his instructions, but she still made a new crease.

'You're rushing it. I'll show you,' Jack said, walking around to Em's side of the ironing board. He put his hand over hers on the iron and guided her. Em felt a warm glow all over that had nothing to do with the steam coming from the iron.

'Now we do the other side. Start at the tip and gently work

your way back again.' Please stop with the dirty talk. Her hormones were in overdrive now. How could ironing be such a turn-on?

Jack seemed flustered too. Or was she imagining that as well? 'Sleeves next,' he said.

'I'll just move to one side so I can watch exactly what you do.'

'Good idea.' He seemed grateful for the suggestion. Perhaps she hadn't imagined it then. 'I'll demo one, and you can do the other.'

As soon as he'd finished the sleeve, he left her in charge of the iron and returned to a safe distance on the arm of the sofa. He patiently talked her through ironing the rest of the shirt.

Em held up the finished article proudly. He was right. It was strangely satisfying when the end result was perfect.

'Do you want to do that again?' Jack asked.

Em resisted the temptation to say "yes but without the iron".

30

Em was walking to Jack's car the following morning when a text from Lucy arrived.

    How was your Netflix and Chilli session !?!!

There was no way Em was going to tell her about the ironing lesson. Lucy would be on the phone straight away if she did. The rest of the evening had been enjoyable but not in the way Lucy was thinking. Em and Jack seemed to have made an unspoken agreement to keep physically apart, sitting opposite one another at the dinner table and then watching the new Swedish crime drama from separate sofas. Em typed out a short reply.

    Nothing to report

She could see Jack strolling over to the car while she was texting. 'Hello, you. Busy?'

Em noticed his perfectly ironed shirt and started to feel hot again.

'Lucy's checking up on me.'

Off to the beach now for another portrait
session with Jack and the wreck. Speak later.

Jack and Em had agreed that featuring the wreck in his portrait made sense, given the important part it had played in Jack's career choice.

'No sketchbook?' asked Jack as they got into his car.

'No. Just photos this morning. This breeze will play havoc with the paper. And I thought you might feel self-conscious standing in a public place for a long time.'

'Thank you,' he said, easing the car into gear and setting off up the drive.

As soon as they'd parked in the harbour car park, Em headed towards the beach. Some children were playing around the wreck.

'Shall we go to Mary's while we wait for them to finish?' Jack asked.

'We could ask them to move?'

'No. Let them enjoy it. And the sun might come out soon.'

'I'm hoping it doesn't. It would cast strong shadows. They'd hide your handsome features.' *Why did you say that? You're supposed to be getting him to relax. Don't make it awkward again now!*

Jack raised his eyebrows.

'Light cloud cover is perfect for portraiture.' Em continued, hoping he'd forget about that last remark.

They headed back up the steps to the cafe.

'Nancy tells me that the grand unveiling of her portrait is all planned.' Jack sounded like he wanted to change the subject.

'Yes. She's got over 40 people on the guest list. She has given you your invite, hasn't she?'

'Yes. I'm on drink duties.'

'What does that involve?'

'Making sure everyone is kept topped up.'

'It seems a bit unfair to give you a job.'

'I don't mind. I don't know most of them, and the ones I do know will probably be amazed at how much I've grown. They always remember me as the cute little boy in short trousers, even though they've met me several times since then.'

'I'm sorry. If you want to be elsewhere, I can cover the drinks instead.'

'No, you can't. You're the star of the show. And I want to be there to support you.'

That was a relief. Apart from Nancy, Jack would be the only person Em knew at the party. When Nancy had shown her the guest list, there were a few names she'd recognised - people who'd popped into Dashford Grange for a chat with Nancy - but Em hadn't spoken to them except in a superficial 'Hello, nice to meet you' way.

'Thank you. I'd love you to be there. Most of them seem to have titles. It's intimidating.'

'Why? They're just human beings. They'll love you. We all do.'

'Do you?' *Why did you say that? You've made him feel awkward again!*

'Yes, we all do,' he said thoughtfully. 'I'll get some drinks.' He quickly strode into the cafe.

31

Monday morning. Em had packed her overnight suitcase ready for the trip to London last night. The train times were awkward, so Jack decided to drive.

'It's a long way - are you sure?' Em would have preferred to go by train. It would give them more opportunities to chat. Connor was not a big talker when he was driving on long journeys. She wondered if Jack would be the same. He'd been reasonably talkative on their day out the previous Sunday, but this trip was much longer.

'Yes, we can take a couple of breaks. I've done it plenty of times before.' Jack said, putting their luggage in the boot of his car.

It was sunny again. Em sneaked a look at Jack, looking cool behind the wheel in his shades as they pulled out of Dashford Grange's drive at 7.30 am.

'If the traffic's good, we should get to Nancy's flat in plenty of time for lunch. There's a little bistro that does tapas just around the corner. Will that suit you?' Jack asked.

'It sounds lovely, but is it safe to go out?'

'I don't think Isabella is planning to kidnap me. I hope not, anyway. '

By midday, they were driving through the outskirts of

London, and it wasn't long before the satnav announced they had arrived. Jack neatly parallel-parked on the street. He looked at his watch. 'Perfect. We've got more than enough time to unpack and get something to eat.'

Em looked up at the 1960s brutalist building which dominated the road. 'Is this it? I was expecting an old house conversion.'

'Nancy inherited the Grange, but this one she and Xander bought themselves. I think Xander wanted something more modern than the big house.'

A few minutes later, he was leading Em into Nancy's flat on the second floor. It was spacious and as expensively decorated as the house in Devon, though in mid-century sleek furniture in keeping with the architecture.

'Nancy has excellent taste,' said Em.

'This was more Xander's home than hers, though it was her family money that bought it.'

It must be the flat where Xander had died.

'You pick a bedroom.' Jack put their bags down in the hall. 'Let me know which one you want, and I'll put your case in there.'

Em hesitated. She didn't want to sleep in the bed where Xander had taken his last breaths. It might be best to avoid the biggest bedroom.

She inspected the first one. Small, with a double bed and not much else. A bit too cosy.

The next one had a king-size bed, a balcony with a fabulous view over the square, a freestanding bath and an ensuite shower room. It must be the bedroom where he had died, though how had someone handcuffed him to the plain fabric headboard?

Jack walked into the room. 'Nancy completely redecorated, including buying a new bed.'

'How did you know what I was thinking?'

'Because everyone who comes here for the first time looks like they're wondering about it.'

'I've never asked Nancy about Xander. Mary told me the gory details.'

'Mary takes great delight in telling everyone at the first opportunity. That's why Nancy let her go. She didn't want any more of her business spread around the village.'

'Nothing to do with dogs or soup tureens, then?'

'Those accidents didn't help, but they were just timely excuses.'

'It must've been awful.'

'Xander's demise? Nancy took it very well, apparently. She knew he was having affairs - she'd turned a blind eye to them for years. That part wasn't surprising, but she expected him to live longer. He didn't look like your typical heart attack victim. Mark was pretty upset, though.'

'I can imagine.' How awful must it have been to hear your father had died and learn that he had a kink at the same time? She imagined how she'd feel if her dad conked out at a swingers' night. *No, do not think about that!*

'You'll be fine in this room. It is the best one, and it isn't haunted, I promise. I've slept in here a few times,' he said. 'And there are aggressive sheep on the wall in the other one,' he whispered into her ear.

'Are you winding me up? No one has sheep on their wall unless they're three years old.'

'Apparently, they do. It's wallpapered with a rural scene featuring curly-horned rams repeated roughly every 12 inches. See for yourself.' He indicated the door across the corridor.

Em walked across the plush hall carpet and looked inside the final bedroom, expecting to see more plain walls. But he wasn't joking. Three walls were painted dark aubergine, but the wall behind the bed did have expensive-looking monochrome paper featuring realistic drawings of fields, cows, birds and, of course, the dreaded rams with expressions every bit as aggressive as her nemesis on Dartmoor. There were loads of them. The same pattern was on the curtains too. Their eyes seemed to follow her around the room.

Em took a sharp intake of breath.

'I did warn you,' Jack said, walking in and putting his suitcase on the bed.

'It looks like I'll have to take my chances with the ghost.'

'I'll be in here if you need me to help with any strange sensations in the night.' He looked away, appearing to be embarrassed by what he'd just said. 'You know what I mean.'

Jack had been right about the tapas bar. Their lunch was delicious. He insisted on paying and then suggested they head off to the Uni. 'You can take some photos in my office before the lecture.'

His office was only a couple of streets away in an imposing building that looked like it dated from the 1920s, judging by its Art Deco entrance doors.

'I'm on the third floor,' Jack said as they entered the foyer. 'Stairs or lift?'

The rickety metal lift doors looked as if they were as old as the building. They didn't fill Em with confidence. 'The stairs will be fine,' she said, heading up the wide stone staircase.

'A wise decision,' Jack said, following her.

His office was at the end of a long, narrow corridor. The office was long and narrow too. One wall was lined with packed bookshelves. A few oversized volumes were shoved on their side on top of the other neatly vertical books. Jack's desk was clear except for one unruly pile of paperwork. Em looked around the rest of the room. Near the door, there was a small round table with a few mismatched chairs, presumably for his meetings with students.

It had a distinctive smell which wasn't unpleasant: a mix of the mustiness of old books and a reassuringly familiar hint of Jack's aftershave. Not surprising, considering it must have been shut up for several weeks.

But Em's main concern was how gloomy it was, despite the tall window and the bright sunshine outside.

Jack must have thought the same. He pulled the blind up further to let in more light. 'That's better. Let's get some fresh air in as well.'

He opened the window. The sound of traffic was suddenly overwhelming.

'How do you work in here in the summer? It's so noisy!' Em asked. The piercing siren of a passing emergency vehicle emphasised her point.

'Peaceful rural Devon has spoiled us. That's why it seems so loud. Once I've been back a few days, I won't notice it any more.'

Had London been this noisy when she lived here before? 'I guess I'm missing Dashford already.'

'You're turning into a country bumpkin, as my mother would say. Not that that's a bad thing.'

'I thought I'd like to live in a big city again, but now I'm not so sure. I suppose you have to live in a city if you're a professor.'

'Not all universities are in the middle of big cities. I guess I've got into the habit of working here. But I could move if I needed to.'

What did that mean? He tore his eyes away from her and looked at his watch. 'We've only got 15 minutes before I have to head to my lecture.'

'Let's get on with it then.'

Jack had brought his professional camera for Em to use. She quickly got it out of its case, cleaned the lens and changed a few settings. She held her hand up and moved around the office, looking at her palm.

Jack looked bemused. 'Is this some weird ritual?'

'Yes, I'm summoning the gods to bless your portrait,' she laughed. 'Or I could just be checking how the light is casting shadows so I can work out the best place for you to sit. It's more efficient than asking you to keep moving.'

He looked impressed.

'Let's try here.' Em moved his chair near to the window but far enough away to be out of the patch of direct sunlight. Jack sat down with the bookshelves behind him.

'No dodgy titles I need to move?' Em asked.

'No! Does that happen often?'

'You'd be surprised,' she said, remembering tidying her dad's bookshelves for the interview. 'If you could look outside.'

She took a couple of shots. 'Now look into the lens.'

He turned towards her again. Another click. She checked the photos she'd taken. Those intense blue eyes.

'Your collar's a bit wonky. I didn't notice until I saw it on the back of the camera.'

Jack attempted to correct it.

'No, still not quite right. I should've brought a mirror.'

'You better do it then,' he said.

Em put the camera down on the desk. Tidying his collar was going to bring her into the heart-stopping zone.

She leant in so she could reach. It would be so easy to move just a little closer and kiss him. *Stop behaving like a heroine in a Victorian novel. You'll be fainting next.* Perhaps it was the wine they'd had at lunchtime, but Jack seemed flustered by how close they were as well. She smoothed down the offending collar.

'Better?' he asked.

'Yes, perfect.'

They locked eyes just as the office door opened, breaking

the spell. A petite, neat-looking woman with short grey hair marched in. She did an unconvincing double-take worthy of a local amateur dramatics production.

'Oh, Jack. I didn't know you were here. I would've knocked otherwise.'

'Hi, Audrey. I wasn't expecting you to be in today.' Jack smiled at her, but his voice didn't match his expression.

'So I see.' Audrey looked like she was sucking a particularly sour lemon.

'Em, this is Audrey, our departmental administrator. Audrey, Em's painting my portrait.'

Audrey now looked as if she'd swallowed the lemon and was struggling not to regurgitate it.

'Of course she is.'

'Nice to meet you, Audrey.' Em gave the woman her best smile, realising too late that she still had her right hand on Jack's shoulder. She quickly offered it to Audrey. It seemed awkwardly formal. Audrey gave her the weakest handshake Em had ever experienced.

'I was returning this.' Audrey pulled a textbook from under her arm and squeezed it onto the nearest shelf. 'Have you been having a good summer break, Jack?'

'Yes, fine, thank you. I'm not back properly until September. How about you?'

'Good, thanks. We'll talk properly in September, then.' Audrey excused herself.

'Odd,' said Jack after Audrey closed the door behind herself.

'Is it?'

'Yes. That's not my book.'

32

'Been busy, I see?' Jack had just returned to Nancy's apartment after his lecture and a brief visit to his own flat to pick up any post. He leaned on the island between the kitchen and the dining room, watching Em make a pot of tea.

'Yes, I thought I'd make the most of the shops.' Em looked over at the pile of bags on the kitchen floor: books, art materials, and a new dress. Having a free afternoon in London had been too much temptation after the limited offerings of Dashford shops - the house deposit saving fund would have to wait this month.

And she'd taken Lucy's advice and treated herself to some new lingerie. After the looks she'd exchanged with Jack in his office earlier, he appeared to be having second thoughts about just being friends too. If she was right, she didn't want him running away at the sight of her functional, well-worn Marks & Sparks underwear.

'I thought you were going to the Summer Exhibition?'

'I didn't have enough time. I'll do that while you're lecturing tomorrow morning.'

Jack looked like he was debating whether to say something or not. Perhaps he disapproved of the mess.

'I'll put this lot in my room,' she said.

'No, no, it's fine.' He started drumming his fingers on the work surface. 'I um... I wonder if you would like to come with me to the cinema tonight?'

Considering they'd spent most of their evenings last week watching television together, she wondered why he was nervous about suggesting they go to see a film. *Perhaps he's treating this as a proper date?*

'They're showing a film about Mary Shelley. I thought you might enjoy it given your interest in early 19th-century women's literature.' Jack continued when Em didn't respond straight away. 'It was either that or Incredibles 2,' he added with a nervous laugh.

Full marks for remembering she'd been reading Jane Austen. 'That would be lovely. Mary Shelley, that is.'

He looked pleased.

The cinema was only a 10–minute walk away. Jack had mentioned that it did proper food and drinks so they could eat there as well, but he'd not said anything about the cosy two-seater sofas. He'd booked one on the back row too. It was looking like a date. Em sat down at one end of the sofa.

Lucy had texted her several times for an update on their trip. Em had time to reply just before they'd set out to the cinema. Lucy was ecstatic.

Mary Shelley had an affair with a married man. Jack's subtly trying to get you to do the same!

Em:

I don't think so. He's a historian. He probably watches this sort of film all the time. And what else are we going to do on a Monday evening?

Em wasn't quite ready to admit to Lucy that she hoped Jack would want to be more than friends this evening.

Lucy:

I can think of a few things - wink. And some steamy sex on the screen might get him in the mood to unfriend zone you.

Em:

It's a 12 certificate.

Lucy:

They're still allowed to include tasteful lovemaking.

Em hadn't thought about that. She wasn't sure how she'd feel watching the actors get their kit off with Jack next to her. There'd been none of that in the Nordic noir series they'd been watching together last week. But it was too late to suggest the Incredibles now.

'Food's on its way.' Jack handed her the mojito she'd ordered at the bar, then settled down next to her. The sofa wasn't big enough to allow them to sit together without their thighs touching. Not that she was complaining. It felt much more pleasant than the last male thigh that had been next to hers. Em shuddered at the memory of drunken Si that night in the pub garden.

Jack looked concerned. 'Sorry, it's a bit cosier than I remembered.'

He must have thought she was uncomfortable sitting this

close to him. To be fair, it wouldn't have been this cosy when he was sharing a sofa with stick-thin Isabella.

'I'm fine, honestly.'

'Are you cold?'

'A bit.' She'd put on jeans and a long-sleeved shirt to allow for the cooler evening, but the cinema's air conditioning was making the interior feel more like an icy winter's day.

'Here. Have my jumper.'

'But you'll be cold then.'

'No, I'll manage.' He gently helped her put it on.

'Thank you.'

'You look warmer already.'

'I am, thanks.' The glowing feeling from being enveloped in soft Jack-smelling wool had helped considerably.

Jack gave her another meaningful look just as the waiter arrived with their food. Lady Luck seemed determined to stop anything more from happening today.

Perhaps you ought to take the hint. No, Em wasn't giving up on Jack that easily.

Em stifled a sob. She didn't want Jack to see her getting emotional about the story on screen.

'Are you ok?' Jack whispered, putting a reassuring arm around her.

'It's just sad, that's all,' she whispered back. She took the opportunity to nestle into his shoulder to see how he reacted. He pulled her in closer. A good sign. *He is a hugger, so don't read too much into it.* In the darkness of the cinema, she closed her eyes, imagining it was just the two of them. She put her hand on his chest. She could feel his heart beating fast.

She opened her eyes again. Mary and Shelley were getting it on in the bedroom. She kept her eyes firmly on the screen. Jack seemed tense too. The camera panned away before things got steamy.

The conversation about Shelley's wife felt more awkward than she expected. And as the film progressed, the story became anything but romantic. Perhaps the Incredibles would have been a better choice after all.

As the credits rolled, Jack sat up. 'What did you think?'

'I enjoyed it. Thank you for suggesting it. How about you?'

'It certainly puts Frankenstein in context.'

'Do you want your jumper back?'

'No, It looks better on you,' he smiled.

He can take it off you when you get back to the flat. Her inner voice was starting to sound like Lucy. But Em wasn't sure she wanted it to go that far now. Seeing how the men in their lives treated Mary and her sister was enough to make retreating to a nunnery sound attractive. But she was being ridiculous - Jack wasn't a selfish Regency poet.

33

It was 9 pm when they left the cinema, but the road outside was still too busy to cross. Eventually, the traffic lights changed, and everything ground to a halt. Jack grabbed Em's hand and led her between the stationary vehicles to the opposite pavement. He kept her hand in his as they turned into the side street. It felt comforting.

Forget about the 19th century. This is 2018, and sleeping with Jack won't get you cast out of society. That would be Lucy's opinion. And her inner voice was right. Why not have some fun? But the effects of the mojito had worn off. She could do with some liquid courage to go through with it.

'Do you fancy a bottle of wine? We could see what that supermarket has?' Em nodded towards the brightly lit shop over the road.

Jack liked the idea. Five minutes later, they walked out of the shop, Jack carrying a bag containing some croissants for breakfast and a bottle of chilled Pinot Grigio. He suddenly stopped as they got to the kerb.

'Everything ok?' Em asked.

He bent down to whisper in her ear. 'That man over there. I'm sure he was in the cinema. Same row as us at the end by the exit. We had to walk past him to get out.'

Em casually glanced across the street. A man was standing with his back against some railings. He had his head down, looking at his phone. Nothing unusual there. 'Could be. Perhaps he's waiting for a lift?'

'Yes, probably. It's just I think I've seen him before. A while ago.'

'Where?'

'Leaving work, back in the winter. He followed me all the way home. I only realised he was still there when I was drawing the curtains. He was hanging around across the street. I had a break-in the following day.'

'And you think he did it? What did he take?'

'That's just it. Whoever it was rummaged through drawers and cupboards, but nothing was stolen. I reported it to the police. But they weren't particularly interested. They thought the intruder had probably been disturbed.'

'That's awful. He doesn't look sinister, though.' He was middle-aged, a bit tubby, and had short brown hair. He wore a plain grey t-shirt, jeans, and trainers. The only thing that stood out about him was the brown leather messenger bag slung over his shoulder.

'What are you expecting a thief to look like?' Jack whispered.

'I wasn't expecting him to have a striped jumper and a bag with swag written on it.' She could see by Jack's expression that he wasn't in the mood for humour. Em tried reassuring him. 'He just doesn't look desperate enough to be a burglar. And why's he here now? He can't be following you. He couldn't have known we'd be at the cinema. You haven't tweeted about it or anything?'

'No.' Jack still looked uncomfortable. 'I guess it's just a coincidence.' But he didn't look convinced.

They couldn't stand there all evening, but Jack seemed to be frozen to the spot. Em was going to have to take the initiative. 'Just in case, let's not lead him to Nancy's. We'll head back towards the cinema and see if he follows. And there are more people around on the main road.'

'Good thinking.'

'I'm a woman. Unfortunately, we have to think like that regularly. Perhaps not in Devon, but definitely in Birmingham and here.'

Jack put a protective arm around her shoulder. Em slipped her arm around his waist. If it weren't for their potential stalker, this would be enjoyable.

When they got to the corner of the street Em turned to look in a window.

Jack seemed baffled at Em's sudden interest in the mobility aids shop. 'Are you in the market for a Zimmer frame?'

'Look at the reflections.' Em whispered.

'Oh, I see. Where is he?'

'He's walking on the opposite pavement back towards the cinema. And now he's noticed we've stopped, he's slowing down.'

'He is following us.' Jack was spooked. 'What do we do?'

Em was feeling nervous as well now. 'We need to lose him.'

'How are we going to do that?'

A black cab pulled up right in front of them and a man got out. Perfect timing. Em dived inside. Jack followed her.

'Where to?' The taxi driver asked.

Jack hesitated.

Em filled the silence. 'King's Cross Station.'

Jack looked puzzled. 'That's in the opposite direction.'

'We need to lose him. It will be busy at King's Cross, even at this time of night. We can make sure he's not followed us, then get another cab back to Nancy's.'

'You've read too many thrillers,' Jack was trying to make light of the situation now, but his expression was still serious.

Em turned around to look out of the back window of the

cab. The man wasn't attempting to follow this time. But he was staring after them and talking on his phone.

Jack had said nothing on the taxi ride to King's Cross, nor during the journey back to Nancy's. He was still on edge as he opened the front door to the apartment building.

Em put her hand on his arm to get him to chill out. 'You can relax now. No one's followed us since we got in the taxi by the cinema.'

He took no notice. 'Stay here. I want to check everything's alright in the flat.'

He ran up the stairs two at a time. Em looked up the stairwell and watched him throw open the door to the flat as if he were expecting to surprise the stalker in the hallway.

'Looks ok.' He shouted down to Em. She followed him upstairs, shut the flat door behind her and walked into the living room. Jack was by the window, looking down at the street.

'No sign of him outside.' He pulled the curtains across the windows. 'I just want to check the bedrooms.'

It all felt over the top, like something from a spy film rather than real life. Em got a couple of wine glasses out of the kitchen cupboard. The Pinot Grigio might help relieve the tension.

'Everything alright?' She asked as he walked back into the living room.

Jack nodded. He sat down on the sofa and put his head in his hands.

'Jack, have you any idea who this man is?' Em put his glass of wine on the coffee table and sat beside him.

'No. That's why it's so unsettling. I don't understand why he's interested in me.'

'Perhaps he fancies you?' She gave him a nudge and a wink to try to break the tension.

'It's not funny,' Jack's expression clouded over. 'The last five years, I've lurched from one nightmare to another. I thought that was going to be over now.' He looked like he was on the verge of tears.

'Oh, Jack. I'm so sorry. I was only trying to lighten the atmosphere.' She stroked his back. 'Could it be something to do with Isabella?'

'Possibly.' He picked up the glass and swirled the wine around but he didn't drink any. 'I don't understand what, though. And why would she get someone to break into my flat?'

Em sat back and took a sip of her wine. Why would she do that? 'Are you sure nothing was taken? There was nothing there that could've been useful to her?'

'No, nothing. Just a load of books, my clothes, a few model ships - she hated those, and some old photos from the pre-Isabella days. It's all my stuff, not Isabella's. I've let her keep everything else.'

'We're just speculating, aren't we? There's nothing else we can do this evening.'

'No, you're right.' He was still nervous, though, drumming his fingers on the wine glass now. 'I'm just worried about what might happen next.'

'We're safe here tonight. You've checked there's no one else in the flat.'

'Someone could still get in.'

'How? We're on the second floor. I've bolted the front door.'

'Easy enough to climb up the balconies, break a window pane and open the window.'

'Only if you're as fit as James Bond. Our stalker looks like he'd get out of breath climbing a flight of stairs.'

'I'm still worried. If he's broken into my flat before, why wouldn't he try it here?'

'If it was him who broke in - and we don't know it was - he

did that while you were out. Would you be happier if we went to a hotel?'

'No, that seems extreme. You're right. We're fine here. But you've got the bedroom with the balcony, so perhaps I should sleep in there tonight? Can you manage with the sheep in my room?'

Em's hope that Jack would spend the night in her bed was about to come true, but not in the way she'd envisaged.

34

Em used the expensive bath foam she'd bought yesterday to fill the large bath in the main bedroom with citrus-scented bubbles. She lay back on the bath pillow and glanced across at the clock on the bedside table. 3.30 pm. Jack would be finishing his last lecture in half an hour. Her ankle was aching from walking to the Royal Academy and back this morning. Another 15 minutes or so of chilling out would help.

The water was starting to cool. She turned on the hot tap, enjoying the feeling of warmth that spread through the bath. But it wasn't just the warm water that was making her glow. She was remembering snuggling up to Jack in the cinema. If only that man hadn't followed them, she was sure the evening would have ended more romantically.

When they got up this morning, there was still no sign of the stalker. Jack seemed more relaxed, but he'd made her promise to ring the police straightaway if she suspected anyone was following her.

There was a knock at the door.

It was too early for Jack to be back. And he had a key, so why would he be knocking? What if it was the stalker? Perhaps she should ignore it.

Another knock, several, in fact. More insistent this time.

Whoever was trying to attract her attention was irritated. Hopefully, it was just a neighbour, as anyone else would have been ringing the bell downstairs. Or the stalker had somehow got in. She couldn't relax now.

Em got out of the bath, grabbed the huge towel, and wrapped it around herself. What if it was the stalker? She picked up her phone from the bedside table in case she needed to dial 999. She tentatively went out into the hallway and peered through the spy hole in the front door. A 30-something woman was standing in the corridor. She was slim, stylish and expensively dressed. Definitely not the stalker, and unlikely to be an axe murderer.

Em opened the door slightly, conscious she was naked under the towel.

'Hello?'

'Where's Jack?' The voice was upper class but harsh. The woman was the same height as Em but somehow managed to give the impression she was looking down her nose at her.

It suddenly dawned on Em who this woman was. The long blonde hair had thrown her. But if she imagined her with a mid-brown messy updo, she would be a match for the woman in Jack's wedding photo - Isabella. Em needed to buy time to work out what to do. 'Jack?'

'Yes, Professor Carver. I was told he was here.'

'Who told you that?'

'A friend.'

'Well, it's just me here.' It wasn't a lie. Jack was currently several streets away.

'And how long have you been here?' Isabella was looking her up and down disapprovingly.

Em ignored the question. 'My bath's getting cold. I'm sorry I can't help.' Em started to shut the door, but Isabella's reflexes were quick. She pressed her hand on the outside of the door and put her foot in the gap.

'I'm coming in.'

'No, you're not.' Em pushed back on the door, determined not to let Isabella into the flat.

'I want to see my husband.'

'But he's not here, so you need to leave NOW, or I will call the police.' Em pushed harder on the door, briefly trapping Isabella's foot before the pressure forced her to pull it away.

'How dare you,' Isabella shouted from the landing. 'I'll be suing you for grievous bodily harm. Tell Jack to phone me.'

Say nothing. Em leaned her back against the other side of the door listening for sounds of movement. There was no noise except the pounding of her heart for a few seconds then she heard the tap tap tap of Isabella's stilettos clipping along the tiled landing floor. They sounded regular. No damage to Isabella's foot then.

It seemed to take forever for the sound of Isabella's footsteps to die away. Had she really gone? Em wouldn't put it past her to have sneaked back barefoot. Em turned around and tentatively looked through the spy hole. All she could see was the empty hallway. She slipped the bolts across the door to be extra sure, then texted Jack.

35

'How has Isabella found out where I am? It must be the stalker. I guess he's a private detective.' Jack was sitting on the sofa in Nancy's apartment, looking shell-shocked.

'But how did she get through the communal front door?' Em asked

'That's easy. You can tailgate someone. Or press a few doorbells, say you're delivering something, and some helpful soul will let you in. I did it myself to surprise Mark when he lived here years ago.'

'Could Isabella have seen you at your flat yesterday?'

'I was only there long enough to pick up the post and check if the place was ok. I couldn't have been inside for more than 10 minutes. Unless she's got someone staking the place out 24/7?'

'Is that what our stalker was for?'

'But we shook him off before we got back here.'

'Could he have followed you home from the university yesterday?'

'Possibly. I was in a rush to get back. I wasn't paying much attention to my surroundings.' Jack looked thoughtful. 'But she can't be paying someone to watch my office every day on the off chance I'll come in. And the summer school schedule is only available to participants.'

'It's nothing to do with Audrey, is it?'

'Why do you say that?'

'You said she behaved strangely yesterday. And I could tell she didn't like the look of me. Could Isabella have persuaded Audrey to tip her off if you came back to your office?'

'Possibly. They were pally in a very one-sided way. Isabella was incredibly rude about her behind her back, but she liked to be charming to her face. She could have got Audrey to spy on me, I suppose. But Audrey doesn't know I'm staying here.'

'She doesn't have to. Audrey tells Isabella you're back. And Isabella gets her henchman to go to the Uni and wait for you to leave. Then he follows you to find out where you're staying.'

'Ok. But why did he follow us last night as well?'

'Perhaps she wanted to know whether you were with anyone? '

'Possibly.'

'Let's look on the bright side. At least that means he's not a psycho.'

'True. But your theory doesn't explain the break-in.'

'Perhaps that was a coincidence.'

'Possibly.' Jack looked thoughtful. 'Well, well done for getting rid of her.'

'I'm quite proud of myself for a change. Once upon a time, I'd have let her in.'

'Being more octopus?' Jack smiled.

'Yes, definitely being more octopus.'

'I know we were planning to eat out again tonight, but would you mind if we headed back to Devon now? I have a horrible feeling Isabella will be back.'

'Ok then.' Em tried to hide her disappointment, but Jack was right. 'But only if you promise to treat me to a burger at the motorway services instead.'

'It's a deal. You're a cheap date, Gillespie,' he laughed.

36

Wednesday lunchtime. Em had been trying to work on Jack's portrait now they had decided on the composition. They'd agreed not to use the photos from his office but to stick with the beach scene instead. But it was still a constant reminder of the events in London. In the end, she decided to focus on painting some of the cliffs in the background - they were less fiddly, so she didn't have to concentrate so hard.

Em's phone buzzed - a phone call from Lucy. Em could do with a chat.

'I've got five minutes between meetings.' Lucy said. 'I hope your radio silence for the last 36 hours is a good sign.'

'Not exactly.'

Em filled Lucy in on the stalker putting pay to any romance on Monday night and Isabella's visit on Tuesday, leading to her and Jack heading back to Devon earlier than planned.

'I can understand not wanting to wait around for Isabella to reappear. But surely he wanted to be with you when you got back home last night?'

'No. The traffic was awful. There was an accident on the motorway. We were both knackered after seven hours on the road. We hugged good night, and that was that.'

Lucy went quiet.

'Are you still there?'

'Yes, I'm just running through what you said, looking for clues that he still fancies you. He definitely said a date?'

'A cheap date. It's just a phrase. I don't know. I think it's just wishful thinking on my part. He's embroiled in all this mess, trying to extricate himself from his marriage. I don't think hooking up with another woman is high on his to-do list.'

'But he must be wondering when he'll get his next shag.'

'Not everyone has a sex drive as rampant as yours.'

'Men think about sex several times an hour. You want him to be thinking about getting naked with you, not someone else. You need to be more obvious. He's probably holding back because he thinks you're still getting over Connor.'

'I would have thought snuggling up to him in the cinema and holding hands whenever we had a chance was obvious enough?'

'Given that he's not been tearing your clothes off, no. Try kissing him.'

'What if he doesn't want to be kissed?'

'I don't mean snog his face off. A chaste peck on the cheek should be enough to show him you're interested.'

Em went back to her easel after Lucy's phone call. It was getting hot in the flat, and the paint was drying too quickly. She packed all her brushes and materials away. Lunch outside in the shade would be good. She headed to the garden with a sandwich and the crime novel she was keen to finish.

'Mind if I join you?' Jack walked towards her with a bundle of papers and a mug.

'Be my guest. What's all the paperwork?'

He sat down at the table and pulled a red pen out of his

pocket. 'I've finished the first edit on the laptop. I usually do the second one on paper. I spot more errors that way. Sorry, it's antisocial, but I wanted some fresh air.'

If Lucy were here, she'd say it was an excuse for him to be with Em, but she must stop thinking like Lucy. It was perfectly reasonable for Jack to want to work outside on a hot day without having a hidden agenda.

They both sat reading in companionable silence.

Ten minutes later, Em finished her book and put it on the table with a sigh.

Jack looked up. 'Good ending?'

'No - it was a bit of a cop-out. I was convinced there would be another twist in the final chapter, but it turned out to be the person I suspected in Chapter 3. You can borrow it if you like.'

'After that stunning review, I think I'll pass.'

'How are you getting on?'

'I've got to do another five pages to keep on schedule.'

'Do you want some tea?'

'That would be lovely. I could make us both one if you like?'

'No, you carry on with your editing.'

A few minutes later, she was back, carrying two mugs.

'Your phone buzzed while you were in the kitchen,' Jack said.

She checked it. A new text had arrived.

'Oh wow!' Em exclaimed

Jack looked up. 'Good news?'

'It's the owner of the gallery down by the harbour. He's asked me to bring some of my work in for him to look at.'

'You're a good artist. Don't sound so surprised.'

'It's just that I emailed him weeks ago and heard nothing. I assumed he wasn't interested.'

'Phil gets a lot of emails.'

Phil? How did Jack know that? 'Do you know him?' she asked.

'Yes. He's the same age as me. His family had a holiday home here when we were kids. He used to join Mark and me on the beach sometimes. I hadn't seen him for years until I walked past the gallery the other day. He lives down here permanently now. What's he asked you to show him?'

She read out the last part of the text message. ''Please bring three originals with you.' He says to phone for an appointment.'

'Have you got three you want to sell?'

'Yes, but they won't all fit in my car. I'll have to take some of the smaller ones.'

'Will they fit in my Volvo?'

'I guess so.'

'I haven't got any set plans this week. Book in with Phil, and I'll drive you down there.'

37

Phil had been keen to meet Em as soon as possible, so the following morning, she and Jack went down to the gallery before it opened to the public.

Phil put Em's canvases on easels and stood back to look at them. He didn't say anything. He moved closer, studying them in more detail. It was impossible to tell whether he was impressed or not. Em realised she was holding her breath.

He stood back again.

'These will sell easily,' he said, indicating the two paintings she'd made of Dashford seafront on a sunny day. 'People like a souvenir of their holiday. You've captured the late afternoon light perfectly. Vibrant, colourful. They are exactly what tourists like to take home to brighten their dreary city lives.'

Em nodded, dumbfounded that he wanted to sell any of them.

He moved in front of the stormy seascape. 'This one is excellent.'

Em had painted it when she first arrived. When she selected it yesterday, she could see she'd channelled all her frustrations with Connor into it. Not a good reminder. It was time to let it go.

'But I don't think it will sell now. It might work in the

winter. We get visitors who come here for the drama of the sea then. Big waves crashing on the shore. Dark, stormy skies. Bring it back in November; someone will buy it for Christmas. Have you got any prints or cards?'

'No, I've been concentrating on creating originals.'

'No matter. I can help with organising those. Always useful to have some cheaper items as well as originals.'

Phil went over to his desk and handed Em a clipboard with some A4 sheets on it. 'Here are my standard terms and conditions. I'll give you a few minutes to read through them. Then we can get you signed up.'

'I told you she was good.' Jack smiled at Phil.

Em and Jack walked back to the car with the stormy canvas.

'That went well,' Jack said.

'Did you do that for me?' Em asked.

'Do what?'

'Get me into Phil's gallery.'

'No, you did that for yourself.'

Em looked sceptical.

'Honestly. I bumped into Phil last week. We got talking, he showed me around the gallery, and I said your work would fit perfectly. He vaguely remembered getting an email from an Emily Gillespie. He said he gets offered a load of dross most of the time, so it's quite disheartening wading through his inbox. He promised to find your submission and see what he thought. That's all.'

'Thank you - for thinking of me.'

'I'm always thinking of you.' Jack looked uncomfortable. 'Sorry, that sounded creepy. But I like to help if I can.'

What had Lucy said? Be more obvious. They were close together now as Jack was opening the boot of the car. Em leant over and gave him a quick peck on the cheek. 'I appreciate it.'

That look again. It looked like Lucy was right. He was going to kiss her this time.

'Jack! Yoo-hoo! Jack! ' The unmistakable form of Mary came trotting across the car park towards them, waving a tea towel as if she needed to make herself any more visible.

'Sorry,' Jack whispered, turning towards Mary. 'Mary. What can I do for you?'

'Well, it's more what you could do for one of my customers,' she said. Jack closed the car boot as Mary sidled up to him and slipped her arm through his, trying to look appealing. 'He was asking about you just now. I think he's a fan. He wanted to know where the shipwreck was as he'd read about it in one of your books. Then he asked where he might find you as he'd like your autograph. I said you were stopping up at the big house for the summer, and he was bound to bump into you if he popped into the cafe a few times this week.'

'Good for business to have a repeat customer,' Em said.

'Yes, which is why I was wondering if you could keep away for a couple of days and perhaps pop in on Friday?'

'So you don't mind losing our business then?' Em laughed.

'He spends more than you two. He had the extra large full English this morning with two cappuccinos,' she said, emphasising the two.

Jack was looking uncomfortable. 'What did he look like?'

It dawned on Em why he was asking.

Mary shrugged. 'In his 30s. Lovely aftershave. Charming. Beautiful teeth.'

They weren't going to identify him from that description. 'Thin or tubby?' Em asked.

'Neither. He looked like he worked out.' Mary had a dreamy look. 'Hot, I'd say. And he had a fancy tiger tattooed on his arm.'

Jack relaxed. 'Not our friend from London then,' he said to

Em.

Mary looked interested, but Jack cut in before she could ask for more details.

'If the best way of supporting your business is drinking elsewhere, then Em and I will go to the Fisherman's Arms for coffee today.'

'And tomorrow?'

'And tomorrow,' he laughed.

Em was sitting opposite Jack inside the Fisherman's Arms, watching the raindrops bouncing off the tables outside. They'd gone for a walk on the beach after Mary's interruption, but it had started to drizzle before they got very far, so they had adjourned to the pub to wait for the storm to blow over.

Jack was stirring his coffee distractedly. Em looked across at him. He looked tense.

'You're miles away,' she said.

'No, I am very much here.'

'Are you wondering if the autograph hunter has anything to do with Isabella?'

'Possibly.' He put the spoon in the saucer and started tapping his fingers on the table. He was on edge. 'Do you miss Connor?'

Why was he suddenly asking about Connor? 'No, I haven't thought about him for weeks. I'm happy here. The happiest I've been for a long, long time.'

'So you're enjoying being single?'

'Yes. I can recommend it.' *Why did you say that? Don't let him get the idea that you want to stay single forever.* 'But I'm coming around to having someone special in my life again. What about you?'

He was looking at her intently now.

The waitress collected Em's empty cup. 'Would you like me

to get you another drink?'

Jack looked exasperated. 'No, thanks,' he answered before Em could say anything.

Em raised her eyebrows as the waitress walked away. 'I wouldn't have minded another cup.'

'I'm sorry. There's no peace here. Can we go back home? I'll make you some tea there,' he said.

They headed towards the door. It was still pouring with rain.

Em hesitated in the doorway. 'We're going to get soaked.'

Jack had sensibly bought a jacket with him. He took it off and held it over his head. 'Under here,' he said.

They ran together across the road to the car. He kept the coat over Em as he opened the passenger door so she could get in, and then he hurried round to the driver's side.

Jack pulled out of the space and headed back up the hill.

'To answer your question,' he said, smiling across at her as they reached the edge of the village, 'I do want to have someone special in my life again.'

38

They spent the rest of the journey in silence, Em pondering what to do next.

Jack parked in his usual spot in the courtyard. 'Shall we do another portrait session now?' He suggested.

Em had enough sketches and photos to work from, but after their conversation earlier, she wasn't going to turn down an opportunity to be alone with Jack. 'Yes, that would be good.'

They got out of the car and retrieved Em's canvas out of the boot.

'Jack! Jack! I've got something for you,' shouted Nancy walking across the courtyard and waving a large envelope.

'All the local women are after you today.' Em teased him.

Nancy was next to them now. 'There's a letter for you. A man dropped it off just now. Feels quite chunky.'

'Probably your autograph hunter,' Em said to Jack.

'Autograph hunter?' Nancy sounded interested.

'Mary said someone was looking for Jack earlier. What did this man look like?' she asked Nancy.

'Early 30s. Looked like he spent a lot of time in the gym. Tiger tattoo on his arm.'

Jack peeled back the flap on the envelope. There were lots

of sheets of paper inside. 'I better open it properly indoors,' he said, heading towards his cottage.

'I'll get my sketch pad. I'll be over in a few minutes.'

Jack looked furious when he opened the door to Em a few minutes later. 'She's accusing us of adultery.'

'What?' Em said as she followed him into the living room.

'Isabella. She's accusing you and me of having an affair. Look.' He handed her a set of photos blown up to A4 size.

Em leafed through the photos, amazed. They were all from their London trip.

Jack holding her hand as they crossed the road outside the cinema.

Jack and Em with their arms around one another as they walked away from the supermarket on Monday evening.

The stalker must have had a camera in his messenger bag. She carried on looking through the prints.

The next one showed both of them loading their overnight bags into Jack's car on Tuesday evening. There were several more of those. Jack had been teasing her about the amount of stuff she'd bought. They were standing very close to one another and laughing. Em had to admit they looked pretty loved up.

There was even a fuzzy photo of Em wrapped in the bath towel near the bedroom window, taken from across the road.

She didn't know what to say for a moment. 'Apart from the fact that we haven't done anything, I didn't think anyone played the adultery card now. You didn't do it to her.'

'I could have done if I hadn't been foolish enough to take her back. And it's one thing finding me in London, but how does she know I am stopping here?'

'I guess her private detective found out who owned the flat we were staying in. A quick look at the land registry records would reveal that. Isabella recognised Nancy's name and guessed you might be stopping here.'

'Then my tattooed fan took the opportunity to talk to Mary to confirm I was at the house to save himself a wasted journey up here to deliver the papers.' Jack sighed.

Em looked at the solicitor's letter printed on expensive paper with an embossed logo and hand signed with what looked like fountain pen ink. 'This must be costing Isabella a fortune.'

'She has deep pockets, or rather Daddy does. He never hid his dislike of me. He'd have much preferred her to marry some high-flying banker. I can imagine that if she went to him pleading for help to divorce me, he would be more than happy to oblige.'

'On a positive note, at least she wants to divorce you now.'

'But on her terms, with me painted as the evil, cheating, manipulative husband.' Jack was reading through the petition documents. It sounded as if Isabella had gone to town with her claims. 'I haven't responded to her pleas for forgiveness, so now she's turned nasty. At least she hasn't put your name on the divorce documents.'

'I'm surprised. She didn't exactly take to me when we met.'

'It makes things more complicated to name the co-respondent these days. I asked my solicitor when I first talked to her about divorce.'

He started putting the photos and the letter back in the envelope, but something was stopping them from sliding to the end. He looked inside and pulled out a small envelope. He turned it over. It had his first name handwritten on the front.

'What's that?' Em asked.

'I don't know, but it's Isabella's handwriting.' He roughly tore it open. A small black and white photo fell out onto the floor. He picked it up and looked at it.

He went ashen. 'Fuck!'

Em had never heard him swear before. 'What's wrong?'

'Can we leave the portrait sitting for now? I need to digest all of this.'

'Shall I put the kettle on?'

'No, thanks. I need to be on my own, please.'

39

Why had the photo spooked Jack so much? Em couldn't stop thinking about it all day.

It was nearly 8 pm now, and she still hadn't seen or heard from him.

Time for a text.

```
Fancy a walk before it gets dark?
```

He was usually eager for an excuse to get some fresh air when he'd been inside all day. He responded straight away.

```
No thanks
```

Disappointing. Then she saw the three dots appear

```
Sorry - can we talk?
```

At least he was engaging now.

```
Yes, please. Here or at yours?
```

Three dots again.

```
I'll come to you.
```

She looked out of the window to see him already walking across the courtyard. He was running up the steps as she opened her front door.

'Hello, you.' Only a half smile this evening.

'Are you alright?' Em asked as he walked in.

'Hmmm. Can I defer answering that one?'

'Is it the photo from Isabella?' She knew it must be, but she was hoping to coax him into talking about it.

'Yes. There was a handwritten note with it too. I've been obsessing about it all day. I tried to do some editing to take my mind off it, but I failed miserably. I'm sure the chapter I finished will need redoing.' He sat on the sofa, tipped his head back against the cushions and closed his eyes. His stomach rumbled loudly.

Poor Jack. 'When did you last eat?'

'I don't know. Breakfast, I guess.'

'We could go up to the Kingfisher? I've already eaten, but you could still have something.' Perhaps he'd be more relaxed after a meal and a drink.

'No, better not.'

What did that mean? 'Do you want me to cook you something?'

He didn't respond. She was expecting some teasing about her culinary skills, at least.

'I have leftover lasagne that Nancy gave me. I could microwave it?'

'Yes. I better eat something. Thank you. Sorry, I should've brought a bottle of wine with me. We ought to be celebrating your gallery success.'

'There's some in the fridge. You sort out a couple of glasses while I heat through your lasagne.'

Giving him something to do might take his mind off

whatever was bothering him. Jack followed her into the kitchen.

'I'm sorry for being so dismissive this morning. I was just so shocked by Isabella's latest move.' Jack handed her a glass.

'What has she done?'

'Stolen an old photo of me from when I was a student.'

'I don't understand.' Why would a photo from that long ago make Jack so upset?

'She or her private detective must have taken it from my flat.'

'That was what the break-in was for?'

'It would appear so. It was in an envelope of photos. That's why I never noticed it was missing. The envelope with the rest of the photos is still there.'

'Couldn't you take her to court for breaking and entering?'

'I don't know. She's banking on me not wanting that photograph to become public.' He took a deep breath and looked at Em warily. 'It's me in a compromising situation. She must've been through my things when we were living together. I'd completely forgotten it existed. Otherwise, I'd have destroyed it years ago. She's threatening to send it to the university vice-chancellor.'

Em's imagination was running riot now. Did he have some weird fetish? Had he robbed a bank? Or worse? It was amazing how many images could flash through your mind in only a second or two. Jack put her out of her misery.

'I'm snorting a line of coke.'

What a relief. Not legal, but not that unusual for a student either. 'Is that all? But I thought you didn't do drugs?' They'd had that conversation in the car on the long journey to London.

'I don't. But I did experiment when I first went up to Oxford. I didn't enjoy it. That's why I've never done anything since.'

'But why have you got a photo of you doing it?'

'One of my flatmates was a photographer. She took loads of photos documenting our first year at Uni. She was still shooting on film - digital cameras weren't good enough then. She used to turn our bathroom into a temporary dark room and do all her own developing and printing. She gave me a set of prints. I put my favourites in an album. Not that photo, obviously. It stayed in the envelope with a few others, and I forgot all about it.'

'Why would the vice-chancellor be bothered about something that happened that long ago? There are even government ministers who've admitted to doing coke.'

'She's vehemently anti-drugs. And she's put me in charge of a campaign to cut drug use on campus.'

'So Isabella thinks it might ruin your career prospects?'

'Yes.'

'And will it?'

'I don't know. I wasn't honest when the VC discussed the job with me.'

'Did she ask you outright whether you had taken drugs?'

'Yes, and stupidly I said no. It wouldn't be an issue if I'd owned up to it. Now she'll know I've lied and wonder what else I've not been honest about. It's not a sackable offence, but she might think twice about getting me to do other high-profile projects.'

'What do you have to do to stop Isabella from sharing the photo?'

'Agree to accept my unreasonable behaviour as the grounds for the divorce, so she comes out of it all blame-free.'

'I guess you've got no choice then.'

'I do have a choice. I can tell her where to go. Enough is enough. If she goes through with her threat, I'll survive. And if she doesn't consent to a divorce, I will get one eventually. It just means I will have to wait a lot longer. What I'm more worried about is what she'll do next. I don't want you to get hurt.'

'What could she do to me? She's only spoken to me for a few moments?'

'I don't know. But she's very creative when she wants to be vindictive. She's given up on trying to win me back. Now she's moved on to inflicting maximum pain as punishment for me not complying with her wishes. '

Em could understand that. She'd seen her mother punish her dad enough times for less serious rebellions than wanting a divorce.

Jack started drumming his fingers on the table. 'Look, I don't really want to suggest this, but I think we shouldn't be seen together. Not until this is all sorted out. She probably still has her spies out looking for us, and if she hasn't, she will have once she reads my response.'

'Have you sent it?'

'No. I was in the middle of writing it when you texted. I'm going to go back now and finish it. I'll email it to her solicitor so we can get this sorted as soon as possible.'

'But if she refuses, it could be years.'

'I know. I'm hoping I'll think of something to persuade her.'

40

Em sat on her sofa when Jack left. What an up-and-down sort of a day. Gallery representation, at last, a glimmer of hope that Jack wanted to be more than friends and now this. She topped up her wine glass and downed it in one.

She needed Lucy's advice. She picked up her phone, found Lucy's contact details and selected video call. No response. She poured another glass of wine and turned on the television.

Her phone rang an hour later.

'Hi, Luce.'

'You're slurring your words. Are you drunk?'

'Slightly.' Em looked at the empty wine bottle on the table. Apart from the glass Jack had had, she'd drunk it all. There were just a few sips left in her glass now. She slid it out of sight of the camera.

'That's not like you. What's happened?'

'Isabella.' She updated Lucy on the day's events.

'But if she doesn't agree, it will take five years before he's divorced. Is he expecting you to wait that long?'

'I don't think so. I'm not even sure he's expecting me to wait at all. I'm so confused. One minute he looks like he's about to make a move on me, and the next ... oh, I don't know what he wants.'

'Vag teaser.'

'What?'

'Jack. He's a vag teaser. Gets you turned on and then runs a mile without delivering the goods.'

'He's just trying to be considerate. I think. Or maybe I've been misreading the signals.'

Did she honestly believe that? Those intense looks. The snuggling up together in the cinema. They'd have all led to a passionate session in bed if it had been Connor doling them out. And then there was the way they looked together in the photos that Isabella had kindly provided.

'Good job we've got your slag off the stag weekend tomorrow. You can escape from Jack and his nightmare wife and have some proper fun with us girls. Sounds like you've got two men to forget about now.'

'No, only one. I realised Connor was a waste of space weeks ago.'

'Thank god for that. I could've told you that at the start.'

'Why didn't you?'

'You seemed happy with him. What would you have said if I had?'

'Probably told you to mind your own business.'

'There you go then.'

'Do you think Jack's a waste of space?'

'He hasn't endeared himself to me this week. But he is going through the mill emotionally. I'll let you know when I have met him in person.'

Em faintly heard a man's voice coming from somewhere in Lucy's flat. 'Darling, are you coming back to bed?'

'Sorry, I should've asked if you were busy.'

'I didn't want to mention Lars, given what you're going through.'

'Still with Lars? How many dates is that now?'

'I've not been counting.'

'I better leave you to it.'

'Only if you're ok.'

'I'll be fine. Honestly. See you tomorrow afternoon.' Em smiled and waved as she ended the call.

She would be fine. A weekend of madness with her besties, miles away from Jack, was just what she needed. She only had to get through the next 16 hours, and then they'd be off.

41

The following morning Em threw herself into getting all her chores done. She'd tried starting a new series of paintings last night when she couldn't sleep. But the results were shaping up to be the sort of stormy pictures that Phil had been less keen on. Today, packing for the weekend away and sorting out the guest changeover was keeping her occupied.

She walked into the kitchen, carrying a pile of laundry.

Nancy looked thoughtfully at her. 'Have you got a moment? I want to talk to you about Jack.'

She patted the stool next to her at the island. 'He's told me about the photos and Isabella. I want to make sure you're ok?'

'I'm fine. Why wouldn't I be?'

Nancy raised her eyebrows. 'You two have become such good friends over the last few weeks. And now you're not bothered that he's decided ignoring you is a good idea?'

What was there to say? Whatever she said would no doubt get back to Jack.

'I'd prefer it if he weren't avoiding me, but it's not as if we've fallen out. And I'm away this weekend anyway.'

'I thought you might be upset?'

'You don't approve of his approach?'

'No, I don't. That's what Isabella wants him to do, in my

176

opinion. She's isolating him from his friends again, and she's not even here. I've told him life is too short. I'm glad you're away this weekend. It might make him rethink things if he's wondering what you're up to.'

'I'm not sure what you mean.'

'He cares about you. He doesn't want to lose you.'

'Did he say that?' Em hoped she didn't sound too excited at the prospect.

'No, but I can tell from the way he talks about you.'

So this could just be Nancy matchmaking again.

'Perhaps a bit of distance would be good for both of us.'

Em let herself into the empty cottage. Just this one to clean and prep, and then she could finish getting ready for her non-hen do weekend. She went upstairs and opened all the windows to let some fresh air in.

While she was putting clean linen on the main bed, she heard Jack's voice outside. 'I know I said I wouldn't come back to London yet, but this changes everything. I don't want you to be on your own.' He sounded worried. Em couldn't hear anyone reply. It must be a phone conversation.

Em tried not to listen, but he was speaking so loudly that it was difficult not to hear what he was saying. He must be standing right under the window.

'A fresh start would be good.' Another silence, then, 'Yes, you're right. I get why you don't want to fight anymore. Fighting's hard work. I think we can agree on that. '

Another gap.

'I've got to go. Are you sure you'll be ok until I get back home?'

Em was frozen to the spot. Home?

'I've missed you too. I'll see you very soon. Love you.'

Love you? Jack didn't usually say love you. Relax! He could have been talking to his mother. Em could hear footsteps on the gravel, then Nancy's voice. 'I've just been speaking to Olivia. I can't believe it.'

So his mother had been on the phone to Nancy, not Jack.

'Bit of a surprise after everything,' he said.

'Jack - I hope this is the right thing to do.' Nancy said.

'So do I, Nancy. So do I.'

'When are you leaving?'

Their voices were fading now. They must be walking over to Jack's cottage or the main house. Em moved nearer to the window and looked out. They were in the middle of the courtyard now.

'After Em's left for her hen do. Don't say anything to her. I don't want her to worry about Isabella and me.'

Em moved away from the window in case they saw her. What would make her worry about Jack and Isabella? Oh god - he was going back to Isabella. After everything he'd been through, he'd given in again. Jack, don't be so stupid.

She needed to know for sure, but how would she find out if she wasn't supposed to be seen with Jack? Though, surely that rule didn't apply now Isabella and Jack were a couple again.

Sod it. Em quickly finished upstairs and went outside. She marched across the courtyard and knocked on Jack's door. It took him a while to answer.

He didn't look pleased to see her. 'Em. I thought you'd be packing for Newquay?''

'I should be, but I realised I'd forgotten to give you clean towels this morning. '

He looked puzzled. 'I picked them up from the kitchen like I normally do. I've got a few things I need to finish. I'll pop outside and wave you off when your friends turn up.' He started to close the door.

Jack was shutting her out of his life already. Charming! 'I'll see you later, then.' she said as she walked off.

42

Em stood in the courtyard with her overnight case, waiting for Lucy and her friends to arrive.

'Hello, you.'

Em's heart skipped a beat. *For God's sake, you've not even looked at him.* She turned in the direction of the familiar voice.

'I know you said you wanted to wave me off, but I thought we weren't supposed to be seen anywhere near one another,' she said, wondering if that would get him to reveal anything.

'I just wanted to wish you a good journey. That's allowed, isn't it?'

'You tell me. You're the one who set the rules.'

The words came out more harshly than Em had intended. Jack looked uncomfortable.

'Sorry,' Em said. 'I don't want to fall out with you. I've had a busy day. A weekend away with my friends will do me good. The minibus will be here any minute. Lucy's just texted me.'

'Ok.' He still looked worried.

'What are you doing this weekend?' Em asked.

'I haven't got anything special planned.'

Apart from moving back in with your wife. Should she challenge him about it? The minibus turned into the drive and screeched to a halt. Six giggling women spilt out. No chance to ask him now.

'Are you Jack? Lucy's told us all about you,' said Sylvie, never backwards at coming forward.

'Has she?' Jack looked at Em.

'Let me introduce you.' Em said hurriedly. 'This is Sylvie. She used to work in the call centre with me.'

'And I'm still there.' Sylvie sighed. She turned to Em. 'Cheryl's gone, though. It's much better without her. I'll tell you all the goss later.'

'Neema and Lydia shared a flat with me at Uni. Freya and I used to work together in London. Charlotte is an old school friend. And this is Lucy, who probably needs no introduction by now.'

'Pleased to meet you at last, Jack.' Lucy was leaning casually on the minibus, weighing him up.

'What about me?' Ella got out of the driver's seat. 'Hello, Jack.' Ella put on her best sultry voice, offering her hand for Jack to kiss, which he obligingly did.

'And this is Ella, who is engaged to Sam, Connor's best mate. She's meant to be the sober one. '

'I am the sober one. Not a drop has passed my lips, which is more than can be said for the rest of them. They've got through half the weekend's alcohol supplies already. You've got some catching up to do, Em.'

'It's been a long journey,' Charlotte said. 'The traffic's been awful.'

Ella rolled her eyes. 'How would you know? You slept through most of it!'

Jack was charming. 'Lovely to meet you all. I hope you're going to look after Em.'

'Of course we are.' Lucy hugged Em. 'I've planned some very genteel activities for our non-hen do. We've got a private chef cooking us dinner tonight, a relaxing yoga session, some pampering, we're going to learn how to basketweave, and then we'll finish each day with an early night with mugs of cocoa. '

'Is that so?' Jack looked amused, if not entirely convinced. 'That sounds delightful.'

'Absolutely,' Lucy grinned. 'Nothing to worry about at all.'

'Have fun,' he said as he loaded Em's bag into the minibus. 'Let me know how you get on. I've heard basket weaving can be very strenuous.'

'Come on, Em!' Sylvie yelled from the minibus. They were all back on board now. 'We have drinking to get on with.'

'I better go,' Em said.

'Take care. I'll miss you.'

Did that mean this weekend or forever? Em felt her chest tighten. 'I'll miss you too.' She better get on the bus before she said something about Isabella.

They all waved as Ella drove out of the drive. Em's last view of Jack was him wincing as the bus narrowly missed the gatepost.

'What are we doing then?' Em was sitting next to Lucy on the minibus as Ella manoeuvred it back onto the main road. She needed something to take her mind off Jack. Lucy handed her a copy of the plan.

Em glanced through the list of activities. 'We really are doing basket weaving?'

'Yep. Everything I told Jack was true, apart from the early nights. I was Googling how to host the perfect hen party, and it recommended a relaxing creative activity for the last morning after the excesses of Saturday night. A delightful lady teaches basket weaving in the village hall just down the lane from our cottage, which means Ella doesn't have to drive until we head home in the evening. Perfect!'

Lucy went through the rest of the list.

'Tonight, our personal chef is cooking dinner for us at the cottage.

'Tomorrow morning, we're easing ourselves gently into the day with some yoga in the garden or the conservatory if it rains.

'Then we've got a beauty therapy team visiting us for an afternoon of pampering ready for our Saturday evening out.

'Dinner at an Italian restaurant. I know we said Indian but Sylvie doesn't do spicy. Followed by a night club. Lots of hot surfer dudes in Newquay. You might get lucky there.

'Basket weaving to keep us amused on Sunday morning, followed by a late lunch at the village pub, and then we head home, dropping Freya and Lydia off in Bristol so they can catch the train back to London from there. Will that do?'

'Superb - thank you so much.' Em hugged Lucy. 'You're the best non-maid of honour a non-bride could have. I'm going to enjoy this weekend so much.'

'You deserve it after what that shithead did.' Sylvie wasn't pulling any punches.

'Sam's had to cancel Connor's stag do,' Ella shouted from the front of the bus. 'Connor reckons he can't afford it. He's pretty pissed that we're still going away.'

Em laughed. 'What a shame. I'm sure he'll be spending the weekend consoling himself with fondling Astra's nipple piercings.' Why had she said that? She would have to sandpaper her eyeballs to get that image out of her head.

'I'm not sure everything's ok between those two.' Ella continued. 'There was a weird atmosphere when we went out with them last weekend. Not exactly frosty, but I could tell something wasn't right. You never know. You might be able to win him back.'

Em looked disgusted at the prospect.

'We need to find you another man to take your mind off it,' said Neema.

'What about Jack?' Sylvie gave Em a wink. 'I wouldn't kick him out of bed for eating crackers.'

'Jack's not available,' Em said.

Lucy raised her eyebrows.

'It's true. There are limpet mines that are less clingy than the current Mrs Carver. He's moving back in with her.'

43

Lucy had surpassed herself. The AirBnB cottage she'd booked was more like a manor house, with five huge bedrooms, a large garden which led down to the dunes and beautiful furniture. Em was thrilled. 'How can we afford this?'

'It was a new listing. I think the owner was desperate to get some bookings. I didn't mention it was a hen party.'

'Technically, it's not now.'

After much discussion about who snored (Freya), who insisted on getting up at 6 am to go for a run (Charlotte) and who couldn't possibly share with anyone else because they had restless legs (Neema, though the rest of them thought it was just a ploy to get exclusive use of the best en suite), they'd finally agreed who was sleeping in each room. Em was in with Lucy, which suited both of them.

Em lay on her side of the double bed and sighed, relaxing into the soft mattress. It was bliss. No one to clean up after, no admin to do and no worrying about Jack. Stop it. She had made a pact with herself not to think about him all weekend.

Lucy was busy unpacking. 'I know you said you didn't want to talk about Jack, but I just wanted to say he has a certain charisma. I can see why you fancy him.'

'You could tell all that from your two-minute encounter earlier?'

'Yes. I always trust my instincts. Just a pity he's going back to his wife. Are you absolutely certain about that?'

'I overheard him telling Nancy earlier.'

'How long do you think that will last?'

'I don't know. But I wish he'd told me. Im going to miss him.'

'Oh, Em.' Lucy hugged her. 'And I thought this weekend was about forgetting Connor.'

'I know how to pick them, don't I!'

'You're no worse than the rest of us.' Lucy looked thoughtful.

'Is everything alright with Lars?'

'Yes. That's just it. It feels too good to be true.'

'Are you scared it's getting serious?'

'Possibly.' Lucy laughed.

'What's he doing this weekend?

'Catching up on his sleep, hopefully. He's spent the whole week at mine.'

'Were you holding him prisoner?' Em grinned.

'No. I let him go to work in between shags.'

They heard a vehicle pull up on the drive.

'I'll go.' Lucy seemed keen to get downstairs quickly.

Em lay thinking about what Lucy had said about Lars and, of course, Jack.

'Our chef has arrived,' Lucy shouted up the stairs. 'He wants to run the menu by you, Em.'

She could hear giggles from her fellow non-hens. Up to something, obviously.

'Coming!' Em yelled.

The sight that greeted her at the foot of the stairs was an interesting one. Their chef was at least six foot four, square-jawed, with mid-brown wavy hair neatly combed back and deep brown eyes. He looked as if he spent all his spare time in the gym. He was sporting a white chef's hat and a full-length apron but, judging by the reflection in the mirror behind him, he wasn't wearing anything else.

'Karl, at your service.' He smiled and bowed his head.

'Hi, Karl.' Em had a fixed grin on her face. 'Lucy. Can I have a word?'

'I'll be in the kitchen if you need me.' Karl gave her a come hither look as the other women trooped after him offering help.

'I thought we agreed no strippers,' she whispered to Lucy.

'Technically, he isn't a stripper. '

'He's stark bollock naked under that apron.'

'Yeah, but he didn't strip. He arrived like that.'

'Isn't it a health and safety issue, cooking naked?'

'I don't think he does much cooking. He only reheats things. Anyway, the agency said he's insured.'

'Against what?'

'I'm not sure. Fire, flood, STDs??'

Em rolled her eyes. It was too late to do anything about it, and she had to admit Karl was easy on the eye. They headed towards the kitchen.

'Oh, and we're not allowed to touch him,' Lucy said as they walked along the hallway.

'Why did they need to say that?'

'I think being touched up is an occupational hazard. I did tell the others when we booked him.'

They walked into the kitchen, where Karl was surrounded by her friends, who all appeared to have turned into his adoring fans, particularly Charlotte, whose hand seemed to be on Karl's left buttock.

Em whispered to Lucy, 'I think you need to remind them.'

Karl proved to be excellent at reheating the pre-prepared

dinner, which was delicious. He remained the perfect gentleman as he expertly dodged a few drunken wandering hands and posed for photos. And he could mix a good cocktail. Em had to admit he was making this evening a great start to the weekend.

Lucy clocked Em eyeing up Karl. 'Am I forgiven?'

'Yes, but it still feels a bit uncomfortable with everyone letching at him. If they offered a service where men were ogling an almost naked woman, there would be outrage.'

'It's just a bit of fun. He doesn't seem to mind.'

'It is quite distracting.'

Karl caught Em looking at him and gave her a wink. It might have been the effect of the mojito she'd just downed, but she was starting to fantasise about what he would be like in bed.

Em took some of the used plates back into the kitchen. 'Have you done this before?' She asked Karl as she watched him packing up his cooking utensils.

'A few times,' he grinned. 'And I'm meant to be doing that for you.' He took the plates off her and loaded them into the dishwasher.

'I'm not very good at being waited on.'

'Now's the perfect time to practise. You seem a bit wistful for a blushing bride-to-be?'

'Didn't Lucy tell you? The wedding's cancelled. But we decided to go ahead with the hen do anyway.'

He looked genuinely shocked. 'I'm sorry. The agency didn't say. Are you alright?'

'Yes. It was me who called it off three months ago. I've got used to it now.'

'Your groom must be gutted to lose you.'

'No. He was cheating on me.'

'That's lousy. I know how that feels.'

'Karl! Karl! We've finished our cocktails.' Lydia's slightly slurred voice called from the dining room.

'I'll be right with you, ladies.'

Karl closed the dishwasher door. 'So you're single then?'

Em hesitated. Of course, she was single. Jack would be back in London now with his wife. She was starting to think that she'd imagined that he had any feelings for her at all.

'Yes. I'm back on the market.'

'Well, if you want some additional entertainment over the weekend, let me know.'

'Is that part of the package?'

'No. It's a free extra just for you. But don't mention it on the feedback form - dating clients is strictly forbidden.'

'My lips are sealed.' She gave him a cheeky grin.

Karl raised an eyebrow. Judging by the look he gave her, they wouldn't be sealed for much longer if Karl had anything to do with it.

'What are you doing tomorrow?' he asked.

'Lucy has arranged a full day of yoga, pampering and partying.' Which was a shame because a night out with an attractive man would keep Em's mind off the Jack situation.

'How about tonight, then?'

'I'd love to, but it seems rude to abandon my friends.'

'Judging by their current state, I don't think they'll notice. They'll be asleep before long. I don't think I should make them another round of cocktails.'

Em looked back into the dining room. He had a point. After the head start to the celebrations in the minibus, they had begun to flag. Charlotte had already slid off her chair. Even Ella, who hadn't started drinking until they arrived, was struggling to stay awake. Sylvie was trying to get everyone else engaged with starting a karaoke session, a sure sign she was drunk. Lucy had more staying power, so that might be more tricky. But Em doubted she'd object. She turned back to Karl.

'Are your intentions honourable?'

'No. Are yours?' He laughed.

Cheeky but appealing. 'Where shall we go?'

'We could have a drink. Get to know one another better. There's a late-night bar on the high street around the corner from my flat.'

'What's it called?'

'Carlo's'

Em checked the map on her phone. It was a ten-minute walk away.

Lucy shouted from the dining room, 'Em! Can you give me a hand with Charlotte?'

'Coming.' She turned back to Karl. 'I'd like to see more of you. I'll meet you at Carlo's.'

'I'm looking forward to it.'

'Was that some flirting going on in there?' Lucy asked as she and Em helped a barely conscious Charlotte upstairs.

'We're going for a drink.'

'You don't hang around. Good for you. If I hadn't got Lars, I'd have gone for him myself. He has an appealing twinkle in his eye. Just a drink?'

'I'll see what happens. But don't wait up.'

'You're normally Miss "keep them waiting until the third date"?'

'A change is as good as a rest, they say. Anyway, I don't think Karl's the third date type. I wouldn't object to being another notch on his bedpost. Or perhaps he'll be one on mine.'

'He's probably had so many notches, he hasn't got any bedpost left. You're not going to regret this, are you? What about Jack?'

'Jack is back with his wife. The only thing I might regret is abandoning the rest of you tonight.'

'I doubt anyone else will notice,' Lucy said, looking at Charlotte, who was now spark out lying facedown on her bed. 'I'll cover for you if anyone says anything.'

They left Charlotte gently snoring and headed back to the dining room. Lucy suddenly stopped halfway down the stairs. 'What if Karl has terrible dress sense? For all we know, he might like wearing elasticated polyester slacks and a Hawaiian shirt when he's off duty.'

'Does he look like he buys his clothes at garden centres? Stop trying to put me off.'

'Don't say I didn't warn you.'

'Warn you about what?' Karl was in the hall now, fully clothed in a figure-hugging navy blue shirt and jeans that showed off all his assets.

'Garden centres. Very dangerous places,' said Lucy enjoying the view. 'But you look like you don't frequent them too often.'

'No.' He looked bemused. 'I haven't got a garden.'

He looked at Em expectantly. 'I'm just about to leave.'

'I'll meet you at Carlo's in half an hour then.'

'It's starting to rain,' he said. 'I can give you a lift?'

44

Karl parked his car outside a very modern-looking block of apartments.

'I need to put all this stuff in my flat before we go to the bar.'

'I'll give you a hand,' Em offered.

'You don't have to.'

'I don't mind. The sooner it's done, the sooner we get to the bar.' She was curious about where Karl lived. From the outside, it looked quite swanky.

'If you insist.'

He handed Em a box of cocktail glasses. She followed him inside and into a lift. Karl let her into his flat on the second floor and indicated a door on the left.

'This is impressive,' she said, walking into a massive living room. One wall was filled with full-height windows overlooking the bay.

'Yeah, the view is even more spectacular in the daylight.'

'Naked cheffing must pay well,' she laughed.

'Not well enough to afford to live here. It's a friend's flat. I'm house-sitting for her while she's working abroad. I get the place rent-free. She won't be back until Christmas.' Karl took the box of glasses off her. 'I've got one more box to bring up from the car. Make yourself at home.'

Em settled down on the sofa, sinking back into the ample cushions and closing her eyes.

'You look comfortable there.' Em sat bolt upright. How could Karl be back so quickly? She must've nodded off.

'I'm so sorry. I've had a long day.'

'If you're tired, we don't have to go to the bar.'

'What would we do instead?' Em tried flirting again.

'We could play a game.'

'Any particular game?'

'Depends what you're in the mood for. Chess, bridge or something less intellectual?' he said with a cheeky grin.

'You need four for bridge.'

'That's a bit racy, even for me. Shall we stick to games for two?' He sat down next to her on the sofa.

'Does that line work on all the women you bring back here?'

'You're the first woman I've brought back here.'

'Are you telling me you live like a monk?' Somehow she didn't believe that was true.

'I wouldn't say that.' He slid his arm behind her along the back of the sofa. 'Can I kiss you?'

'I was hoping you would,' she said.

He leaned over and gently pressed his lips against hers. No fireworks, but it felt nice in a strangely comforting way. She pulled him towards her, feeling his hand move under her top, his tongue parting her lips.

He pulled back. 'Are you ok with this?'

She responded by pushing him back against the sofa and sitting astride him.

'Is that a yes?' he laughed.

'Yes.' She whispered in his ear.

He expertly undid her bra and started caressing her

breasts. She pulled her top off to give him easier access. He carefully removed the bra and started covering her breasts in gentle kisses.

'You've got me at a disadvantage now.' She said, unbuttoning his shirt.

'You've been checking out my naked arse all evening. I think you've had a head start.'

'I thought I was being discreet.'

'I could see your reflection in the dining room mirror.'

So much for being subtle. She pulled away from him slightly to admire his bare chest.

'I haven't seen this view before.' She slid her index finger slowly down his torso to the top of his trousers.

He gently held her hand to stop her from going any further.

'Hold that thought. I need something from the bedroom,' he whispered in her ear. He held her tightly as he stood up while she was still on his lap.

'Impressive.' She wrapped her legs around him.

'I hope you'll be even more impressed in a minute,' he said as he carried her across the room.

Em was relaxing in Karl's arms as they lay exhausted in his bed.

'Jack's a fool,' he said.

'Jack?' Em tensed. How did Karl know about Jack?

'Your ex. You moaned 'Oh Jack' at the moment of truth.'

'Did I? I'm so sorry.' Had she really said that? Em was mortified. She hadn't intended to, but somehow as soon as Karl had put her down on the bed, all she could think about was Jack, imagining it was his hands gently caressing her in all the right places, his breath blowing softly in her ear, his lips covering her neck in delicate kisses.She decided not to correct Karl's assumption about who Jack was. The truth would sound even worse.

'I'll let you off.' Karl smiled. 'I often imagine I'm making love to my ex, though not tonight.'

'What was she like, your ex?'

'Sophie looked a lot like you. We were together for over two years. I thought she was the one. But somebody else thought that too. Someone with a fuck off big house and a Ferrari. I couldn't compete with that.'

'She must be a fool as well.'

'Thanks.' He gently put a stray lock of Em's hair back behind her ear.

'How long since you split up?' she asked.

'Eleven months and five days. Not that I'm counting.' He lay back on the pillow.

'Would you take her back?'

'She married him on Valentine's Day. And now she's pregnant, so that ship has well and truly sailed.'

'I'm sorry.'

'Nothing you can do about it. Apart from taking my mind off it.'

'I was thinking I ought to leave you now so you can get some sleep.' Em sat up.

'I don't want to go to sleep just yet.' He started kissing her neck again, easing her back onto the bed.

She arched her back in pleasure as he slowly worked his way down her body. 'If you insist. I promise I'll only think about you this time.'

45

Em left Karl sleeping. She decided to walk back along the beach to the cottage. The cool breeze cleared her head. The beach was nearly empty. The sea and sky looked beautiful in the early morning sunlight. A perfect start to the day. She felt more alive than she'd done for a long time.

The view would make a good painting. She stopped to take a few photos.

She took the path up the dunes, hoping to sneak into the cottage unnoticed via the back door. No such luck. Lucy was in the kitchen when Em walked in.

'Well?' Lucy put down her coffee mug and grinned at Em.

'Well, what?'

'Don't play the innocent. It's 7 am. Are you going to tell me you spent all night star gazing with Karl's telescope?'

'Is that what they call it now? You know I don't kiss and tell.'

'Must've been disappointing then.'

'Far from it. To use one of your more delicate phrases, he gave me a good seeing to,' Em said as she inspected the contents of the fridge. 'Several times.'

'You've not fallen for him, have you?'

Em put a yoghurt on the counter and got out a spoon.

'No. He's lovely, but he doesn't have the same effect on me as Jack.'

'You mean he doesn't leave you feeling frustrated?'

'He didn't ask for my number, and I didn't ask for his. And I said Jack's name at the crucial moment. I think I can safely say I'll never see him again. '

'See who?' Charlotte walked into the kitchen looking far too bright and perky for someone who'd been as far out of it as she had been last night.

Em flashed Lucy a 'don't say a word' look. 'Just someone I met in Newquay.' She said as Charlotte got a glass of water from the dispenser on the fridge.

'Oh. I thought you were fucking Karl last night.' Charlotte said as she walked back out of the kitchen.

How on earth did she know? 'What makes you say that?' Em called after her.

'The way you were looking at one another. And his car's on the drive.'

Em looked at Lucy. 'I don't understand.'

'Shall I check it out?' Lucy offered.

'No. I better go.'

Karl was getting out of the car when Em opened the front door. He gave her a big beaming smile as he walked towards her.

'I'm not stalking you. You left this. It was on the floor by the bed.' He handed her a diamond earring. 'If anyone else had answered the door, I was going to say I found it in one of the boxes I took home last night.'

'That's very kind.' She turned the earring slowly over in her hand. 'There's one slight problem.' She grinned at him. 'It's not mine.'

'That's awkward.' He had the grace to look embarrassed.

'Perhaps it belongs to your friend who owns your flat,

seeing as you haven't invited any other women back there?'

'Yes, it must do.'

She handed the earring back to him, feeling disappointed.

'I'd have given you a lift back here this morning if you'd asked,' Karl said.

'I didn't want to wake you. Thank you for last night.'

'We could do it all again tonight? I know you said you're out with your friends, but you could come round to mine afterwards. You're worth waiting up for.'

'I think it's best I don't. I don't want to hurt you.' Em didn't want to get hurt, either.

He looked disappointed. 'That's a shame. If you're sure?' That cheeky grin again.

'Yes, I'm sure.' In her head, her dad's voice was saying 'Don't settle for second best', and Karl was definitely second best.

'If you change your mind, I'll be home from 10 pm.' He gave her one last smile as he walked back to his car.

Em waved him off and closed the door.

Lucy was eagerly waiting in the kitchen. 'What was all that about?'

'I'm not sure.' If it hadn't been for the earring mistake, she would have taken Karl up on his offer. 'But it's confirmed that I'm a rubbish judge of character.'

Lucy had been over-ambitious, thinking they could cope with a morning yoga session after a heavy night's drinking.

Lucy kept up reasonably well, Em had a decent stab at it, but the yoga teacher called it a day after half an hour when she encouraged them to do child's pose, and they all fell about laughing at Lydia's farts.

The pampering session after lunch went better. Lucy had booked three therapists so they could all take turns having a facial, a massage and a manicure.

Em was last on the list for the massage. Having someone work on all the knots and tension in her shoulders and neck was so soothing. Em felt her body relax into the couch.

'Who's Jack?' Ivanna, the massage therapist, asked as she wiped the massage oil from her hands.

'Sorry?' Em said, confused. Why was this woman asking about Jack?

'You said his name while I was massaging you. I think you were asleep, yes?'

Not again. How embarrassing. So much for not thinking about Jack. Em's subconscious clearly couldn't let him go. 'He's just a friend.'

'A very close friend, I think.' Ivanna gave her a knowing look as she passed Em her robe. 'He's good at massage, no?'

'I've no idea.'

'But you are hoping he is.'

'Possibly,' Em got off the massage couch.

'I hope you and Jack are very happy together,' said Ivanna as Em left the room.

Lucy was sitting on the sofa in the living room. 'What was that about you and Jack?'

'What do you mean?' Em sat down next to her.

'I heard Ivanna say she hoped you and Jack would be very happy together.'

'I nodded off during the massage, and apparently, I was talking to Jack in my sleep.'

Lucy shook her head. 'What are we going to do with you?'

'I don't know. I just hope that by the time I get back to Devon, he's decided to see sense about Isabella because it seems I'm incapable of forgetting about him.'

46

The rest of the weekend passed without any major incidents. The meal at the restaurant was good. They all had a great time dancing at the club till the small hours of the morning. The basket weaving was far more fun than it sounded. And their Sunday lunch was as delicious as the TripAdvisor reviews for the pub had promised. But as they packed their luggage back into the minibus, Em started to think about Jack again.

'Are you with us?' Lucy asked. 'You seem miles away.'

'Sorry. I'm trying to work out what could have made Jack go back to Isabella.'

'Don't waste any more energy on him. He's moved on. I know it's hard, but you're going to have to forget about him.'

'I know. I'll get there. It's just been a shock. I never thought he'd do that.'

Lucy hugged her. 'I'm sure Nancy will fill you in on the details. Then it might make sense.'

Three hours, and a traffic jam on the M5 later, Ella parked the minibus in the middle of Dashford Grange's courtyard.

Em stood up. 'Thank you so much for a lovely weekend, everyone. I needed that so much.'

She hugged them all one by one.

'We should do this more often,' Freya said.

'I'm not planning on marrying anyone ever again,' said Em. 'One of you will have to tie the knot next time.'

Lucy handed Em her suitcase and got off the minibus after her. She looked around the courtyard. 'No sign of Jack.'

'No,' said Em, looking over at his cottage, which was in darkness with the curtains closed. Another car was parked in his usual spot. 'He's gone.'

'Come on, Lucy,' Ella shouted from the driver's seat. 'Lydia and Freya have a train to catch.'

'I'll phone you tomorrow,' said Lucy, jumping back on the bus.

Em waved them off.

She looked sadly at Jack's cottage again. It wouldn't be easy getting used to him not being there.

47

Em was so tired she slept through the alarm on Monday morning. Not that it mattered on her day off.

There was still no sign of Jack when she got up. She bumped into Nancy in the courtyard.

'Good weekend, Em?'

'Yes, very good, thanks.'

'You look a lot more relaxed. A trip away with friends is a great mood booster, I always find.'

'Did I miss anything?'

'No. It's been very quiet. Saturday's guests were all lovely, and they turned up on time. And Jack had to go to London to see his sister, Kate.'

'Sister?' Em wasn't expecting that.

'She left her husband on Friday. Got on a train to London with her three children and moved into Olivia's. Awful situation - her youngest is only four months old. Jack went to help her until Olivia got back from holiday last night. I think he was glad of an opportunity to see her. Isabella always objected to visiting Kate in Edinburgh so he's not seen her for several years. Are you feeling alright?'

Em must've looked stunned. She didn't know whether to be relieved that Jack hadn't gone back to Isabella or annoyed with him for not revealing what he was actually doing. 'I'm just surprised he didn't mention it.'

'He didn't want you to worry about Isabella hunting him down. He told me not to tell you until you got back.'

So he was trying to be considerate to Em and helpful to his sister, all while Em had been throwing herself at Karl. What a mess. 'When's he coming back?' Em asked nervously.

'He was supposed to be driving back today, but he texted me this morning to say he's decided to fly to Italy. He needs to do some research for his book. I thought he'd finished writing it, but there's something he wants to check, and he can't do it online.'

At least Jack would be coming back, but she had no idea what she was going to say to him when he did. 'Whereabouts in Italy has he gone?'

'Tuscany. He's stopping with an old friend out there. She's got a villa. But he'll be back in time for the portrait party on Friday.'

She? Em tried to keep her composure. No Isabella to worry about but now there was a mysterious woman friend instead. 'He's never talked about having friends in Italy.'

'He's got academic contacts all over the world. I'm sure he'll tell us all about it when he comes back.'

Em was back in her flat that afternoon, doing her best to paint another cheery view of Dashford to replace the one Phil had sold at the weekend. She should be working on Jack's portrait, but she couldn't face it. Her phone rang. Lucy. Em put down her brush, wiped her hands on her apron and answered it.

'How are you? Recovered from the weekend?' Lucy asked.

'I've had a lie-in, and I feel fine now, thanks.'

'You sound a bit down to me.'

Em was fed up but Lucy sounded like she had some news

to share. 'I'm fine. How are you? You sound like you're excited about something?'

'I am. Lars has invited me to go with him to visit his folks in Canada in September.'

'Wow! He is serious then.'

'Looks like it.'

'And you're ok with that? I remember what you said in Newquay.'

'Yes. I was having a wobble. We had a serious relationship conversation when I got back last night. I think we're on the same page.'

'I'm so happy for you.'

'We just need to get you sorted now.'

'I'm considering joining a convent. It would be a whole lot simpler.'

'Lars is going away on a stag weekend at the end of next week. I'm guessing you'll be working, so can I come and stop with you? We'll see if we can find you the perfect man.'

'Good luck with that.'

'You're not going to find him staying in Dashford Grange. Any news on Jack and Isabella?'

Em filled Lucy in on why Jack had gone back to London.

'That's great news! Not for Jack's sister, obviously, but you're still in with a chance.'

'Am I? I'm not sure I'll be able to look Jack in the face after that night with Karl.'

'Why? You didn't cheat on him. You and Jack have never got together properly. And you thought Jack was back with Isabella. Plus, you were fantasising that Karl was Jack. You have absolutely nothing to apologise for.'

'I still feel bad about it. I don't think Jack will see it that way. He was off being a saint while I was having a one-night stand. Anyway, he's left the country to spend the rest of the week with a mysterious woman.'

'He's doing what? Tell me more.'

48

It had been a long week without Jack to talk to. Friday finally arrived, but there was still no sign of him. Em had checked the times of flights between Italy and all of the London airports to see if it was feasible for him to get home in time for the party. It was, but he should have landed by now, and she thought he would've texted her or Nancy if he was on his way.

'You've folded and unfolded those towels at least three times in the last five minutes. What's bothering you?' Nancy asked.

Nancy and Em were getting one of the guest bedrooms ready for Nancy's rock climbing friend, Daphne, who was stopping over after the portrait party that evening. 'It's not Jack, is it? I'm sure he'll be back today.'

'It's not just Jack. I've had nightmares all week about the party. Last night I dreamt no one turned up.'

'I've had 30 positive RSVPs, so I'm expecting at least 20 of them to turn up, plus a few who've forgotten to reply. That's how it usually works out. People do enjoy my parties, you know.' Nancy smiled. 'What other disasters have you dreamt up?'

'Everyone hated the portrait. One person hated it so much

he put one of your cake forks through it and ripped it to shreds.'

Nancy chuckled. 'I love my portrait, and so do all the others who've seen it. Even Nigel was impressed when I sent him a photograph. He's usually the first to find flaws in anything. So I don't think it's at risk of being damaged by an irate art critic with a cake fork or any other item of cutlery, for that matter. '

'I know it's mad. On Monday night, I dreamt I didn't get any enquiries, and you were annoyed with me for wasting your time. And on Tuesday night, I got so many enquiries I was writing them all down incorrectly, and everyone was angry with me and phoning up later to cancel their orders. It was like being back in the call centre again. It was so stressful I woke up in a cold sweat. Then I went back to sleep and dreamt everyone died from inhaling poisonous fumes from the frame.' Em laughed at the number of things she was finding to worry about.

'You've taken overthinking to a new level,' said Nancy. 'Just relax. Whatever happens, I can catch up with some old friends, and a few more people in Devon will be aware of your artistic skills.'

They heard a car door slam in the courtyard. Nancy looked out of the bedroom window. 'You have one less thing to worry about. Jack is back.'

Em walked over to the window. He must have sensed her watching. He looked up and smiled. Not his usual megawatt smile. It looked a little uncomfortable if anything. But perhaps she was imagining it or projecting her own guilty feelings onto him. He was sporting a deep brown tan. He hadn't spent the whole time in Italy indoors then. Perhaps the woman he was with was the outdoorsy type? That conjured up a load of images that she didn't want swirling around in her head.

Jack unloaded his suitcase from the boot of the car and headed towards his cottage. He wasn't rushing in to see her, then.

Em went back to helping Nancy.

'I think that's everything done now,' said Nancy.

Em looked at the gorgeous sunshine outside. Exercise might help her relax. 'I'm going to go for a walk on the beach. I'll be back in time to help you sort out the drawing room.'

'Hello, you.' Jack pulled out the chair next to Em outside Mary's cafe. 'Nancy said you might be here,' he said, sitting down.

'You're looking well. Italy suited you.' She was pleased he'd come to find her. He still didn't seem like his usual self, though.

'Hmm. I guess. I needed a break. It was all a bit confusing here.'

'Confusing' was an interesting word to use. 'I thought we weren't supposed to be seen together in public.' Em said.

'I've changed my mind. Is that allowed?'

'Isabella hasn't put me on a mafia hit list, then?'

'I hope she hasn't. When I thought about it, I figured she's more likely to go for me first - she can claim my life insurance payout then.' He did a half laugh, but the expression in his eyes was serious. 'How was Newquay?'

'Fun.' Em didn't want to offer any more details. Better to keep off that topic completely. 'How was Italy?'

'Fun.'

So he was playing the same game, but she was dying to know more. 'Nancy said you were stopping with a friend out there?'

'Yes, someone I used to be at university with. Clara's got her own holiday home in Tuscany. She invited me for a few days.'

'That's lucky, getting an invitation like that.'

'It wasn't luck. I phoned her.'

So he was making a point that he'd deliberately made contact. Now it was Em's turn to feel confused.

'Lots of sunbathing, by the look of it?' she said.

'Some. Not much sunbathing for you in Newquay?'

'No, it was sunny, but Lucy kept us so busy there wasn't time.'

'And Karl's not into sunbathing, I suppose? I guess he has to be careful with tan lines in his line of business.' He gave her a long hard look.

'Yes, probably.' How did he know about Karl?

Jack must've read her mind. 'I saw some of your friends' Instagram posts.'

Oh god. What had they posted? Em had checked Lucy's feed, which wasn't incriminating, but she hadn't bothered with everyone else's as they kept their accounts private. She vaguely remembered them taking photos with Karl. One of them must have accepted Jack as a friend.

'I'm glad you had a good time,' he said. 'With Karl.' That stern look again.

He could talk, but then she didn't know what had happened in Italy. 'And I'm glad you had a good time with Clara. Is she coming over here?'

'No. I doubt I'll see her again for a while. She prefers to spend the summer in Italy. Is Karl planning to visit you?'

'No. I haven't spoken to him since Saturday. You weren't tempted to stay longer in Italy?'

'No. I didn't want to overstay my welcome. And I was missing life here.'

Life? Not Em specifically, then.

Mary materialised at their table. 'Can I get you a drink, Jack?'

'I didn't know you did table service.' Jack gave Mary a

beaming smile. So he'd not forgotten how to do those. He just wasn't using them on Em.

'Only for my favourite professor,' Mary winked at him flirtatiously.

Em stood up to leave. 'I don't want to play gooseberry.'

'Don't go just yet.' Jack sounded anxious.

'I think I should.' Em walked away and didn't look back.

49

Nancy's portrait stood in the drawing room in its new gilt frame on an old ornate display easel which Nancy had found in the attic. It was the first time Em had seen the picture since it went to the framers.

'Pleased?' asked Nancy.

'Very.' Em had to admit that it did look good.

'Excellent. Let's get the rest of the room ready.'

Nancy had her own ideas about where the drawing room furniture should go to maximise seating space and give an unhindered view of the painting.

'Are you going to say a few words this evening?' Nancy asked Em as she pushed one of the armchairs in front of the fireplace.

'I've no idea what to say. I thought I'd let the painting do the talking for me. '

Nancy put her hands on her hips. That was obviously the wrong answer. 'The main reason we're having this party is to get the great and the good of North Devon to ask you to paint their portraits. You need to subtly show off your skills so they come to the conclusion that they can't live without their own Emily Gillespie masterpiece.'

'What do you think I should say? I'm not very good at

blowing my own trumpet.'

'That's fine because blowing your own trumpet is the last thing you should do.' Nancy picked up a couple of the family photos on the grand piano. 'You could talk about how you helped me choose a location, tips for deciding what to wear, how you put your sitters at ease. Those sorts of things. Then they will start visualising working with you and how it will be an easy, enjoyable experience.'

'I can back that up if you like?' They both turned to see Jack walking into the room.

Em had been grateful that prepping for tonight's party had been taking her mind off the whole Jack situation, and now here he was. 'I enjoyed being painted by you. I'm missing it now we've stopped.'

'What an excellent idea. The more testimonials, the better.' Nancy replied. 'Jack, you can give Em a hand moving that heavy sofa.'

'Why are we moving that?' Em asked, glad of the excuse to change the subject away from progress on Jack's portrait.

'It blocks off access to the piano,' Nancy said. 'I thought you could lay out some of your preparatory sketches there to give people a better idea of the process. I've made some room.' She walked over to the Chinese cabinet in the corner and put the photo frames she was holding inside.

'I could put my sketchbooks out for your guests to look through, I suppose.'

'Perfect. And put your business cards next to them, of course.'

'Business cards?' asked Jack.

'Yes. Nancy suggested I get some printed. Here.' She picked up the box of cards from the coffee table and handed one to him. It had a print of Nancy's portrait on one side and Em's contact details on the other.

Jack turned the card over in his hand. 'Well, Emily

Gillespie, portrait and landscape artist, these look extremely professional.'

'Thanks.' Em busied herself with putting the rest of the cards on the piano.

Nancy headed for the hall door. 'I'll leave you two to move that sofa nearer the bookcase while I make some tea.'

Jack waited until Nancy was out of earshot, then turned to Em. 'Truce?' He said tentatively.

'I wasn't aware we were fighting.'

'I felt we didn't part on good terms earlier. And you didn't seem that pleased to see me when I came in just now.'

She felt awkward. 'I'm sorry I walked off at the café. You're a guest here, and I should've treated you better.'

'I hope you'd have wanted to treat me better because we're friends.' He looked downcast. 'But I should have treated you better as well. I'm sorry I kept on about Karl.'

He sounded genuinely apologetic.

'Can we just forget about that conversation?' Em asked.

'That suits me.' Jack smiled. 'Honestly, forgetting everything that's happened this week would suit me. '

'Same here.' Em smiled back at him. They made eye contact for a moment.

'Haven't you moved that sofa yet?' Nancy returned with a tray of mugs.

Jack nodded to the sofa. 'You grab that end, Em.'

50

Half an hour before the official party start time, Em was nervously nursing a cup of tea in the privacy of her own living room, trying to pluck up enough courage to go over to the main house.

Her phone buzzed. A FaceTime call from Lucy, no doubt following up on the text Em had sent her an hour or so ago, filling her in on today's events. Better keep it quick. She ought to be in the drawing room helping Nancy make sure that everything was ready.

'I've been checking out this Clara woman,' Lucy said.

Em rolled her eyes. 'I'm not interested in who Clara is. If he's had a brief fling with her, that's his business. I can't complain after Karl.'

'But it has upset you.'

'Yes, it has. But he says he wants to forget about everything that's happened in the last week. I'm hoping that means he wants to forget about her too.'

'Remind me, when did he go to Italy?'

'Monday morning, according to Nancy.'

'So it was probably in response to seeing you with Karl on Instagram.'

'I guess that would explain his use of the word

"confusing",' Em conceded. 'Are you making excuses for him?'

'I'm just frustrated that you both seem to want one another, but you don't seem to be able to make it happen! It shouldn't be this difficult. Is he at the party tonight?'

'Yes. He said he'd say a few words about working with me.'

'Being supportive. That's a good sign. Make sure you thank him properly afterwards.'

'I'm not sure what you mean.' Em had a very good idea of what Lucy meant, but she wasn't sure that Jack would appreciate it now she was back in the friend zone.

'Try the peck on the cheek again. That would've worked last time if you hadn't been interrupted. And if he doesn't respond, you know where you stand.'

Em had already decided she wouldn't be the first to make a move this time. If Jack wanted her, he could say so. She heard a door slam in the distance on Lucy's end of the conversation.

'Got to go,' Lucy said. 'Lars has arrived. I'll email you the Clara dossier. It's entirely up to you whether you read it. Good luck with the party. I hope you get lots of interest.' Lucy winked at Em as she ended the call.

'That went well.' Jack walked into the kitchen at Dashford Grange and put down a tray of leftover party food on the island.

Em looked up from loading the dishwasher and beamed at him. 'Yes, I've had two enquiries, and they both seem very keen.'

She was thrilled. Deep down, she'd thought getting one person interested in having their portrait painted would be a resounding success. To get two was amazing. Plus, everyone who had said they were coming to the party had turned up, there had been no poisonous fumes to worry about, and no one had felt the urge to destroy the painting. She smiled to herself.

'What's amusing you?' Jack asked.

'I was just thinking about all the stupid things I came up with that could have gone wrong tonight.'

'Nothing went wrong, did it? Your talk went really well, and everyone was raving about how good Nancy's portrait was.'

'No, it was all perfect.' Em said.

And the best part of the evening was that she and Jack seemed to be back to being best buddies. He'd been attentive and supportive. No awkwardness and no more digs about Karl. He'd said he'd wanted to forget about the last week, and he'd stuck to that. And she'd managed to do that too until now.

She thought about last Friday night and Karl. This evening's party had been a much more genteel affair than last week's - no chance of any hot sex tonight.

'Em?' Jack's voice brought her back to now.

'Sorry, I was miles away.' Thinking about whether you're as good between the sheets as Karl, but she decided not to mention that.

'Do you want another drink?' Jack was waving a half-full bottle of Pinot Grigio at her.

'No, no more thanks.' Or I might rip your clothes off.

Nancy's friend, Daphne, walked in.

'Don't mind me. I just want some water to take up to bed.' Daphne got a glass from the cupboard and walked over to the fridge.

'I must say that was an excellent party. Well done, Em.'

'It was all Nancy's doing, really.'

'I'm sure you contributed too. And well done to you, Jack. The way you extracted poor Em from Mrs Forrester's clutches was a masterclass in diplomacy.' Jack had spotted Em trapped in a corner by a local councillor who was giving her chapter and verse about a painter who used to live in Dashford in the 1950s. 'She has a heart of gold, but she never knows when to shut up. I, on the other hand, do know when my presence is no longer wanted.' Daphne grinned at them as she left the kitchen. 'You two make a lovely couple.'

Em noticed Jack smiling to himself. 'By the way,' he said, 'I haven't heard anything from Isabella.'

Interesting that Daphne's comment had made him think about the Isabella situation.

He put the wine in the fridge. 'Now we're friends again.' Em noticed that he'd emphasised 'friends'. 'Would you like me to cook you dinner tomorrow night? I thought you might be exhausted after the party and sorting out this week's holiday changeovers?'

51

Em was exhausted after the stressful week. She was glad to be standing in Jack's kitchen while he prepared their evening meal.

'Lucy's coming to stay next weekend,' she said as she sipped a glass of wine while Jack chopped mushrooms.

'Just Lucy? No Lars? I thought they were inseparable?'

'They are. But he's going on a stag weekend. I think this visit is as much about taking her mind off that as it is about seeing me. '

Jack stopped chopping.

'Are you ok?' Em asked.

'Yes. I was thinking about Mark. I miss having a close friend.'

'No chance of you making it up with him?'

'I don't know how I'd feel seeing him again. Or if he'd even want to see me.'

'When was the last time you saw him?'

Jack looked at her with a 'When do you think?' expression.

'Sorry - I wondered if you'd spoken to him since.'

'Just an angry text from me telling him what I thought of him, with a reply from him begging forgiveness. I blocked him after that. '

'Nancy blames Isabella.'

'She's right. But he didn't have to … ' Jack couldn't bring himself to say it. 'It's not like she drugged him.' He went back to chopping but more aggressively this time.

'Everyone makes mistakes.'

Jack stopped again. 'But could I trust him when I get a new partner? How would you feel if you'd caught Lucy in bed with Connor?'

'I'd be horrified. Confused. Upset. Think I'd slipped into an alternative universe as she can't stand him. Probably fantasise about murdering her.'

Jack raised his eyebrows.

'Only fantasise!' Em emphasised. 'But I hope I'd want to talk to her about it. Find out why, if nothing else. We've known each other since nursery.'

Jack finished chopping the last few mushrooms. 'It's a lot of friendship to lose, isn't it? '

'Yes, it is. Would another girlfriend use him like Isabella did?'

'I won't make the mistake of giving my heart to a woman like that again. You think I should contact him?'

'I don't know. You're more generous than me - you took Isabella back. I didn't give Connor a chance to explain.'

'Do you regret that?'

'No, I don't. It had been going on for months. Perhaps if it had been a one-night stand - a drunken lapse - I might have been more forgiving. No, Connor was having a full-on affair. I could never take him back.'

'Whereas Mark and Isabella was a one-off deliberately timed by her so I would catch them and get rid of her closest rival for my attention,' he said thoughtfully.

Jack started melting butter in a frying pan. 'Thank you - that helped,' he said, scraping the mushrooms off the chopping board and into the pan.

52

When Em walked into the kitchen on Tuesday morning, Nancy was singing to herself.

'You sound happy.'

'I am, and I think I have you to thank.'

Em looked baffled.

'Mark's coming home - just for the weekend. Jack contacted him. Offered an olive branch.'

So that's why she was so chirpy. 'Wow! I'm pleased for you. This weekend?'

'Yes! We're going to be very busy with your friend Lucy coming as well. Come here, darling girl. I'm so glad our paths crossed.' Nancy gave her a big hug. 'You're the daughter I never had.'

And Nancy's the mother I wish I'd had. Em teared up. She held her breath for a moment to get back in control.

Nancy must have noticed. 'Come on. We haven't got time for sentimentality. I need to get Mark's room ready. Would you be an angel and give me a hand?' Nancy passed Em a tissue and headed out of the kitchen.

Mark's bedroom was at the far corner of the house, with windows overlooking the garden and out over the fields to the sea in the distance.

'How long since he lived here?'

'Nearly 16 years. Once he left university, he officially moved out, but I kept his things so he'd feel at home whenever he visited.'

Despite the antique furniture and the expensive-looking drapes and bedding, there was still a studenty feel to the room, thanks to the bookcase full of mismatched books and folders, and the desk in the corner with a notice board above it. Em went to have a closer look.

'Is that Jack?' she said, pointing to a photo of two small boys in shorts and t-shirts standing on a rock.

'Yes - and that's Mark next to him.' Mark, slightly shorter than Jack with curly mid-brown hair, was holding a fishing net while the young Jack was carrying a bucket and spade. 'They used to spend hours rock pooling.'

There were loads more photos of their teenage years and early twenties, by the look of it. Em smiled at the pics of Jack looking less than sober in various bars, and holiday photos from loads of locations. But her eyes kept being drawn back to a sunny shot of the two of them looking tanned and ripped on a tropical beach. Were those abs still hiding under the loose shirts Jack favoured?

'Em?'

'Sorry, what did you say?'

Nancy looked amused. 'I said they were carefree times - I hope we recapture some of that this weekend.'

She handed Em a set of clean bedding. 'Let's get it done, shall we.'

53

Friday dawned sunny and warm. A busy day for Em. Changeover day for Wisteria Cottage, and Lucy was arriving for the weekend too. The sound of a car driving into the courtyard distracted Em from the bookings spreadsheet on Nancy's laptop. They weren't expecting any guests until mid-afternoon, it was too early for Lucy, and Jack was collecting Mark from the airport later. Em looked at the security camera app.

Someone had parked a large black Range Rover in the courtyard. Em watched as the driver got out. The camera footage wasn't clear, but Em could tell it was a woman with blonde hair and a haughty demeanour. She looked very familiar. Em went out through the side door into the courtyard.

'Excuse me,' the woman shouted across to Em.

Yes, it was Isabella. There was no mistaking that harsh voice demanding immediate attention. 'I'm looking for Jack - Jack Carver?'

Isabella walked towards her. 'Don't I know you from somewhere?'

'And you are?' If Isabella didn't recognise Em, then Em wasn't going to show she knew who Isabella was - no need to inflate Isabella's ego any further.

'Mrs Carver, Jack's wife.' Short, snappy and to the point, emphasising the word 'wife'. She looked Em up and down, giving off an air of disapproval.

'He's not here,' Em said calmly.

'I remember now. You told me that bullshit before when I met you in London. Do you think I'm a complete fool? His car is parked right there.' Isabella pointed to the Volvo. 'Where is he?'

There was no point lying. 'He's in the village. He'll be back later.'

'How much later?'

'I don't know.' Em was lying now. Jack had said he'd be back by 11 am, but Em wasn't going to tell Isabella that. She hoped if Isabella thought he would be hours, she'd go away.

'I will wait in the car for as long as it takes.'

Without as much as a thank you, Isabella turned and strode purposefully back to her car. Her stilettos caught in the gaps in the gravel, ruining the haughty effect, much to Em's amusement.

As Isabella reached the driver's door, she turned around. 'You're welcome to him. Our marriage was a nightmare from day one. I warn you; he won't care about you once he's got a ring on your finger. All he cares about are ships, books and Clara bloody Benetti.'

Clara? Em didn't respond. She'd have to read the dossier Lucy had sent her on Clara after all. In the meantime, she needed to warn Jack about Isabella. Grabbing her phone from her back pocket, she went indoors to text him.

    Red alert. Isabella is parked in the courtyard
waiting for you.

Jack rang back almost immediately. 'I was expecting

another solicitor's letter, not a royal visit.'

'She's refusing to leave until she's seen you.'

Jack sighed. 'Lucky me. I'm halfway up the hill. I'll be 10 minutes. It will give me time to get my thoughts together. '

'See you soon. Let me know if you need moral support.'

Nancy appeared in the kitchen just as Em ended the call. 'Moral support?'

'Isabella is outside, demanding to see Jack.'

'Is she indeed? How convenient. I was going to visit her in London next week. She's saved me a trip.' Nancy looked genuinely delighted. 'Olivia and I were only discussing it this morning. And here she is on my doorstep. The universe works in mysterious ways.'

Nancy headed over to the desk by the Aga. 'Would you mind telling her to come in, please? Put her in the drawing room while I find my phone. And then tell Jack not to talk to her until I've spoken to him.'

Nancy was up to something. Em went back outside.

Isabella was reluctant to go indoors. 'I know Jack is stopping in one of the cottages. Why do I need to come into the house?'

'I don't know. But it's the only way you'll be able to see him,' said Em.

She showed Isabella into the hallway. 'Please make yourself at home in here,' she said, opening the double doors into the drawing room.

Once Isabella had settled on a sofa, Em retreated to the safety of the kitchen and phoned Jack again to update him on Nancy's plan.

'What's she up to?'

'I've got no idea, but she's quite gleeful about it. I get the impression she's been plotting something with your mother.'

A few minutes later, Jack stuck his head around the back door. 'Where's my adoring wife?' he whispered.

'I don't know about the adoring one,' Em said, 'but the vindictive one is in the drawing room. Nancy is in her study. I've shut the drawing room doors. You should be able to get to the study without alerting her ladyship.'

'Wish me luck.' Jack headed into the hallway.

The door to Nancy's study clicked shut. A few minutes later, Em heard Jack's footsteps crossing the hallway to the drawing room.

She heard Isabella's raised voice but couldn't make out what she was saying. She couldn't hear Jack at all.

Nancy walked into the kitchen, looking triumphant.

'What did you do?' Em asked.

'London can be a small world sometimes. Olivia heard a rumour that Isabella was having an affair with her personal trainer, Angelo. So Olivia employed Angelo to train her. She's had an exhausting few weeks trying to keep up, poor soul. She's never needed to work out before.'

'Why did she do that?'

'We needed evidence of Isabella's infidelity to give to Jack.'

Em was baffled.

'Olivia watched Angelo type in the code for unlocking his phone a few times, memorised it, and when he left it unattended while he went to get some fitness equipment out of his car, she had a look at what was on there. She slipped the lock on the front door to give herself plenty of time, so Angelo had to ring the bell to get back in the house. Then she went through his camera roll and found some compromising photos of Isabella.'

'Playing Isabella at her own game.' Em admired their ingenuity, but she was worried about Jack. 'Isn't that illegal, though?'

'No, no. She didn't take copies of Angelo's images. She checked Angelo's calendar to see when and where he'd got his next few liaisons with Isabella. Then she employed a private detective to get some photos we could use. Not as x-rated as Angelo's, but proof that Isabella and Angelo are an item. That's what I showed Jack just now. And those are what he's hopefully showing to Isabella.'

'How come Angelo didn't know that Olivia was Isabella's mother-in-law?'

'Olivia removed all the photos of Jack and Isabella on display. And she always uses her maiden name, which wouldn't have meant anything to Angelo either.'

They heard the drawing room door open and the click of Isabella's heels as she marched towards the front door, slamming it as she went out.

Jack walked into the kitchen.

'Dear boy, you look exhausted,' Nancy grabbed his hand and patted it. 'Anyone would think you'd just done ten rounds with Tyson Fury. Did it work?'

He nodded. 'We've reached an agreement.'

'Marvellous. Will you give Olivia the excellent news, or shall I?'

'You do it. I need a few minutes to myself.' He looked like he was about to cry as he headed towards the back door.

54

Em decided not to follow Jack outside. She was desperate to know what had happened but didn't want to pressure him. And Isabella's Clara comment was bugging her. Em had ignored Lucy's Clara dossier, but she wanted to know what it said now.

While Nancy was busy on the phone in her study, Em found Lucy's email and started to read.

```
    Clara Benetti, television presenter, 36,
studied history at Oxford at the same time as
Jack, divorced, no children.
```

No mention of any relationship between Clara and Jack.

Lucy had pasted in a headshot of Clara. Bleached blonde hair, brown eyes, attractive smile. She looked similar to Isabella. Perhaps Jack had a type - one that wasn't like Em.

Lucy had also included a link to a magazine article about Clara's Tuscan home. It was a double-page spread with lots of photos of Clara and her undeniably beautiful traditional Italian house, complete with a swimming pool and a hot tub on a terrace overlooking some spectacular countryside. A lovely location to top up a tan. She visualised Jack lying on one of the double sun loungers with Clara next to him, rubbing suntan lotion on his chest seductively. No, stop torturing yourself! He's not with Clara now. He's a few yards away in the garden.

Em made tea and went outdoors. Jack was sitting on the low wall at the edge of the terrace, his head in his hands.

'For you.' Em handed him a mug. 'Unless you want something stronger?'

He looked up at her. His eyes were red. 'No, that's perfect. Thank you.'

'Do you want me to leave you alone?'

'No. Take a seat.'

Em sat beside him. 'Nancy told me what your mother did.'

'I could have done without seeing those photos.'

'I know that feeling.'

He looked puzzled.

'Connor and Astra?'

'Oh, of course! I know Isabella and I are over, but seeing her kissing another man still feels painful. Is that odd?'

Em shook her head. 'It all gets very confusing. Are you regretting splitting up with her?' Surely he wasn't thinking of giving Isabella yet another chance?

'No! Absolutely not. I guess I'm still in mourning for the relationship I thought we had. But she's agreed to a divorce now on the grounds of my unreasonable behaviour.'

'Your unreasonable behaviour! I thought that's what she suggested in the letter.'

'It was, but she's changed the wording now.'

'How is that fair?'

'It isn't fair. But I have to be pragmatic. She'll never admit that she's done anything wrong. It's better than waiting for five years.'

'So what have you been doing that's so unreasonable?'

227

'We've agreed that I work excessively and I don't socialise with her. I can live with that. It's a big improvement on how she described me in the original divorce papers.'

'So that's it then.'

'It should be. I was beginning to think it would never happen. I ought to be celebrating.'

'I can see if Nancy's got some champagne in the fridge? She usually does.'

'No, I don't want to tempt fate. Let's save the celebration until I get the decree nisi.'

55

'I'll just get this out of the way, and then I'll help you with the sofa bed,' Em called out to Lucy, who was in Em's bathroom, unpacking her toiletries.

It was Friday evening, and the new guests had settled in. Lucy had arrived ten minutes ago, and now they were getting ready to enjoy the weekend. Em was ironing a blouse to wear tonight.

'I thought you hated ironing?' Lucy said as she walked back into the living room.

'I used to because I never made a good job of it. But Jack's given me some tips, and it's much easier. My clothes look like I've ironed them now.' She proudly held up the crease-free garment. 'He's teaching me how to cook as well.'

'Have you got some weird pupil-teacher relationship going on?' Lucy looked horrified. 'Have you taught him anything?'

'How to fold fitted sheets neatly. And how to put on a duvet cover easily.'

'Oh, my god. You've only known him for a few weeks. You're meant to do all this domestic bliss stuff after you've got bored with fucking one another's brains out. You haven't been secretly fucking one another's brains out, have you?'

'No. You know we haven't. And I hope it would take a bit

longer than five weeks to get bored with that.'

'You got fed up with that hot Argentinian in three weeks.'

'He had to go back to Argentina. And it was never going to turn into a long-term relationship.'

'So apart from swapping domestic tips and hints and kidding yourselves that neither of you is ready for another relationship, what have you and Jack got in common?'

Em started putting the ironing board away. 'Not much but it's easy being in his company.'

'You could say that about a dog.'

'You were the one who was pushing me to seduce him.'

'I wasn't expecting it to get this mundane this quickly. I wanted some excitement for you, not someone you could discuss housekeeping techniques with.'

'It's not mundane!' Was it? It did look that way to an outsider, Em supposed. If they ever did get it together romantically, would it get boring quickly? Bloody Lucy, sowing the seeds of doubt in her mind. She was usually more positive than this. Em was starting to wish Lucy had stayed in Birmingham.

'You said you could see what I saw in him when you met him the other week.'

'I think I must've been looking at him through rose-tinted glasses.'

'You'll get another chance to meet him on Sunday. He's cooking lunch for us all in the main house. His old best friend will be there too.'

'The mysterious Mark?'

'Yes, though I'm not sure he's that mysterious. He shares loads on Instagram. '

Em showed Lucy Mark's Instagram feed.

'Ooh - nice. If I hadn't got Lars, I might give him a try.'

'Have you heard from the lovely Lars?' Em asked, relieved to get an opportunity to steer the conversation away from

Jack and his friend.

'No.' Lucy looked deflated. That might explain her mood.

'What's he meant to be doing?'

'Enjoying the scenery in Mallorca.'

'On a stag do?' That sounded highly improbable.

'He promised he'd behave himself. They were up in the mountains this afternoon. One of his mates posted a photo to his Instagram story.'

'Ok.'

'I'm being a fool, aren't I?'

'I don't know him. He might very well be more interested in mountains than Magaluf. What do you think?'

'I think he's probably shagging someone as we speak.'

'Do you know that?'

'Something's keeping him busy. He's not responded to any of the texts I've sent him since he flew out yesterday evening.'

'Perhaps he hasn't got a phone signal?'

'It's Spain, not Mars. They even have a 4G signal on Mount Everest now.'

'You fucking arsehole!'

'Well, that's nice!' Em had just come out of her bedroom.

'Not you - that bastard Lars. Look!' Lucy thrust her phone in front of Em's face. Em backed away slightly to focus on the image that filled the screen. A shot of Lars with a blonde woman draped across his lap. The woman's swimsuit left nothing to the imagination.

Em wasn't sure what to say. 'He's being helpful. With a skimpy design like that, her boobs probably need extra support from those big hands of his. And look, he's cleaning her ear with his tongue too. What a generous man he is.'

'Don't make excuses for him. And look at this one.'

Em peered closely at a picture of the stag clutching an empty yard of ale. 'Is a yard of ale even a thing in Spain?'

'Never mind that. Look who's in the background.' Sure enough, there was Lars, snogging the face off a different woman. 'Two can play at that game.'

'Aren't you just going to dump him?'

'I want revenge first.'

So much for their plans for a quiet meal in Dashford. Lucy wanted to go out partying.

56

As Lucy put it, going on the pull might be tricky in Dashford, which only boasted a few sleepy pubs. Em had driven them 20 miles to the next big town. They were now sitting outside a busy bar by the harbour in the twilight drinking with two men, thanks to Lucy, who never had any trouble getting male attention.

'Jason and I are just going for a walk. Is that alright?' Lucy said to Em.

'Yes, fine.' Jason's friend, Luke, seemed nice enough.

'She strikes me as a bit of a man-eater, your friend,' Luke said to Em as they watched Lucy and Jason walk along the harbour wall.

'Sometimes. I hope Jason is not easily hurt.'

'He's a player - he'll be fine. You didn't say why you were here?'

'Lucy fancied a night out. I'm here as driver and moral support.'

'I meant in Devon.'

'I work here now.'

'What do you do?'

Em hesitated slightly. 'I'm an artist.' It felt good to say that. With the sales from the gallery and the portrait enquiries from Nancy's party, she didn't feel like she was stretching the point.

'How long have you been doing that?'

'Not long. I used to work in a call centre until this spring.'

'I used to do that,' Luke said. 'I'm so glad I got out.'

They shared call centre horror stories. Luke was an entertaining raconteur. She could picture the scenarios and personalities he described perfectly.

They must've been talking and laughing for at least 20 minutes when Em felt her phone buzz. Probably Lucy.

'Sorry, can I just check this?' She said to Luke.

Jack. Why was he texting?

```
Do you need my Taekwondo skills?
```

Odd.

```
No, I'm fine. Why are you asking?
```

A speedy reply from Jack

```
I thought he looked too close to you.
```

Jack must be somewhere nearby. Em looked around.

'Everything ok?' asked Luke.

'Yes, it's just a friend. Looks like he's here tonight.'

She texted Jack back.

```
Where are you?
```

'Just here,' Jack said, walking towards their table. His voice sounded deeper than ever. He didn't greet her with his usual welcoming smile. Was he trying to play the alpha male?

'I didn't expect to see you here.' Em said.

'Obviously,' Jack's voice had a certain husky menacing

undertone. 'I thought you and Lucy were going for a quiet meal in Dashford?'

'Change of plan, thanks to Lecherous Lars.'

'Lecherous Lars?'

'Yes, he's playing away from home in Spain.'

'Mark and I were just reliving our youth. Mind if we join you?' Jack sat down next to Em without waiting for an answer.

It was Luke's turn to look annoyed now. Em noticed Mark standing behind Jack, looking amused.

'Pleased to meet you, Em.' Mark gave her a peck on the cheek.

'And you at last. I've heard a lot about you.'

'Most of it bad, I'm guessing? I've heard a lot about you too.'

Em smiled, wondering what Jack had been saying.

Luke got up. 'I'm just going to get a refill. Want to come with me?' His body language made it clear that the invitation was aimed at Em only.

'She's fine here,' Jack said.

'I'll be the judge of that, thank you,' Em said, glaring at Jack. It wasn't anything like the situation with drunken Si. She'd been having a friendly conversation with Luke. It wasn't as if she and Jack were officially dating.

'I'd love to come with you, Luke,' she said. 'Excuse me, gentlemen. We'll catch up properly tomorrow, Mark.'

She could feel Jack's eyes burning into her back as she walked into the bar with Luke.

'Is Jack an ex?' Luke asked.

'No, just a friend.'

'Are you sure? He looked jealous to me.'

57

Em dragged herself out of bed at 8 am to sort out the guests who were leaving early. Lucy was still in a deep sleep on the sofa bed. Em got dressed quietly and went over to the main house to get a drink to avoid waking her. It would also give her some peace and quiet to think about last night's events. Her feet hurt from dancing until the early hours. She'd enjoyed letting her hair down again.

While Em waited for the guests to drop off their keys, she looked at Lucy's photos on Instagram. It looked like they were all having a riot of a time. She saved a few to her camera roll. Luke had exchanged numbers with her before saying good night. He was good fun, but there weren't any fireworks. Not like when she was near Jack.

She heard footsteps on the staircase. Mark walked into the kitchen, looking dreadful.

'You're not seeing me at my best,' he muttered.

'Coffee or paracetamol?' Em asked in a stage whisper.

'You're an angel. Both, please. What time did you get in?'

'Lucy and I left at 2. I thought you and Jack had already gone.'

'Yes, we left well before then. This hangover is mostly attributable to the bottle of whisky Jack forced me to share with him when we got back.'

'Are you two friends again?'

'Yes, as far as I remember. Though my head and my liver currently loathe him. Are you still friends with him?'

'That depends on what sort of a mood he's in today.' She put a glass of water and the packet of painkillers in front of him.

'Thanks. I thought after his heavy-handed interruption last night, you might have gone off him. Is Luke a fixture now? Jack's worried he might be.'

'And why would that worry Jack? I do have a vacancy for a boyfriend, which Jack doesn't seem keen to fill.'

'Don't believe everything he says. Shall I tell him you're interviewing?'

'You could ask him to submit his CV.'

'Morning!' Nancy walked into the kitchen before Mark could reply. 'And how are you both on this beautiful morning?'

'Good god, Mother, do you have to be so impossibly bright and breezy?'

'I see Em's sorted you out,' she said, spotting the paracetamol. 'Still not a morning person then, darling?' She gave him a rough hug.

Mark groaned and held his head. 'I should report you for child cruelty. I'm going back to bed.'

'I don't think Social Services care when you're 36.' She shouted after him.

Nancy started making a pot of tea.'You got back late.'

'Sorry, did we wake you?'

'No, I wasn't asleep. I heard your car pull up while I was reading in bed.'

'We were out dancing.'

'And so you should be on a Friday night at your age. Is Jack a good dancer?'

'I don't know. I wasn't dancing with him.'

'Oh,' Nancy seemed surprised. 'I just assumed you two were out with the boys.'

'No, we went out separately.'

She wasn't sure if Nancy disapproved or not.

58

It was nearly 1 pm, but Jack's curtains were still shut. And he hadn't answered the text Em had sent him to check he was ok.

'Stop worrying about him. If he was on the whisky last night, it's not surprising he slept in.' Lucy was in a better mood this morning, having had a conciliatory text from Lars. She was currently letting him stew.

'Mark got up.'

'And went back to bed. If you're that concerned, why don't you go over to his cottage?'

'Good idea." Em was concerned about Jack, but she was also regretting the CV comment she'd made to Mark. She wanted to catch Jack before Mark did. Em headed out of her front door towards Jack's.

She knocked on his door several times. No answer.

She shouted through the letterbox. 'Jack! Jaaaaaack!' There was a sound of something falling over inside.

'Hang on. Hang on. I'm coming.' It sounded like she'd woken him up. Thank God he was alive. *Don't be such a drama queen*.

The door opened to reveal a bleary-eyed Jack wearing the same shirt and trousers that she'd seen him wearing last night, but looking a lot more crumpled, with the shirt half hanging out of his chinos. Bed hair and stubble set off the look perfectly. Bizarrely, he still looked appealing. *How desperate are you?*

'I was worried about you,' Em said.

'Thanks.' Jack indicated for her to come in.

There were not one but two empty bottles of whisky on the coffee table.

Jack must have seen her looking. 'They weren't full before last night, and I did have some help from Mark.'

'Yes, I know. I saw Mark at breakfast.'

'Breakfast? He could always handle his drink better than me.'

'Not much better by the look of him.'

She wrinkled her nose. 'Shall I open a window?' Judging by the stale air and the messy blanket on the sofa, Jack hadn't made it as far as his bedroom last night.

'Have you spoken to Mark this morning?' She asked as she drew back the curtains.

Jack flinched at the bright sunshine. 'Not yet. Why?'

'No reason. Just making conversation. If he mentions anything about a CV, ignore him.'

'CV?'

'It doesn't matter. Have you thought about what ingredients you need for cooking Sunday lunch?'

'What time is it?'

'1 o'clock.'

'We were supposed to go to the supermarket this morning. Sorry!'

'Just give me a list of what you need. I'll ask Lucy to go while I sort out today's new guests. Perhaps have a shower first? It will help improve the ambience in here.'

'Sorry.'

'I'll make you a bacon butty while you're getting washed.'

'Thank you.' He slowly headed for the bathroom, taking his phone out of his pocket and leaving it on the kitchen counter.

'Actually, a ham sandwich will do,' he said. 'I'm not sure my head will cope with the noise of the smoke alarm today.' He managed a smile.

'Cheeky!' At least the hangover hadn't dampened his sense of humour.

While she was looking for butter and ham, Jack's phone buzzed. Em ignored it. A few seconds later, it buzzed again. Curiosity got the better of her, and she casually glanced at it on the way back from the fridge. He'd left it unlocked. There was a text on the front screen.

```
hi jack darling are u free later daisy xx
```

Darling? Daisy? Kisses? Who is Daisy? Em's mind started racing. Play it cool. Don't jump to conclusions. It could be anyone. Jack had probably bumped into an old summer holiday pal with Mark last night.

Jack looked more compos mentis when he emerged from the bathroom five minutes later. Em was casually arranging the sandwiches on a plate, trying to look innocent.

'Your phone buzzed while you were in the shower.'

'Thanks.' Jack picked up his phone, looked flustered and quickly shoved it into his bathrobe pocket.

'There's your sandwich. I've got to go.' Em headed to the front door.

'Off to meet Luke?'

She turned and looked at him. 'No. Are you going to see Daisy today?'

He looked puzzled. 'No.'

She didn't respond to that. As she opened the door, he called after her.

241

'Thanks for the sandwich, darling um, Em'.
Darling? Em needed a consultation with Lucy and fast.

59

'You look like you've got all the worries of the world on your shoulders, ' Lucy said as Em walked into the living room of her flat. 'What's wrong?'

'I'm an idiot. I've just given the game away that I've read one of Jack's text messages.' She filled Lucy in on what had happened.

'He called you "darling"? Isn't that a good thing?'

'Not when he immediately regretted it. The mysterious Daisy called him darling too. He was thinking about her. I'm just so confused. I don't know what to think any more.'

'This has got to be the most complicated non-relationship ever. We need to go back to basics. Do you still fancy him?'

'Yes. I've always fancied him since that very first day.'

Lucy raised her eyebrows.

'I never said I didn't fancy him, just that I didn't want a new relationship.'

'Do you want him?'

'I didn't at first. I didn't trust anyone after being blindsided by Connor. And I thought Jack wasn't available. But since then, I've grown to enjoy being with him. He makes me feel safe and cared for. And there's still that massive heart-racing spark whenever I'm near him. He was even in my head when

I was with Karl. Then we danced with Jason and Luke last night, and I suddenly felt young and free again.'

'So Jack doesn't make you feel young and free?'

'No. I suppose it's because he's older. We do calm grown-up things. We're friends.'

'Because he friend-zoned you. So is Luke a better bet?'

'He made me laugh, but there wasn't that spark. I'm sure we'd have fun. I'd have given Luke a chance if I hadn't met Jack. But I want to see where that chemistry with Jack leads when we let it. Otherwise, I'll regret it. I've never had that feeling with anyone else other than Jack.'

'So Jack's in the lead over Luke. Does Jack fancy you?'

'I think he does. We've had several moments where I thought he was going to kiss me, but he always backed away from it. He was distant after Isabella's threats. But he was very proprietorial last night around Luke. And then there's what Mark said this morning, which implied he did want me to be his girlfriend.'

'So what's stopping him from making you his girlfriend?'

'Perhaps he's gone off me, but the other evidence doesn't suggest that. Or, as he's said before, he wants to get the divorce sorted before he gets into another relationship.'

'If he's flirting with other women and giving them his phone number, he's ready. Or he's trying to make you jealous to see if you're ready.'

'Daisy might just be a family friend?'

'I think you're clutching at straws there. She's calling him "darling" and asking him out. Have you checked their Instagram feeds?'

'Whose?'

'Jack's and Mark's?'

'No. I've only just found out about her.'

Lucy was already tapping away on her phone. Em looked over her shoulder. The last post from Jack was from the trip to Dartmoor. A photo of the house and some teaser text about his new book. But he kept it strictly work-related, so that wasn't a surprise. Nothing in his stories.

'Now for Mark, ' said Lucy. 'Much more interesting.'

Mark had shared one photo from last night - a picture of him and Jack, arms around one another. Jack had a pint in his hand. It was broad daylight, so it must have been early evening. The caption read, 'Back home with my best buddy'.

'Let's check his stories. 'Devon girls are the best' written across a photo of Mark with his arm around two women, a similar age to Lucy and Em - too young to be old flames from school days. Jack probably took it. It looked like it was by the harbour, and it was dark, so it was after they'd bumped into Em and Luke.

A selfie popped up, showing Mark with one of the women from the previous picture. Then it moved on to someone else's stories.

'Nothing useful there,' said Lucy.

'Hang on. Go back. Who was behind Mark?'

'Ooh, you're right.' Lucy looked more closely. 'That's Jack.'

The image of him was fuzzy, but it appeared to be Jack laughing with his arm around the other woman.

'I bet that's Daisy.' Em felt jealous. She was gazing into his eyes. 'I wonder if he has the same effect on her as he has on me.'

'Let's see if it is Daisy.' Lucy went back to the photos in Mark's feed. The one of Jack had 23 likes. She looked through the list of likers. Iamdaisydashford was one of them.

Iamdaisydashford 's account was public. She was the woman Jack had his arm around - her story had a selfie with a tipsy-looking Jack. Lucy took a screenshot of it. 'For future reference,' she said.

Lucy carried on scrolling. Em looked dazed. What should she do now?

'Looks like she's a teacher at the local secondary school,' said Lucy. 'A history teacher, specialising in 19th-century ships.'

'What?'

'I thought that would make you pay attention. She is a history teacher, though.'

She is attractive, and she has something in common with Jack, even if she isn't obsessed with ships. I've lost him!

'I need a plan.' Em said.

'No, you don't,' said Lucy. 'You just need to tell him how you feel as soon as possible.'

Ping. A text from Jack.

'And there's your chance,' Lucy said.

Em didn't unlock her phone. 'He probably thinks I'm a psycho after the Daisy text revelation.'

'But that's easily explained away. Mark's Instagram feed led us to find out about Jack and Daisy, not the text.'

'True! Thank you.' She checked the notification.

'It's just his last-minute shopping list for Sunday lunch.'

'The one I'm graciously going out to buy for him? He's got us both waiting on him now.'

'He's not in a state to drive, and I've got guests to sort out. I didn't think you'd mind as you'll enjoy eating it.'

'Give it here. I'll write it down in my notebook.'

'I can text it to you.'

'No, I prefer paper. Hand it over.'

'We've got a double date tonight!' Lucy gleefully announced as Em returned to the flat from doing her concierge job for the day.

'Jason and Luke?'

'No, Jack and Mark.'

'Seriously?' What had Lucy been up to?

'Yes, Jack's booked a table at that restaurant we were

originally going to last night.'

'I'm surprised he got one at short notice on a Saturday night.'

'He said Nancy knows the owner. She called in a favour. They usually keep a couple of tables free for walk-ins.'

'When did all this happen?'

'He popped over half an hour ago while you were busy. You're right - there is something even more appealing about him when you're talking to him one to one.'

'I'm not going to be fighting you for him, am I?' Em was worried enough about Daisy as a potential rival, but if Lucy set her heart on a man, she usually got him.

'Of course not. I've got my eyes on Mark.' Lucy tended to be a serial monogamist, but this was moving fast even for her.

'Lars is a goner then?'

'Yes, I just haven't told him yet. Now, let's get down to business. Can I borrow your straighteners? I left mine at home.'

60

 Jack had volunteered to drive. The restaurant was gorgeous, and they had been given the best table with views over the bay. The food was delicious. Mark entertained them with stories of his adventures in Spain. And, best of all, Jack was being attentive to Em again. It was shaping up to be an excellent evening. They could go for a romantic walk on the seafront afterwards, and she could talk to Jack while Mark and Lucy went on ahead.

They were working their way through their main courses when Lucy started coughing. 'I think I've got a bone stuck in my throat,' she managed to say.

Mark attracted the waiter's attention. 'Could we have some water, please?'

Lucy gulped down a pint of water, but the bone was still stuck.

'Would you like to try some bread?' the waiter offered, keen to get the situation resolved as soon as possible because the other diners were starting to stare.

The bread didn't work either. And neither did the ball of rice that the waiter brought from the kitchen.

'Do you want to go home?' Jack asked.

'No, don't spoil the evening. I'm sure it will move in a

minute. You have your desserts.'

Lucy tried some more water. Still no joy.

'I think we should go.' Em said. Jack and Mark agreed.

Lucy was quiet on the drive back to Dashford Grange.

'It's starting to seriously hurt,' she whispered to Em.

Jack must've heard her. 'We need to get you to hospital,' he said. 'We can drop you off at home first, Mark?'

'Don't make me spend Saturday night with my mother. I haven't done that since I was 15. We'll all go.'

Jack turned onto the main A road towards Barnstaple A&E, 20 miles away.

Half an hour later, they were all sitting in a row on hard plastic hospital chairs, waiting for Lucy to be seen.

'I'm sorry. I've ruined everyone's evening,' Lucy said, almost crying.

'It's not that bad. A&E on a Saturday night is quite entertaining,' Jack said as they watched a man walk in wearing a long winter coat and dragging a Hoover next to him.

'Odd to wear that coat when it's 25 degrees outside.' Em said.

'You're more worried by the coat than the hoover?' Jack said.

They watched the clock tick around for at least an hour.

Em started to nod off on Jack's shoulder. She felt him put his arm around her.

'Lucy Thomson?' a nurse shouted. Em was suddenly wide awake again.

'Do you want me to come with you?' Em offered.

'No, it's fine. You look comfortable there. Don't move.'

'I'll come with you,' Mark volunteered.

Em was sure she heard him say, 'I don't want to play gooseberry' to Lucy as they walked away.

'Did you ask them to do that?' Jack asked.

'Do what?'

'To give us some time alone.'

'No. I thought you must have said something after your plan was foiled.'

'My plan? You're the one who insisted on our evening out.' Jack laughed.

'No, you did. Lucy said you came over to suggest we all went out.'

'Perhaps I should ask a doctor to look at you as well. You seem to have forgotten the text you sent me this afternoon.'

'The last text I sent you was to check you were ok this morning.'

'No.' Jack looked genuinely concerned. 'Don't you remember suggesting we go out?'

She shook her head. Em was starting to doubt her own memory now.

Jack got out his phone and showed her the message thread. After his shopping list text, there was a reply from Em:

```
    thanks for the list darling id love to go out
this evening, how about a meal at Sashas xx
```

Jack:

```
    Much as I love spending time with you, it
seems a bit off leaving Mark and Lucy alone.
```

Em:

```
    they could come to
```

Jack:

> OK. I'll see what I can do. Are you alright?

Em:

> yep - looking forward to seeing you xx

'I didn't send those. Look at the spelling and the punctuation.' Em got out her phone to check. Yes, there were the same messages.

'I did think that was odd, but I thought you might be tired from last night. So who did send them then?'

The penny dropped. 'Lucy! She took my phone from me to write down your shopping list. She told me you'd suggested Sasha's. I thought how thoughtful of you because I missed going there last night.'

So it hadn't been his idea, which was a shame. It had still been a good evening, though.

Jack laughed.

'You must've thought your luck was in with all these women calling you darling,' Em said.

'What do you mean by that?'

'Well, Daisy and fake me.'

'You've been reading my messages.' Jack wasn't laughing now.

'You just showed them to me.'

'I didn't show you the message from Daisy. I wondered how you knew about her.'

Don't panic. 'Lucy was looking at Mark's Instagram pictures. We worked it out from there.'

'And how did you work out that she called me darling from a photo on Instagram? You read Daisy's message while I was in the shower!' He was angry now.

The woman opposite, with a sleeping child lying across her lap, scowled at him. 'Would you mind keeping your voices

251

down? We don't all want to listen to your domestic, thank you.'

'I would've thought you'd have learnt your lesson about reading other people's personal correspondence.' His voice was a stage whisper now.

'That's a low blow,' Em hissed back at him.

'I'm disappointed in you. I thought you were better than that.'

'Don't be so bloody pompous. I couldn't help seeing it. You left your unlocked phone right under my nose.'

'Yeah, right.'

'All sorted.' Lucy almost bounced back into the waiting area with Mark in tow. 'No need to look so glum. No damage done. '

'Isn't there? Let's go.' Jack stormed out into the car park.

61

'You look perky. Matchmaking suits you.'

Lucy was already bustling around making breakfast when Em got up the following morning.

'You sussed my little ruse then? I thought it was going well until they'd finished sorting me out in A&E. Why were you and Jack so quiet on the way home last night? The atmosphere was awful. Mark noticed it too.'

Em had gone straight to bed when they got back last night, pleading a headache to get out of their usual post-date post-mortem. She was surprised Lucy hadn't heard her crying in the night. The stress of the stuck fishbone must have worn her out.

'You're very pally with Mark all of a sudden?'

'He's good fun. We have a lot in common. And I'm officially single again. I sent Lars the 'you're dumped' text last night. Life's too short to waste time. But you've avoided the question. What's up between you and Jack?'

Em explained.

'I shouldn't have put darling in the message. Sorry!' Lucy was mortified.

'It's not your fault. I shouldn't have mentioned Daisy. I don't know how we recover from this. He was furious.'

'Probably touched a raw nerve. I can imagine Isabella did her fair share of snooping. I'm sure he will have calmed down by now.'

'I hope so. It's not as if I broke into his phone. It was just there in front of me. I'll offer to help with lunch. Hopefully, we can talk then.'

But Jack wasn't in the mood for talking when Em went over to the main house later that morning, far from it.

'What are you doing here?' was the only greeting she got when she walked into the kitchen. No good morning. No pleasantries at all. He was still pissed off then.

'I work here!'

'Not on Sundays.'

'I thought you might like some help with preparing lunch.'

'As you can see, I've got it all in hand. I don't need your assistance, thanks. I've got Mark to help me.'

'I just need to pop out,' said Mark, drying his hands on a towel and looking like he wanted to be anywhere else but here.

'Can't it wait? We're on a tight schedule.' Mark was getting the full force of Jack's foul mood too.

Mark exchanged a wtf look with Em.

She saw a pile of veg waiting to be prepped. 'I could peel the spuds. Even I can manage that,' she said, trying to lighten the atmosphere.

'One - I'm not convinced you could do that without screwing up. And two - I said I didn't want you here. Just leave us to it.'

'And fuck you too!' Em muttered under her breath as she marched out of the kitchen.

'Pardon?' Jack said.

'You heard.' She slammed the door. Jack 1, Em nil. She needed to work on her composure.

62

The afternoon started with pouring rain with an occasional clap of thunder. The weather matched the mood in Nancy's dining room perfectly.

Em had suggested to Lucy that they skip lunch altogether and go for a drive somewhere instead. But Lucy seemed keen to stick to the original plan. 'You never know. Jack might have mellowed after taking it out on beating the Yorkshire pudding mix.'

But Jack hadn't mellowed. He looked like he would have to make enough Yorkshire pudding batter to feed a small army before he could be remotely decent to Em, though he was treating everyone else with some form of civility.

'What time is your flight, Mark?' Nancy was trying to keep the conversation going as they tucked into their mains.

'Take off is 7.35 this evening. Lucy's dropping me off at the airport on the way home.'

'We thought we'd head off after we've finished lunch,' Lucy said. 'The traffic might be bad this evening, with the rain and the end of the school holidays.'

'That's very kind of you, Lucy. That will save Jack a trip to Bristol and back.' Nancy sounded pleased. 'The weather forecast says it's going to dry up by six. You won't have to miss your usual Sunday evening walk with Em, Jack.'

Nancy stared pointedly at Jack, waiting for his reaction.

'I won't be walking with Em. I've got other plans for this evening.'

'Oh, really?' Nancy sounded surprised. 'You're turning into quite the party animal. That will be three nights in a row. Mark's a bad influence. Doing anything exciting?'

'Hopefully. I'm meeting someone.' Jack glared at Em.

'Daisy, by any chance?' Em asked.

'Yes, actually. You can read the details on my phone if you like.'

Unnecessarily bitchy. It was a good job Nancy had a big dining table. Otherwise, Em would've been tempted to kick him, but after this morning's argument, she didn't want to let him get a rise out of her again. She counted to ten in her head.

'That won't be necessary. How you spend your time is nothing to do with me,' Em managed to say in her breeziest voice. 'Everyone ready for dessert?'

Lucy had packed her bag and was standing in Em's hall.

'I'm sorry how things have worked out. I hope he has a shitty date with Daisy and comes running back to you.'

'Que sera sera. I'm not going to get upset by it.'

'Aren't you?'

'I shall probably sob into my cocoa tonight, but I'll get over it. If he's going to be a moody sod, he doesn't fit in with my grand plan.'

'It's a bit hot for cocoa. I'd try a G&T or three. Remember, the octopus.'

Em smiled. 'Have fun with Mark.'

'I don't know what you mean,' Lucy said with a smirk on her face.

The thunderstorm had blown over. Mark was already in the courtyard hugging Nancy.

'You will come home for Christmas,' Nancy said. 'It's been horrible without you.'

'Yes, I'll be back before then, I think.' Em noticed him exchanging a look with Lucy.

Jack was hanging back.

Mark went over and gave him a man hug.

'Don't screw things up,' she overheard him say to Jack.

'What's that meant to mean?'

Mark looked over at Em, who was helping Lucy load her bag into the car boot.

'Pick the right woman this time.'

Jack ignored his comment. 'Have a good flight.'

'See you, Em.' Mark smiled and waved at her as he got in the passenger seat.

'It was good meeting you, Mark. Hopefully, I'll see you again soon.'

Em stood next to Nancy, as they both waved Lucy and Mark off. Jack kept his distance.

'I've got some urgent work to do,' Nancy said, hurrying into the house, leaving Jack and Em alone, no doubt deliberately.

Jack looked like he was going to say something, then changed his mind and walked back to his cottage.

63

Monday afternoon. Em was working on a new landscape painting to replace the ones that the gallery had sold last week. She stood back to look at it. She'd planned to paint a sunny day, but it kept turning into a storm. Time to put the paints away until she was in a better mood. A text from Lucy popped up on her phone.

```
Any news on Jack?
```

Em sighed and started typing her response.

```
No - his car wasn't back till 8 am this
```
morning. Haven't seen him all day.

Em had noticed Jack's curtains were still closed at lunchtime. He couldn't have had much sleep last night. She didn't want to dwell on why that might be.

```
You weren't spying on him, were you?
```

Em wasn't going to admit to that.

No, I was already up. I heard his car tyres on the gravel. Did Mark catch his flight?

Em was curious about the situation with Lucy and Mark.

Yes. Got there early. Had time to get to know him better before he left.

Best not to think too hard about what Lucy meant by that.

Keeping in touch with him then?

Three dots appeared then

He's coming back to see me in 3 weeks. Don't tell Nancy

64

There was a break in the rain at last. The week was dragging without Jack to talk to. Em usually did admin on Thursday mornings, but the weather forecast predicted rain again that afternoon. Nancy was going to be out all day learning to hang-glide with her WI friends, so Em could do the admin later.

She grabbed her sketching bag. Car or walk? Her ankle could still be dodgy sometimes. And if she drove down into the village, she'd have an extra 20 minutes of drawing time. Car then.

Fifteen minutes later, Em was sitting outside the beach cafe.

'You've not been down here on your own for ages. Man trouble again?' Mary sat down at Em's table and pulled out her vape.

Em put down her pencil.

'Yeah. I'm beginning to think they're not worth it.'

'I thought something was up. His lordship was asleep in his car when I arrived on Monday morning.'

'His lordship?'

'Your Jack.'

'I don't think he's ever been my Jack.' Sadly, whatever she'd kidded herself.

'I took him a coffee to make sure he was alright.'

'And was he?'

'He said he'd been walking on the beach since sunrise and wanted to think. He just needed a nap before he drove back home. I couldn't get anything else out of him. He looked upset.' Jack must have better resolve than she had if Mary had failed to extract any gossip. 'Is that it then for you two?'

'I think so. I haven't seen him since Sunday. He's avoiding me.'

'Shame - you made a lovely couple. You could tell he was in love with you.'

'Could you?'

'Yes, the way he looked at you. And he was so impressed by your paintings. He was telling me about the ones you sold when you two were here last week. He couldn't wait to see the portrait you were painting of him. I can't remember why you weren't there. I think you'd gone to the gallery to talk to them about something.'

'He's got a new woman now, so it doesn't matter any more.'

'What woman? You don't mean Daisy?'

'What made you suggest her?'

'I saw them walking together on Sunday evening. You don't need to worry about her. She prefers bad boys. She's been seeing one of the surfers all summer. She's not with Jack,' Mary said as she headed back inside the cafe.

Em tried to put Jack out of her mind. Despite what Mary had said, he was still avoiding her.

It was Friday lunchtime. Em had sorted out Rose Cottage. But there was still one cottage to do. Em looked at the pile of towels and bedclothes on the table in the kitchen.

'Are those Jack's?' Nancy asked.

'Yes. He normally collects them.'

'I would offer to take them over, but I think you need to offer an olive branch. I much preferred the friendly, relaxed atmosphere we had before last weekend.'

'Was I in the wrong, though?' asked Em.

'Would you like it if he'd read a text someone had sent to you?'

'No. But if I'd left my phone where he could see it, it would be a different scenario to him deliberately unlocking the screen to snoop. I guess neither of us is right.'

'With anyone else, I'd tell you it was his loss but remember how Isabella treated him. He's bound to be sensitive if he thinks he's been spied on.'

Nancy was right. Em picked up the clean linen and headed out into the courtyard. She knocked on Jack's door.

'Your fresh towels and sheets, Professor Carver.'

'It's lovely to see you.'

'Why? Have your sheets seen so much action this week that you're desperate for new ones?' *Oh God, why did you say that? He'll know you're jealous now.*

'You know that's not true.' Jack looked downcast.

'Daisy might have been over. I don't monitor your cottage 24 hours a day.'

'Daisy and I aren't together.' So Mary was right.

'I'm sorry Sunday's date didn't go well. Not that it's any of my business.'

'I didn't have a date with her on Sunday. We went for a walk. Nothing else. She wanted advice about a history degree application for one of her pupils. I thought it was an excellent opportunity to make you jealous.'

'Well, you succeeded. How old are you?'

He laughed. 'Old enough to know better. And you?'

'It's impolite to ask a woman's age. I'm sorry I read one of your texts. I promise it was an accident.'

'I'm sorry I overreacted. Can we pick up where we left off?'

'Barnstaple A&E is 30 minutes drive away.'

'You could sit next to me on the sofa, and we can imagine that a man with a vacuum cleaner stuck on his cock has just walked in.'

'Was that why he had his coat on?'

Jack laughed. 'Shall I cook dinner for us tonight?'

'Yes, please. I've been living on salads and ready meals all week.'

65

Em heard a car pull onto the drive. Hopefully, the final set of guests. After a busy day cleaning and organising, she was desperate to be waited on by Jack.

She looked out of her window to see three energetic young boys spill out of a big SUV. They began throwing gravel at one another. An exhausted-looking man got out of the driver's seat and made no attempt to stop the mini-riot.

A woman emerged from the passenger side. She looked considerably younger than the driver and voiced her annoyance loudly. 'I don't know why I agreed to come on holiday with your children. It's only been four hours, and I've had enough already. We should have gone to Rhodes on our own.' The man made no effort to respond.

Em checked her clipboard. The Smiths. *Heaven Knows I'm Miserable Now* started playing in her head. How appropriate. It looked like they were going to have a fantastic week. Em opened the door to greet them.

With the Smiths settled into Lavender Cottage, Em headed next door to Jack's.

He'd cooked her favourite meal: lasagne with garlic bread and salad.

'I've missed this,' he said as they sat opposite one another at his dining table.

'Lasagne?' asked Em.

'No. Eating with you.'

Em smiled. 'This is so good.'

'Eating with me?' Jack gave her a cheeky grin.

'No. The lasagne. '

They both laughed.

'My mother's recipe,' he said. 'I'll have to teach you how to make it.'

'I'd like that.' Em cleaned up the last piece of lasagne from her plate. 'There's one thing that's been bugging me. Why did you wait for me to come around with your clean linen today? Why didn't you come to see me once you'd decided to forgive me?'

'Because I hadn't entirely decided to forgive you. Then when I saw you …' He sighed.

There was a crash from next door and the sound of Mrs Smith shouting. Em winced. 'I hope Nancy's got good insurance.'

'Something tells me I'm not going to get much peace and quiet this week,' Jack laughed.

'I can ask them to keep the noise down?'

'I think you might be asking for the impossible.'

Jack started pushing his last piece of lasagne thoughtfully around the plate. 'Do you want children?' he asked.

Em looked at the wall adjoining the Smith's cottage. Judging by the sounds coming from next door, the riot that had started on the drive was kicking off again indoors. 'Not those ones,' she said.

'But would you like your own?'

'Are we doing all the serious questions tonight?'

'Yes, I thought we could cover politics and religion next.' He grinned.

'You already know my political views, and I'm an atheist.'

'Same here, but you've dodged the family question.'

'Did you and Isabella want a family?'

'I did. I thought she did too, but then it turned out that she thought pregnancy would ruin her figure, so she kept taking the pill without telling me.'

'That's awful.'

'It all came out when I suggested we go to a fertility clinic. But at least it got me to finally see that everything in our marriage was only about her and what she wanted.' He sighed. 'And you've still managed to sidestep my question!'

'You should get a job on Newsnight.'

'Sorry - it's too personal. I shouldn't have asked. It's the wine talking.' He looked at his empty glass. 'Top up?' He picked up the wine. Em nodded. Jack distributed what was left in the bottle between their glasses.

Em swilled her wine around, wondering what to say to him. She might as well be honest. 'The truth is I'm scared I'll be a terrible mother.'

'Why do you think that? I don't get that impression of you at all.'

'My mother didn't set a good example. She was a lot like Isabella, by the sounds of it. I think she only agreed to have a child so she'd have someone to look after her in old age. I worry I'll turn into her. I'm not even sure I know how to be a good parent.'

'But she showed you how to be a bad one. So don't do the bad things.'

'You make it sound so simple!'

'Life often is. It's just us overthinking things that makes it difficult.' He looked thoughtful again. 'Perhaps I should take my own advice.'

'What do you mean? What have you been overthinking?'

He turned to face her. She saw that look of loneliness in

those deep blue eyes again. It made her catch her breath. An almighty bang from next door broke the spell.

They could hear the muffled sound of Mrs Smith through the wall. 'For fuck's sake, Joseph, why won't you do as you're told for once?'

Em sighed. Perhaps she and Jack weren't meant to be any more than friends. Fate seemed to have an uncanny knack of ruining the moment whenever it looked like he wanted more.

Jack looked at the clock on the mantelpiece. 'Why don't we go for a walk and watch the sunset? It will be more relaxing than listening to World War III next door.'

66

'Do I need walking boots?' Em asked as Jack grabbed the picnic rug from the hall stand and shut the door to his cottage.

'No, it's an easy route. There's a short stretch without a path, but you'll be fine in trainers.'

He led the way across the courtyard, through the gate into the paddock and then turned right, heading towards the old open barn in the corner. Tucked behind the barn, partially hidden by an overgrown hedge, was a small gate labelled PRIVATE.

'I've never noticed that before,' Em said.

'Few people do, which suits me as this is where I go for peace and quiet when I want to think.' He opened the gate for her. 'Don't put this walk on Instagram.'

The gate led into a copse and onto a path with a sharp right turn leading deeper into the trees. They walked along the trail, but once they'd turned the corner, Jack stopped.

'This way. Mind your head.' He had to bend double to get under the low branches. Em followed him along what looked like an animal track.

A few seconds later, they came out into the open again.

Em gasped. In front of her was a small field full of tall

grasses and the last few wildflowers of late summer waving gently in the evening breeze. 'It's beautiful, like something out of a dream.'

'It is, isn't it.' Jack smiled at her. 'And you haven't seen the best bit yet. Come on.'

He took her hand and led her through the grass. Em smiled to herself. It felt like she was starring in one of those over-the-top perfume commercials, shot in slow motion in golden evening light, her hair streaming behind her as she ran across a field with her lover. Except her ankle wasn't up to running, and Jack wasn't ...

'Turn around,' he said, bringing Em back to reality as they reached some more woodland on the other side of the field.

Em looked. 'Oh, that's amazing.'

The field fell away steeply, giving an uninterrupted view over Dashford, the cliffs and the beach way below. The setting sun cast a golden glow over the sea.

'I know you said no Instagram, but am I allowed to take a photo just for me?' Em had a feeling she'd want to paint this view in future. Jack nodded.

He laid out the picnic rug and sat down while she took several shots.

When she'd finished, she sat next to him. 'Have you brought many people up here?'

'No, you're the first.'

'Really? Not even ...'

'No - no one,' he interrupted.

'Thank you for sharing it with me.'

'It's a pleasure. You're the only person I've ever wanted to share it with.' He sounded sincere.

'I'm going to miss having you around. This summer's been ...' Em struggled to find the right adjective. 'Interesting.'

'That's one word for it. It's been an emotional roller coaster ride for me. But it's not over yet. I'm still here for another week.'

Somehow they'd moved closer to one another. Em could feel his breath on her cheek. 'What happens when you go back to London?'

'Let's not worry about that yet. I'm more interested in what happens now.' That puppy dog look again. She so wanted to know what his lips felt like on hers. She kissed him tentatively on his jawline. The feel of his stubble against her skin sent shockwaves through her body.

'I know I said we should just be friends,' he said. 'But can I change my mind?'

'I'd like that,' she said.

67

Em stirred as a ray of sunshine squeezed through the gap around her bedroom blind, and warmed her skin.

She looked at the clock. Shit! She normally got up earlier than this on a Saturday. She must've forgotten to set the alarm. Then she smiled as she remembered why.

There was a dent in the pillow next to her. She rolled over and inhaled the distinctive scent of Jack's aftershave. All the memories from last night came flooding back. Making love in the field. Walking back to the courtyard, thinking everyone must know what they'd just been doing. And then heading to her bed to pick up where they had left off until they both fell asleep exhausted.

'Hello, you. Why were you sniffing that pillow?'

Em rolled back onto her side and saw Jack walking into the bedroom wearing her short flowery bathrobe and nothing else. He was carrying two mugs. 'I love the smell of your aftershave.'

She sat up and took one of the mugs off him. 'Hmm. Just the way I like it.'

'I aim to please.'

'You certainly do. I don't have any complaints.' Jack had proved to be a skilled and generous lover.

'Neither do I. Perhaps you do deserve that 5-star review on TripAdvisor after all.'

'Even though I hit you with the hoover?'

'A certain type of client might see that as a bonus.'

'I do have one complaint,' Em said with a serious expression.

Jack looked worried.

'That robe looks awful on you.'

He grinned, put his tea on the bedside table, and slipped the robe onto the floor. 'Better?'

Em took in the view. 'Much better.'

'What time do you need to get up?' He was already snuggling back under the sheets.

'Half an hour ago, sadly.'

He started slowly covering her shoulder in gentle kisses. 'If I promised to help you today, could I persuade you to stay in bed a little longer?' He whispered, taking her mug from her hand and putting it beside his on the bedside cabinet.

'You'll have to work harder than that to persuade me.'

'Oh, will I? I think I'm going to enjoy finding out the best way to get you to agree,' he said, sliding his hand up her inner thigh.

68

Jack helped Em sort out the departing guests. Then they cleaned the cottages in double quick time. Em was about to suggest they have an early lunch together, but Jack said he had to go into Exeter on an errand. He wouldn't say what it was. 'You will find out soon enough,' he whispered in her ear and kissed her goodbye.

Em went into the main house and found Nancy having lunch in the kitchen.

'Movement at the front door,' the video doorbell announced.

Nancy checked the camera feed on her iPad.

'I don't like the look of him.' She showed Em the screen.

Em couldn't see the man's face, but she could tell instantly who it was. Connor! Not today of all days. Sporting his Aston Villa baseball cap, a baggy t-shirt, joggers and trainers, and with a big holdall that appeared to be nearly empty slung over his shoulder, he looked like he was going to rob the place.

'It's ok. I know who it is.'

'Really?' Nancy raised her eyebrows.

'He's my ex.'

'I thought you said Connor was a recruitment consultant?'

273

'He is. He might look more like a drug dealer now, but he does have good taste in suits when he's working.'

'Did you tell him where you were?'

'No, I have no urge to see him again. The last thing I would've done is tell him I was living here.'

'We can't leave him standing there. Do you want me to answer the door? I can say he's got the wrong address?'

Tempting as that offer was, it wouldn't solve anything. 'Thanks, but I better deal with it.'

The sooner Em could find out what Connor wanted and get rid of him, the better.

'What brings you here?' Em didn't bother with any niceties when she opened the front door.

'Great to see you too. Funnily enough, I hadn't got anything in my diary for this weekend after you cancelled our original plans.'

It would've been their wedding day. How could that have slipped her mind? She was surprised Connor had remembered. 'I thought you would have forgotten by now.'

'Not with a fucking great loan to pay off. And that's after I sold the car. I'll have a monthly reminder for the next three years.'

'Why did you waste money on a train fare to come and tell me that?'

'You've blocked me on every social media platform known to man. And you've blocked my phone. How else was I supposed to contact you? Send you a handwritten love letter like someone from your frigging Jane Austen books?'

'It would've been cheaper. Or you could've made your caller ID private and phoned me again.'

A look of annoyance crossed his face. He must be kicking himself for not thinking of that.

'Are you telling me you've travelled 200 miles just to have

a go at me?' Em asked.

'No.' Connor sighed. 'The conversation hasn't gone how I planned at all. I miss you.' He produced a battered bunch of red roses from the holdall.

Em kept her hands firmly on her hips. 'What is it you miss exactly? Having someone to wash your clothes and clean the bathroom up after you? Someone to warm your ice-cold heart in the winter? Do tell.'

'You were more to me than that. It's just not the same without your smile. And your sarcastic take on everything.'

'Where's Micra or Astra or whatever she's called? Isn't she sucking your cock any more?'

'No. She's run off to France with the projectionist.'

'Do cinemas still have projectionists?'

'No. He's a dick. He called himself that because it sounded impressive. They just press a button on a computer now. And then spend the rest of the night serving behind the bar, flirting with Astra. Well, he used to. He's in fucking Paris now fucking that fucking bitch.'

'Three fuckings in one sentence - that must be a record even for you.'

'Oh, I see.' He attempted an upper-class accent. 'Now you're living in a mansion, you're too posh for swearing.'

The conversation was going nowhere useful. Time to tone it down a bit and get rid of him before Jack returned. 'That wasn't the point I was making. I'm sorry you've had a wasted journey. I'm happier now than I've ever been. I don't want to go back to how we were before.'

'It's that bastard Jack, isn't it?'

'What's Jack got to do with it?' How did he know about Jack?

'I knew it. I saw you together in that photo Lucy posted on Instagram last weekend, him giving you the "fuck me now" look.'

Oh, for god's sake, surely Lucy hadn't. But then it was Lucy, so she obviously had and being the thorough social media expert she was, she'd probably tagged the location as well. That explained how Connor had discovered where Em was living. The comment about Jack's look was an interesting one. She didn't think they'd been at all loved up that night. She'd have to check Lucy's Instagram feed later.

'Well?' Em's lack of response had made him agitated.

'It's nothing to do with Jack. Even if you crawled across broken glass and promised to spend ten hours a week rescuing orphaned kittens, there is no way I am taking you back. Just go home, Connor.'

He looked crestfallen. She thought he was going to cry. 'So nothing will change your mind?'

'No, nothing.'

'I suppose that's that, then. There's one slight problem. I can't go home. There isn't another fucking train till Monday.'

Em scowled.

'Sorry, your ladyship.' Connor put the posh accent on again. 'There are no vehicles the railway variety to transport me back to my abode in the shire of the West Midlands until the morrow of Monday - or some such shit.'

'You'll have to find a room in Dashford, then.'

'There are two problems with that milady. 1. It's a two-mile walk in this baking heat, and 2. There are no rooms available. I checked on the train before I got here. There's some gathering of dancing wankers with bells on happening all weekend, so everywhere's booked out.'

The Morris Dancing Festival - Em had forgotten about that. 'Wait there. I'll be back in five minutes.'

69

'For someone whose job is essentially sales, he doesn't do a very good job of selling himself,' Nancy commented as Em walked back into the kitchen.

'You heard all that then?'

'Unfortunately, yes. My uncle used to have a parrot who swore like that. They were fucking annoying as well.' Em was taken aback. That was the first time she'd heard Nancy swear.

'The parrot or your uncle?'

'Both. What is the lovely Connor going to do?'

'I wanted to ask you a favour.'

Nancy looked concerned. 'Much as I enjoyed his description of the Morris Dancing festival, I don't want him in my house.'

'I wouldn't dream of asking you to put him up. But I wondered if I could stop in one of your spare rooms while Connor slept in my flat?'

'I thought you might have somewhere else to sleep.' Nancy raised her eyebrows and gave Em a knowing look.

Em blushed. 'You don't miss anything, do you?'

'I may be old, but I'm not blind. I saw Jack leave your flat this morning. It's about time. I'm pleased for you both.'

'I didn't want to presume Jack would take me in.'

'He's a hot-blooded male. Of course, he'll take you in. Especially if it keeps you away from your ex - though I don't think there's much competition. But if you want a backup plan, you can use the room next to Mark's. Though no taking Jack up there. It's frustrating enough being on my own without having to listen to other people having sex all night. I had enough of that last weekend with Lucy and Mark.'

An interesting revelation. So that's why Lucy hadn't heard Em crying last Saturday night. Something to follow up with Lucy later. But right now, Em needed to concentrate on getting Connor sorted.

The heat was getting oppressive. Thirty-two degrees Celsius, according to the weather app on Em's phone.

'Connor, will you be much longer?' Em shouted through her bathroom door. Today's guests were due in half an hour, and she was desperate to wash and change, ready to greet them.

The sound of the shower stopped, and the door opened. Connor stood there stark bollock naked.

Em rolled her eyes. 'If you think waving your cock around will change my mind, you've got another thing coming.'

'Don't flatter yourself - I need a towel.'

'In the cupboard behind the door.'

He shut the bathroom door again. Em heard the airing cupboard door open and close.

Connor emerged a few seconds later, suitably covered up. 'It's all yours.'

Em walked into the bathroom, locking the door behind her. She undressed, turned the temperature down on the shower, and got under it, letting the cool water wash away the stress. Jack should be back soon, so once the guests were settled in, she could relax with him. Perhaps they could pick up where they left off this morning. She got a warm glow at the thought. She better get a move on. She didn't want to be late. She picked up the shower gel and squeezed it onto the sponge. A tiny drop came out, accompanied by a horrible squelchy noise. Connor must have finished off the bottle.

'Connor!' She shouted. 'Can you get me a new bottle of shower gel, please? It's under the kitchen sink.'

'Just a moment, sweetheart. I will be right with you. I can wash your back if you like?'

Sweetheart? Backwashing? Was he going to have another go at charming her?

'Thanks for your kind offer - but no thanks.'

He knocked on the door a couple of minutes later. She drew the shower curtain around herself, opened the door slightly and took the bottle off him.

'Thank you.'

'Any time.' He grinned. No, it was more of a smirk. What had she ever seen in him?

70

'Have you seen Jack? I was expecting him to be back by now.' Em had gone over to the main house when she couldn't see his car in the courtyard.

Nancy peered over her glasses at her. 'He's been and gone. Didn't he tell you?'

She handed Em a handwritten note. 'This was on the kitchen island along with his key.'

'Key?' Em read the note.

Dear Nancy,

Thank you for putting me up, or should that be putting up with me for the summer. I've appreciated it very much.

I know I said I was stopping until the first week in September, but something unexpected has happened, and I need to go back to London this afternoon. I've left the cottage tidy - not too much to do to get it ready for the next guest.

Hopefully, you'll have time to pop in and see me when you're next in town.

I'm sorry I didn't have time to say goodbye properly.

Love always,

Jack x

* * *

'Do you know what happened?' Em could feel the panic rising in her chest.

'Sorry, I've no idea. I only came back ten minutes ago. Hopefully, nothing to do with that wretched Isabella. I still have the photos if she is playing up.'

Em checked her phone. No text. No WhatsApp message. No voicemail.

'I suppose I've been busy with the guests until now. I hope he's ok.' Em was trying to make sense of it all. Why hadn't he come to find her before he left? What was so urgent that he needed to return home on Saturday afternoon?

Nancy tried to reassure her. 'I'm sure he'll phone you later. He'll be in the car now. You know it takes hours to get to Camden.'

Em looked at the big kitchen clock. 5.10 pm. He'd be on the road until 9 o'clock tonight, at least. But he wouldn't be able to drive all that way without at least one break. If she texted him now, he'd have a chance to reply when he stopped for a coffee.

Her thumbs hovered over the screen, unsure what to type. She finally settled on

```
        Nancy showed me your note. Hope you're ok.
If you need me to do anything, let me know. Xxx
```

Avoiding the L word. Not too soppy. She pressed the send icon. No point waiting for the three dots. It would be ages before he'd have a chance to reply. She put her phone in her back pocket and drummed her fingers on the worktop.

'Are you going to be on edge all evening?' Nancy asked.

'Probably. Until I know what's happened.'

Her phone buzzed. Nancy looked up.

'It's only a text from Connor.'

Both of them looked disappointed.

```
Where can I eat around here?
```

Em replied:

```
There's a pub 5 minutes walk down the hill.
```

Connor's answer was almost instant:

```
Want to join me as Jack's not here?
```

Em suspicions were raised. Why would he know that? 'I'm just going over to my flat, Nancy. I have a horrible feeling Connor has something to do with Jack's departure.'

When Em walked through her front door, Connor was sprawled on the sofa, television on, channel hopping.

'How did you know Jack wasn't here?' she demanded.

'Good afternoon to you as well.'

'Connor - answer the question.'

'I didn't need to use my supernatural powers. I saw him drive off an hour or so ago. Threw a load of stuff in the boot. He seemed in a hurry to get away.'

'Why did he leave?'

'How should I know? I'm not his keeper.'

'Did he pop over here while I was out?'

Connor hesitated slightly. 'No. Have you joined the Spanish Inquisition?'

'It's not like Jack to disappear, and it's odd it happened on the same afternoon that you arrived.'

'Has anyone told you you have a nasty suspicious streak?'

'Only you.' Em scowled.

'He knows when he's beaten.' Connor winked.

'What's that meant to mean?'

Connor shrugged. Em was even more convinced that he was behind this now.

'Perhaps he sensed my alpha male credentials and did a runner.'

'And how would he sense anything about you if you two hadn't met.'

'I didn't say we hadn't met. I said he didn't come round here while you were out.' There was a mischievous expression on his face.

Oh my god! 'Did he come round while I was in the shower?'

'Yep.'

'So you answered the door, dripping wet in a towel. And was that when I shouted for the shower gel?'

Connor just raised his eyebrows, looking pleased with himself.

'That's why you called me 'darling' and offered to wash my back!' Em was enraged. 'What did you say to him?'

'Just hello. He worked the rest out for himself.'

'Take that smug look off your face, you bastard. You think you're so bloody clever. Get out. That's the last time I ever do you a favour. I don't care if you end up sleeping with a dancing wanker. You're not stopping here any fucking longer. Get the fuck out of here.'

'Not so posh now, then.'

She picked up his hold-all and threw it out of the front door.

'Alright, alright, I'm going, you mad bitch.'

Em slammed the door behind him and leaned back on it, wondering how to undo the mess.

Ten seconds later, there was a knock on the door.

Em flung it open. 'What?'

'My phone's on the coffee table.'

'Wait there.' She slammed the door again, marched into the living room and grabbed his phone.

I wonder. Yes, he was still using the same passcode.

She scrolled through his contact list. That one would do perfectly.

'Come on, Em. I thought you wanted to get rid of me?' he yelled through the letterbox.

She tapped out a message, pressed send, checked it had been delivered, deleted it, switched back to the home page, went back into the hallway and shoved the phone through the open letterbox straight into Connor's face.

'Ow!'

Em didn't respond. She breathed deeply. How am I going to get out of this mess?

There was another knock at the door.

'What now!?' Em shouted as she opened the door again.

Nancy was standing on Em's doorstep. She looked surprised.

'Did you try to kill him? There's a trail of blood leading down my drive.'

71

Nancy was unloading the dishwasher as Em walked into the kitchen. 'Nothing from Jack yet?'

'No, nothing at all. I was hoping you might have heard something.' Em took her phone out of her back pocket just in case she'd missed a notification in the 30 seconds since she'd last checked it.

'It's early yet,' said Nancy. 'He's probably having a lie in after all that driving.'

'Yes, probably.' Em yawned.

'Did you get any sleep last night?'

'Not much.' None at all, if she was being honest. Her mind had refused to shut down. She'd lain in bed looking at a crack in the ceiling, running through all the ways she could get through to Jack if he didn't phone. When the morning twilight started to appear around the edge of the blind, she had given up all hope of sleeping and got out of bed. Jack's portrait was by the window, almost finished. She picked up her brushes, unwrapped her acrylics and quietly worked on the bits of the background that needed completing, remembering the sexual tension between them during the sittings. It was the next best thing to being in the room with him. By 6 am, she was happy that his portrait was finished.

Em's stomach rumbled.

Nancy looked concerned. 'I can hear that from here. When did you last eat?'

Em frowned. When had she last eaten? Not since she'd kicked Connor out. And she'd skipped lunch as usual on a Saturday, preferring to get all the cottage cleaning done first.

'I think I had a snack yesterday morning.'

'You can't go on like that. I don't want you fainting on me.'

Nancy started bustling around the hob and the fridge. 'A cooked breakfast is in order.'

'That's kind, but I'll go back to my flat and get some cornflakes or something.'

'No, you won't. You'll sit here while I make you bacon and eggs. I think I'll join you for a change. I haven't made an effort to cook breakfast in ages. Would you like mushrooms as well?'

'Yes, please.' Em couldn't be bothered to put up a fight. And it was nice to be waited on. Just like Jack waited on her. Oh god, don't go there. Tears welled up again.

Nancy looked concerned. She came over and gave Em a hug. 'I'm sure Jack's fine. Once you've had a chance to explain the mix-up with Connor, you'll be back to normal.'

'But what if it's something else? What if he's had a car accident?'

'Aliens could have landed on the M4 and abducted him, though I think Radio 4 might have mentioned that in this morning's news bulletins. You're not thinking straight because you've not slept or eaten. I'll phone Olivia later to see if she's heard anything. It's too early now. She likes to lie in on a Sunday.'

9.30 am. Em was lying on her own sofa, having finally fallen asleep after forcing herself to eat Nancy's breakfast. Not that it wasn't tasty. She just didn't feel like eating anything at all.

Her phone alarm went off. She stirred in her sleep, picking the phone up and putting it down to snooze it. But it carried on ringing. She looked at the screen, struggling to focus. It wasn't the alarm at all. It was a call from Jack. Em was wide awake now.

She'd missed the call. But at least he must be ok.

She tried to call him back. Caller busy. He must be leaving a voicemail. She tried again, her heart beating so fast she could barely hear herself think. It rang out. Please answer.

'Hello.'

His voice sounded gravelly. Had he been drinking? Or perhaps he hadn't slept much either.

'Sweetheart are you ok?' she said. He must've heard the relief in her voice.

'Is that what you call Connor? It's what he calls you.' He spoke so calmly, it was chilling.

'I'm so sorry about the mix-up. I tried to explain last night. Connor came to try to get me back ....'

Jack talked over her. 'I'm not interested in stories. I've spent the last five years hearing Isabella's extravagant tales. It took me a long time to see through them. But I'm an expert at spotting a liar now. If you think you can spin me some feeble yarn to explain away why you screwed him, you can think again. Christ. It was only a few hours after I left your bed. Wasn't I good enough?'

'I didn't screw him. I offered to put him up because he had nowhere else to stay.'

'And I guess you were saving water by showering together? You must think I'm a gullible idiot.'

'I know how it must've looked, but I swear I've not done anything wrong. Ask Nancy.'

'Have you been lying to her as well? I know those tricks. Isabella is an expert. Getting my friends and family on her side. You're just like her. I can't believe I fell for it again. '

' But Jack ...'

' I don't want to listen to you any more. I called to tell you it's over. I don't want to see you or hear from you again. I hope that's clear.' He ended the call.

Em sat back on the sofa. This time yesterday, she'd been on cloud nine imagining their life together, and now he'd pulled the rug from under her feet entirely. She remembered the Luke situation. He had calmed down fairly quickly after that. Hopefully, he'd do the same this time.

PART THREE

AUTUMN 2018

72

It was a misty October morning in North Devon. Em had been out photographing the pockets of fog nestling in the valleys behind Dashford Grange. She had a portrait sitting later that morning; otherwise, she'd have spent much longer outdoors. She did lots of walking these days. Being out in nature calmed her, and concentrating on looking for scenic views to paint took her mind off Jack. It was odd how when she left Connor, she had been able to draw a line under their relationship quickly. She'd barely thought about him at all. Jack was different - unfinished business.

Em opened the front door to her flat and walked in. She felt a rustle of paper under her foot on the doormat. The postman had been. She picked up the envelope.

Her address was printed, but it had a traditional stamp rather than the pre-paid postage that junk mail usually had. There were no other clues other than a London postmark. She should have been loading her painting gear into the car, but the envelope intrigued her. She got a knife from the cutlery drawer and opened it neatly. The paper had the logo of the annual Unity portraits prize at the top.

Dear Ms Gillespie

Shortlisted portraits

Following our email, please find enclosed your official invitation to the prize giving, a label for the back of your artwork and instructions on how to deliver your piece to the gallery.

What were they talking about? There must be some mistake. The letter carried on for another page and a half. She skim-read the rest of it.

It was thanking her for entering their annual competition, but she hadn't entered any competitions, let alone one as prestigious as this. She hadn't had an email either. It must be a scam. She'd have to read it properly when she got back after lunch. One part caught her eye as she put the letter on the coffee table - the title of the portrait: Professor Jack Carver on Dashford beach.

Had Jack entered it on her behalf? But that was ridiculous. He hadn't even seen the finished painting. And he hadn't responded to any communications from her since that last phone call. Lucy had fallen out with Mark, so she hadn't heard anything via that route. Jack had even ignored Nancy. Em felt tears in her eyes, remembering the hurt and frustration.

Her phone buzzed. A reminder to leave for her appointment. She put her art equipment in the boot of the car and set the sat nav.

Nancy was sweeping up leaves when Em got back just after lunch. 'Thought I'd make the most of the autumn sunshine. What have you been up to?' she said, leaning the broom against the wheelbarrow.

'I've been over to Winton Hall again. Another sitting for their portrait.'

'Did the dogs behave this time?'

Em was producing a large portrait of Lord and Lady Dashford and their four boisterous cocker spaniels, who were adorable but completely out of control. She'd have to charge extra for dogs in future. 'No, it was crazy again. I turned Lady Mary into Cruella de Vil - not consciously, of course. I'll have to rely on photos for this one.'

Em started unloading her painting gear back into the flat. Working out how to deal with the dogs had put the letter out of her mind, but seeing it on the coffee table brought all the questions back. Perhaps Nancy would be able to shed some light on the mystery. Em went back outside.

'Nancy. A weird thing happened this morning. I got a letter telling me I'd been shortlisted for the Unity portrait prize.'

'Oh, that's fantastic news. Well done!' Nancy was thrilled.

'But the odd thing is I never submitted an entry.'

'Ahhhh,' said Nancy, looking slightly sheepish. 'Lucy and I might have entered it on your behalf.'

'Might have?'

'Well, we did.'

'Why would you do that?'

'Because you refused to consider it. And we both thought you were more than good enough. Looks like we were correct.'

Lucy's last visit to Dashford had been several weeks ago. She'd been trying to console Em after the breakup with Jack. Em vaguely remembered a conversation about painting competitions, but her mind had been all over the place at the time. She didn't want to bother with anything. It was enough of a struggle to keep her mind on the day-to-day stuff. They must have submitted the entry then.

At least it wasn't a scam. She should be thrilled at having her work exhibited in a top London gallery. And she would have been if only it weren't Jack's portrait.

'I am grateful, but why didn't you enter yours?'

'Who wants to look at a wizened old woman? Jack's is better, so emotional. And we thought he would be a more appealing subject, particularly with his television work. '

Em didn't respond.

'And it would be a good excuse to get you two talking to one another again.'

So they had another agenda as well. Were they in league with Jack, or was it all their idea?

'Did you tell him?'

'No. We thought it would be better if you did that.'

So he was oblivious to their plan, which put Em in an awkward position. 'Telling him will be tricky as he won't take my calls.'

'Have you tried recently?'

'No, the only thing I've been trying is to forget all about him.' She'd been doing well after the first few weeks until last Wednesday. She'd stumbled across one of his documentaries while channel hopping. She'd ended up binge-watching the entire series twice and wondering what might have been if Connor hadn't screwed it all up. *Face it, Emily Gillespie, there is a big Jack-shaped hole in your life and not where Lucy would say it was either.*

'Remind me when the exhibition is,' said Nancy.

'At the beginning of December.'

'So we've got several weeks to get him onside. He could be your guest at the opening night. He'll be promoting his new book in the spring, so he needs to start being more visible, and it gives him the ideal excuse to talk to you again without losing face.'

'Jack has never struck me as someone worried about losing face. And he made it clear he never wanted to see me again.'

'Time mellows people's feelings.' Nancy raised her eyebrows.

'Do you know something I don't?'

'Let's just say I've made sure Olivia knows you're still single and nothing was going on between you and Connor. So I'm confident she will have passed that message on. She really likes you.'

Em ought to be pleased they were on her side, but Jack would see that as Em manipulating his family. And what if she invited Jack and he didn't show or, worse still, he turned up but refused to talk to her? 'I'd rather invite you or Lucy. It's only fair since my work wouldn't be in the exhibition if you hadn't intervened.'

'If I remember the small print correctly, you're allowed up to four guests in addition to the sitter, so we can all go.'

'I'll think about it.'

'Don't think for too long.'

73

Em did think about it. She thought about very little else over the next three days. While a small part of her was furious with Nancy and Lucy for putting her in this predicament, she had to admit she was pleased to have another opportunity to try to get Jack back. But she needed to talk to him before the opening night to find out where she stood. A botched reunion in public would be embarrassing.

She tried phoning Jack, but it went straight to voicemail. He probably had her number blocked, despite Nancy saying he'd answer now.

No point using Nancy's mobile or landline as he was ignoring her too. Then she remembered the advice she had given Connor. She googled how to hide her caller ID. It was simple to do. She phoned Lucy to test it.

'Hello.' Lucy's posh voice. She never used that when she was speaking to Em. It must have worked. May as well have some fun with it.

Em put on her best Black Country accent. 'It's the Wolverhampton Sexual Health Clinic here. I'm afraid one of your ex-boyfriends has come in for treatment, so we need to test you.'

There was a moment of silence.

'Ok. What has he got exactly?'

'Restless cock syndrome.' Em burst out laughing.

'Emily Gillespie, you bitch. Why aren't you calling from your phone?'

Em was sitting on her sofa, her heart in her mouth as Jack's number rang out. After ten rings, it went to voicemail. Damn. She didn't leave a message.

She tried again a few minutes later - the same result. She remembered Jack telling her he often took a break at 12.30 when his morning meetings and seminars were over. She'd give it another go then.

Nancy was out at her pilates class which she usually followed with coffee with one of her friends, so Em was alone all morning. She spent two hours attempting to do admin. It was the longest, most tedious morning of her life.

As soon as the old grandfather clock in the hallway struck half past twelve, Em picked up her phone and dialled.

'Hello.'

He'd answered straightaway. Her heart started racing. She couldn't speak.

'Hello. Who is this?' He sounded out of breath. She pictured him walking up the stairs to his office on campus. Get a grip; otherwise, he will think it's a spam call.

'It's Em. It's work-related. Please don't hang up.' She said it quickly, trying to get it all out before he had time to think about pressing the red button to end the call.

He didn't respond, but he didn't hang up either.

'Lucy and Nancy entered your portrait in a competition.' She was speaking more calmly now. 'It's been shortlisted for a prize, and there's going to be an exhibition. The organisers would like the sitters at the opening night, if possible.'

She heard a woman's voice in the background. 'We're going to be late.'

Jack responded. 'I'm coming.'

'I can't talk now,' he said into the handset. 'Can I phone you back?' His voice was abrupt.

'Yes, please.'

'I don't think I've got your number any more.'

He really hadn't wanted to speak to her again.

'I'll text you with my caller ID switched on so you can reply later. Assuming you haven't blocked my number.'

'OK. And I never blocked your number.'

So he knew exactly how many times she'd phoned in those first couple of weeks, but he still hadn't responded. That was worse than blocking her. Bastard!

'I won't have time to call you until this evening,' he added. 'Bye.'

74

It was getting late. Em had received several texts from Lucy along the lines of 'Hasn't he phoned yet?' but nothing from Jack. Em had almost given up hope. How was her behaviour 'being more octopus'? She felt like a lovesick teenager. It was ridiculous. Then her phone rang.

'Hello.' Jack's voice but monotone. Not his usual greeting either. It wasn't a good start, though perhaps he didn't do the 'hello, you' thing on the phone. They hadn't had many phone conversations in the summer.

'Tell me about the exhibition.' No pleasantries, just straight to the point. It didn't sound as if he'd mellowed that much.

Em filled him in on the details. 'It will be good publicity for you. Hopefully, that will help when your new book comes out. And it would help my portrait business too. I know you don't want anything to do with me, but if you could do that, I would be very grateful.'

'Yes, ok. I can see it would be beneficial to both of us. I'll do it.'

'Thank you. I have one more favour to ask. Could we meet up before the opening? Only for a short while. I want to clear the air between us when we're not in public. I'm in London next Monday if you're free.' Em didn't need to drop the

299

portrait off at the gallery for a few weeks, but she didn't want to wait until the last minute to catch up with Jack. It would be worth making a special trip.

'Sorry, I'm busy. You needn't worry. I'll be on my best behaviour at the opening. I've got to go now. See you on 4th December.' He hung up.

So that was it. Short but not sweet. Em made up her mind. She FaceTimed Lucy.

'I want to know everything he said.'

'That will take all of 30 seconds.' Em filled Lucy in on what few details there were.

'It's not looking promising.' Even Lucy wasn't trying to put a positive spin on it.

'You don't say! I've had enough. I'm ready to accept that that's it. There's no point moping about Jack any more. He's not the man I thought he was. I need to chalk it up as a holiday crush. I'll see him at the exhibition. We'll be civil to one another and then wave bye-bye. I felt so guilty when I talked to him, but I've done nothing wrong. He's as bad as Isabella. Why did I waste so much time and effort trying to win him over?'

'Do you mean that?'

'If I say it often enough, I will believe it eventually.

'He has been an unforgiving arsehole.'

'When there's nothing to forgive. I decided to give up my flat for one night, so my ex wasn't sleeping in a ditch. Jack misinterprets what he sees, automatically thinks the worst of me and then refuses to believe my explanation. I know he's been mistreated in the past, and I've cut him some slack because of that. But he owes me an apology for calling me a liar, if nothing else. Time to 'Be more octopus'. Professor Jack Carver can take a hike.'

75

Em woke up the following morning feeling determined to make some changes. She'd just been treading water, thinking Jack might come back into her life, which was pathetic. And, as she'd said to Lucy last night, she wasn't even sure she wanted that to happen now. A couple of weeks ago, when Em had been feeling particularly down, Lucy had recommended a life-planning questionnaire. But Em had been sceptical at the time.

'It's not one of these woo-woo things where you visualise what you want, and it magically happens, is it?'

'You cynic! Some people swear by the law of attraction. It's amazing what the Universe can deliver when you wish for it, often in unexpected ways,' Lucy said. 'But no, it's not one of those. You score where you are now in various aspects of your life, work out where you want to be, and then come up with some actions to get you there. Simple, but it works. How do you think I got my apartment? I can help you go through it if you want, but it's better to get a G&T and do it on your own, at least at first.'

Em scrolled through her WhatsApp conversation with Lucy and found the link. She tore a blank sheet of paper from her drawing pad and wrote 'Life Plan - October 2018' across the top of the page, then doodled a little octopus in the corner.

Em read the instructions.

Question 1. Score each of these seven aspects of your life on a scale of 1 to 10, where one is awful, and ten is perfect.

She looked through the headings.

Health and fitness. Although she did a lot of walking now, she hadn't run for months, there was no gym nearby, and she hadn't got a bike. But she hadn't got any horrible afflictions. So healthy but not very fit. A middling score, then. She wrote 5 next to the heading.

Finance and security. Not bad. With the extra money from the paintings the gallery had sold for her, she had started to build up some savings. Not in millionaire territory by a country mile, but not poor either. 7. No, be more positive. She crossed out the 7 and wrote 8.

Creativity. An easy one. Lots of time to sketch, paint and take photographs. And she was pleased with the results too. Got to be a 10. Perhaps life wasn't that bad.

Career. Her current job was not a career, but she enjoyed it. She got to meet people, it was rarely stressful, and she had a supportive boss. And it gave her time to work on her long-term career as an artist. The portrait commissions continued to come in. But she needed to do more, so she gave it a 7. Em took another sip of her tea, thinking about what she would have scored that this time last year. A resounding 1! A big improvement.

Love and emotional well-being. Oh, dear. A year ago, she would've probably written 10 in blissful ignorance of what Connor was up to. Best not to dwell on that. She had a great network of friends, plus her dad. They had all supported her when she'd split up with Connor, but they lived miles away. Nancy was supportive too. But no one shared her life as a partner. Don't think about what could've been with Jack. He'd turned out to be an arsehole, so at least she hadn't wasted any more time on him. 5 then.

Fun. See above. She needed to get out more. Way more. A solid 3!

Work-life balance. Easy! At least she could end question 1 with a high score. 10 out of 10.

Em carried on working her way through the rest of the questions. When there was no tea left in her mug, she looked at the clock. She had just enough time left to finish the last question before heading over to the house to do all the admin she'd failed to do yesterday.

Q10. Identify one thing you can do now to improve each of your three lowest scores.

The health and fitness one was easy. She wrote down 'run at least twice a week'.

Love and emotional well-being. Hmmm. Online dating, perhaps? But she'd heard so many complaints from Lucy about her dodgy dates that she wasn't sure she was mentally strong enough to try that yet. Em needed a few months without any emotional turmoil. She wrote 'Review in Spring 2019'.

She moved on to 'Fun'. If you didn't surf, there wasn't much to do locally with anyone under the age of 40. But there must be something, especially if she looked at the neighbouring towns. She settled on 'Research local groups and activities'.

Em felt happier and more in control already. Lucy was definitely on to something with this technique.

Nancy was in the kitchen chopping vegetables when Em walked in.

'Morning!' said Em.

'You sound happy today. How did things go with Jack?' Nancy looked hopeful.

'Not well.' Em filled Nancy in on her conversation last night.

'That's disappointing. But I'm sure he'll come round when he sees you. He's always had a stubborn streak.'

'I've decided I'm not going to wait around for him to change his mind. I've wasted enough time moping about. Time for a fresh start.'

Nancy stopped chopping. 'You're not leaving, are you?' She looked genuinely concerned.

'No, no, no. I love it here. You've been so good to me. I just meant I need to get on with doing new things.'

Nancy started chopping again. 'I'm very relieved. What new things are you planning?'

Em told Nancy about her action list.

Nancy looked serious for a moment. 'If you're looking at getting back into running, why don't you join me and my new personal trainer for a few sessions?'

'I didn't know you'd got a personal trainer?'

'I didn't have one until this week. Thought I needed to up my game if I'm going to make it to the top of Kilimanjaro next year. Dorothy at the WI recommended him. He's coming here next Tuesday.'

'Kilimanjaro?' Climbing Kilimanjaro was news to Em as well.

'Yes, I wanted a new challenge. But I need to be fitter - the air at the top is so thin.'

'I haven't run for ages. I'm not sure I'm fit enough to keep up with you yet.' Which was embarrassing but true.

'You could have a free taster session with him instead? I did mine yesterday down at the beach. He's very good and not too expensive. Do you want me to ask? He's called Ben, and he's about your age. I'm sure you won't be disappointed.'

Something about Nancy's expression gave Em the idea that she might be about to shift her matchmaking efforts to getting her fixed up with Ben. She could do without that. But a personal trainer would be helpful to get her back into running. Em could afford to try a few sessions, at least.

76

Nancy booked the taster session on Em's behalf, and the following Tuesday, Em headed over to the main house in her running gear.

Walking into the kitchen, she saw a man filling a water bottle from the fridge water dispenser. He must be Ben. From the back, she could tell he was well over six foot tall with short medium brown hair and a very cute arse. It bugged her that there was something incredibly familiar about him.

Em took a sharp intake of breath as soon as he turned around. Of course he looked familiar. It was Karl! He grinned at her. Clearly, Em's presence wasn't a surprise.

'Em!' Nancy walked in looking hot and bothered. 'Let me introduce you to Ben. We've just been doing interval training on the beach. He's worn me out.'

'He's very good at doing that.' Em was trying to work out what was happening.

'Do you two already know one another?' Nancy asked.

Karl/Ben jumped in before Em could answer. 'Yes, we met when Em was in Newquay.'

'How lovely. What a small world. I'll let you two catch up while I have a shower. See you next Tuesday, Ben. Same time?'

'Yes, 10 am is fine.' Karl/Ben said.

Nancy left the kitchen.

He went to say something, but Em put her finger to her lips. She waited until she heard Nancy's bedroom door shut. 'Why are you here?'

'I'm training Nancy for her Kilimanjaro trip.'

'No, I meant in Dashford. It's a sleepy backwater compared to Newquay. Did you run out of women to take back to your lair?' She gave him a cheeky grin and folded her arms.

'My friend wanted her apartment back, and I fancied a change of scenery.'

'I thought you said she wasn't coming back until Christmas?'

'She came back early. Unfortunately, so did her husband.'

'Is that why you're Ben now? In hiding?'

'I've always been Ben. Karl was my naked chef name. The company made us use different names so we wouldn't have clients trying to get in touch outside work.'

'And you didn't think to mention that to me before?'

'Just like you didn't correct me when I thought Jack was your ex.'

So he knew more about Jack now. 'What has Nancy told you?'

'That you and Jack were meant for each other, but other people kept getting in the way. And now you've split up.'

'I'm not so sure about the 'meant for each other' part any more, but the rest is true.'

'I'm sorry.'

'And now I have to see him again at an art exhibition.'

He looked puzzled. 'Nancy didn't mention that.'

'It's a long story.'

'I've got time to listen. Sometimes I think I should retrain as a therapist. My clients share a lot when they're training. Shall we get down to business?'

Em raised her eyebrows.

'I meant go for a run,' Ben laughed.

77

Maybe this wasn't such a good idea. Em was setting up her easel and canvas in a corner of Dashford village hall.

'There are some tables in the side room if you want one for your paints and brushes.' Carol, the organiser, bustled over. 'But we have to cover them with plastic. The village hall committee don't like it if they're more colourful than when we started.' She gave a rather pained smile.

With her fitness plan sorted, Em had moved on to tackling her lack of social life. She'd found the art group in the parish magazine.

A supportive social art group for adult artists of all ages and abilities.

We meet fortnightly on Thursdays from 7.30 pm to 9.30 pm.

Phone Carol on 07700 900077 to book your place.

£5 per person to cover room hire and refreshments.

They didn't have an internet presence, not even a Facebook page, but Nancy said she knew Carol from WI and she was a good organiser, so it would be worth a try, especially as they met in the evenings, so it shouldn't just be retirees. But the eight other attendees this evening were at least 70 by the look of it.

Em waved a fiver in Carol's direction.

'I'll collect those later. We usually have a break halfway through for tea and biscuits, and someone talks about their work. We have a rota. It's Jerry's turn today,' she said, pointing at a man with floppy white hair and a paisley cravat who was tinkering with what looked like a painting-by-numbers landscape. 'We're very fortunate. Jerry is an experienced painter. He's been creating art for over 40 years. We love Jerry's tips.'

Em wasn't sure she would feel the same way, but there was no escape now. She may as well make the best of it.

The rest of the painters were engrossed in their work. There wasn't much chit chat considering it was meant to be a social group.

A loud noise disturbed the silence. Em turned to see a tall man in a check shirt and baggy jeans attempting to get a large easel and canvas through the door.

'Sorry I'm late, everyone.' He flashed a big smile from deep inside his bushy ginger beard. He looked about the same age as Em - a breath of fresh air.

'Ooh, a new face.' The way his eyes lit up looked like he thought Em was a breath of fresh air too. 'I'm Matt,' he held out his hand and shook hers enthusiastically.

'Hello Matt, I'm Em.'

'Do you mind if I set up my easel next to you?'

'Be my guest.' Perhaps this evening wouldn't be a waste of time after all. Em wasn't attracted to him, but at least he wanted to be friendly.

Matt's canvas was a large abstract with strong brush marks in shades of red and burnt orange. Em was genuinely drawn to it. 'That's so powerful.'

'Thank you. I'm going through a phase of self-doubt.'

'You shouldn't be. But I know that's easier said than done. I love it. How long have you been coming to this group?'

'It must be nearly three months now. I teach at the local

secondary school. I started in September.'

'Do you teach Art?'

'No, no, no. Too dangerous being stuck in a room of hormonal teenagers with paint and knives around. I prefer History - fewer potential weapons.'

Oh no, another historian. 'You don't specialise in ships, do you?' Em asked.

'No. Why did you ask that?'

'It was just a guess.' She decided to change the subject. 'Is that a Brummie accent?'

'Yes. You sound like you might be from my neck of the woods too?'

They carried on chatting about Birmingham and art and music and books, all much to the disapproval of several of the other artists.

'I thought this was a social group?' Em whispered to Matt after they'd been glared at for the umpteenth time by a spiky-haired woman who was working on a dog portrait.

'Not everyone read that part of the description. There are Trappist monks who talk more than some of this lot.' He whispered back.

'Why do you keep coming back?'

'It makes me paint, and I haven't got anything else to do on Thursday evenings. Well, most evenings, actually. I was teaching at a school in Bristol before, and loads was going on there, but around here, it's a bit sleepy in the evenings.'

'Right, everyone. Tea's ready.' Carol pointed to the hatch into the kitchen.

'You think for £5, they could manage a better selection of biscuits,' Matt whispered to Em as they looked at the bourbons and custard creams arranged on a plain green plate that looked like it had been around since the 1940s.

'At least they aren't rich teas.'

'We had garibaldis last week.'

'I love those.'

'Ugh! Squashed flies. You have no taste.' He screwed his face up in mock disgust.

'When we've all finished analysing the biscuits,' Carol looked pointedly at Matt and Em, 'instead of a talk today, Jerry is going to be giving free critiques of your work.'

'I didn't realise Jerry was a qualified judge?' said Em.

Matt appeared to be having a coughing fit.

'I'm not, Emily, was it?' From the way he looked her up and down, it looked as if Jerry was judging her already. 'But as the most experienced artist in the group, I like to share my expertise to help the rest of you.'

'How kind,' said Em. This should be good.

He started with spiky-haired woman's dog. 'It's very precise, Esme, but I think the eyes look slightly dead. Do you mind? ' he said, taking a paintbrush from her table and adding some horribly bad highlights before she could object.

Em's eyes widened in horror.

But Esme didn't seem to be bothered. On the contrary, she appeared to be thrilled by Jerry's adjustment. 'Oh, that's much better, Jerry. Thank you so much.'

Em and Matt exchanged a glance. Matt looked unimpressed too. 'He's not getting anywhere near my picture,' whispered Em.

Jerry continued his tour of the room with the other artists trailing after him as he dispensed his somewhat suspect pearls of wisdom and occasionally amended their work.

As he neared her easel, Em positioned herself strategically between the canvas and her equipment. There was no way she was going to let him put any paint on her landscape.

'Ah. The new girl's work. It's a good start, Emily. You could do with more control over your paintbrush, though.' He stopped a few feet from her easel, picking up the vibes she wouldn't be receptive to a bit of artistic collaboration. 'I offer one-to-one lessons if you want to progress your art further.'

Old Em would have smiled and not said anything. But, new Em decided not to let him get away with his patronising attitude.

'That's very kind, Jerry, but I have a first-class honours degree in Fine Art from the Slade, so the variation in my marks is a deliberate choice. I feel your own work could do with more variation and contrast to make it more exciting. I'd be happy to give you some lessons.'

Jerry drew himself up to his full height, puffing out his chest like a male bird trying to ward off a rival on a David Attenborough documentary. Matt's coughing fit had returned with a vengeance.

'I'll have you know that my work has been exhibited in the North Devon show every year for the past two decades, young lady. You may not approve of it, but many people in the art world do.'

Young lady? He'd got her back up now. She could hear Lucy's voice whispering, 'Octopus time!' in her head. But she was meant to be making friends, not enemies. A more subtle approach was called for, but she was stumped as to what that was.

'I'm afraid it's time to pack up already, everyone.' Carol seemed anxious to wrap the meeting up before things turned any nastier. 'If Jerry hasn't had time to critique your work, I'm sure he'll do so next time.'

'Unfortunately, Carol, I'm away at my second home in Sardinia for the rest of the year.'

Matt piped up. 'Perhaps Emily could give us some advice instead? She's well qualified.'

Em smiled at him. He'd given her an opportunity for the perfect reply. Bless him. 'I'm afraid I won't be here next time either. I'll be in London. One of my portraits has been shortlisted for the Unity prize, and I'll be at the exhibition's opening night.'

A hush settled over the rest of the group. Jerry stormed over to his easel and tidied away his things in furious silence.

Matt followed Em out to the car park. 'Was that true?'

'One hundred per cent. I wouldn't have crowed about it normally, but Jerry wound me up.'

'You're entitled to crow about it. Who did you paint?'

'Professor Jack Carver.'

'The historian? That's brilliant. I'm in the presence of a genius.' He bowed to her.

'Thank you, but that's overstating it a bit,' she laughed.

'It's way better than the lovely Jerry's North Devon art show! It's been worth all those £5 weekly fees to see him taken down a peg or two. Do you think you'll come back to the group in future?'

Em pulled a face. Apart from having a laugh with Matt, she hadn't enjoyed it. 'I need to think about it.'

'Would you fancy helping me set up a rival group?'

'Are we going to fight this lot in the car park?'

'Oh yes. Paintbrushes at dawn! Fastest drawer wins.' He mimed waving a sword around. 'Seriously though, there were a couple of people who came to a session in October. They didn't enjoy it either. But I've kept in touch with them. We've been talking about organising our own group together. Would you like to join us?'

78

'Time to put your clothes back on,' Em told Ben, giving him a cheeky wink.

'Are you sure? I thought you preferred me naked?' Ben grinned.

It had all started a couple of days previously when Ben and Em had walked into the kitchen of Dashford Grange after Em's latest workout. Ben's training regime was working. Em had finally been able to run up the last part of the hill without collapsing at the top in a breathless heap.

'I'm not sure you need me any more,' Ben said.

Em enjoyed Ben's company. She didn't want to stop training with him yet. 'There's still room for improvement. I might struggle to stick with it in the winter if we haven't got our weekly session.'

'Ah, good. You're back.' Nancy sounded pleased to see them as she looked up from the laptop. 'I've had an idea that I want to run past you. I've been thinking about how to increase our low-season bookings.'

Ben picked up his kit bag. 'Time I wasn't here. I'll leave you to discuss business.'

'Please stay for a little longer if you can, Ben. You're key to all this.' Nancy said to him.

Ben looked bemused. He sat down on one of the high stools.

Nancy turned to Em. 'Ben was talking about the surfing lessons he offers when we were training last week.'

Em raised her eyebrows. 'Are you going to take up surfing now?'

'No, not for me,' Nancy laughed. 'I already know how to surf. '

Of course she did. How could Em have thought otherwise?

'I've noticed some of the holiday lets further down the coast offer surfing holidays. I think we should give it a try.'

'But we already have surfers stay here sometimes,' said Em.

'They're experienced surfers. I'm thinking about beginners. We sell the holiday and the lessons as a package. We do a deal with Dashford surfing school, so our holidaymakers get the accommodation and the lessons cheaper than if they booked them separately. And they don't have to worry about coordinating accommodation, board hire, lessons and so on. We sort it all out for them.'

Em nodded. It did make sense. 'But what if someone in their party doesn't want to surf?'

'Yoga! We offer a yoga option for those reluctant to hit the waves. Or art. Could you give art lessons? What do you think?'

'I know an excellent yoga teacher who lives in the next village,' suggested Ben.

Em grinned at him. 'Is she supple?'

'HE is very supple! Not all my friends are women,' he smirked.

'Excellent. I've already spoken to Gary, who runs the surfing school. He's keen too. How about we start promoting the idea on social media? See what level of interest we get?'

'I've got our Instagram posts scheduled for the next few

weeks,' Em said. 'But we can swap some of those out or add some extra ones. I haven't got any suitable photos, though.'

'That's where Ben comes in. No offence to Gary, but he's seen better days. You would make a much better model, Ben. I'm happy to pay for your time, of course.'

'Another woman who only wants me for my body!' Despite his words, Ben didn't seem too put out by Nancy's suggestion.

'Excellent. When are you available for a photo shoot?'

'Who's the photographer?'

'The lovely Em, of course. You can use my camera.' Nancy said.

Which was how Ben and Em came to be spending a cold Friday afternoon in late November on the beach taking surfing-themed photos.

'I think we've got enough now,' Em said, flicking through the images on the back of the camera. She had a varied selection: action shots of Ben surfing, Ben walking on the beach carrying his surfboard taken from a variety of angles, Ben posing with his surfboard by the surf school building, and a close-up of Ben looking windswept which was worthy of an aftershave commercial, even though Em said so herself.

'Good,' he said. 'Because it's getting cold, even for me. I'll go and get changed.'

'Meet you at Mary's? I'll buy you a hot chocolate?'

Ben gave her a thumbs up as he headed to the surfing school building. Em walked up the beach to the cafe.

Mary smiled as Em walked up to the counter. 'I've been enjoying the view. Nice work if you can get it. He's a bit different to Jack.'

Was Mary looking for an update on her favourite professor? Or just trying to work out how Ben fitted into Em's life?

'All women like Ben.' Em said.

'A lot of women like Jack too.'

'Not me, not any more.' Was that true? It felt uncomfortable saying that.

'I'd heard you were off to London soon with his portrait.'

'Yes, I'm not looking forward to it.' That was true. Em should be excited, but the closer the exhibition got, the more the thought of seeing Jack again was putting a damper on the whole thing. Less than four months ago, the prospect of spending an evening out in London with Jack would have been something she'd have looked forward to. One stupid misunderstanding, and now life was completely different. She was worried that seeing him again would bring all those feelings of attraction back to the surface.

'Two hot chocolates, please,' she said.

Mary looked amused. 'It must be nice to be ordering two drinks again.' So she was fishing for gossip.

'It's not like that,' Em said, picking up the two steaming mugs.

'Shame. I wouldn't kick him out of bed for eating crackers.'

Em walked outside to the nearest table, thinking about the last time she'd heard that phrase. A picture of Jack waving the non-hen do minibus off floated back into her mind. What a year. Still, get the awards ceremony out of the way, then a couple of weeks later, she'd be back in Birmingham for Christmas, and soon there would be a whole new year to carry on building a better life. Roll on 2019.

'Don't wish your life away,' Ben said, sitting beside Em.

'Did I say that out loud?' she said, pushing his mug of hot chocolate towards him.

'Yes, you did. What's 2019 got in store for you?'

'I don't know. 2018's been quite eventful. I could do with a calmer 2019.'

'You'll get bored.'

'Maybe. I'm helping to set up a new art group. I'm excited

about that. It will be something different to do, and it should widen my social circle. And I've had some more portrait enquiries. It looks like next year will get off to an interesting start. What plans have you got?'

'Keep this between ourselves for now, but I'm considering going to Australia. I've got some friends in Sydney. The surfing's excellent, and the sea is warm. I should be able to get a visa for a few months. And I'm hoping being on the opposite side of the world to Sophie will help me move on.'

'Sounds good.'

Ben looked at her thoughtfully. 'Why don't you come with me?'

'Ben said what?' Lucy looked flabbergasted on the other end of Em's phone.

'He asked me to go to Australia with him.' Em settled down on her sofa.

'And are you going to go?'

'Of course not.'

'But that's an amazing opportunity.'

'If you like funnel web spiders and baking hot weather.' Em shivered and pulled a blanket over herself. It was the first frosty night of the autumn, and her flat was chilly. Moving to a warmer climate might not be a bad idea. 'Anyway, I could go on my own if I wanted to.'

'More fun with Ben in tow, I would've thought.'

'Oh yes, with everyone thinking you're dating a hot surfer dude. Meanwhile, he's off shagging anything in a bikini.'

'Has he worked his way through many women lately?'

'Not that I've noticed.'

'Perhaps he's turned over a new leaf?'

'I think it's more due to lack of opportunity around here. Stop trying to get me fixed up with him. He said that he was inviting me as a friend. We'd both had a stressful few months and "it would be nice to go somewhere completely different" was how he put it.'

'How have you left it?'

'I told him it was lovely he'd asked me, but I was happy here.'

'And what did he say?'

'If I changed my mind, to let him know.'

'He sounds keen to me.'

'Everyone sounds keen to you.'

'He obviously wants you to go. When are you seeing him again?'

'We're doing weights at a local gym tomorrow.'

'I thought there weren't any local gyms in Dashford?'

'I didn't think there were, but apparently, there's a private one near the church. One of his surfer mates hires it out.'

'£5 says he asks you about Australia again.'

'You're on because I'm confident he won't.'

79

Ben leaned against the gym wall, watching Em do press-ups. 'Have you thought any more about Australia?' That was £5 down the pan if she fessed up to Lucy what he'd said.

'I haven't changed my mind. I might do New Zealand one day, but Australia's too hot for me.'

'Or I'm too hot for you,' Ben chuckled.

Em got up and threw her towel at him. 'Vain sod.'

'You can do another ten of those for your cheek,' he laughed. 'I'm going to look at flights next week, so I thought I'd mention it.'

'So soon?' Em would miss Ben, but not enough to go halfway around the world with him.

'I'm not going to go for a few months yet. But I want to get it all booked in.'

'Will you be alright on your own?'

'I'm a big boy now. I'll manage.' He looked serious for a moment. 'Promise me something.'

'What?'

'That you won't stay here on your own.'

'What do you mean? I'm happy here.'

'Life could easily pass you by, living in Dashford. You deserve more fun than that.' He turned and headed towards the weights machine before Em could respond. She followed him.

'You're miles away,' Ben said as he set up the weights.

'I was just thinking about what you said.'

'Just that? You were like it earlier on as well.'

'I keep worrying about the prize giving on Thursday. I'm dreading it.'

'Why? You'll get made a fuss of and potentially win a fancy award that could seriously help you grow your art business. It's a fantastic opportunity.'

'I know. But I hate being the centre of attention.'

'Is that the only reason?'

'No. I don't want to see Jack again.'

'I thought so.' Ben could be perceptive at times. 'I'm sure he'll behave like a perfect gentleman.'

'I'm sure he will. I'm just worried it will stir up old feelings. How would you feel if you had to socialise with Sophie again?'

'The same, I guess.' Ben was quiet for a moment. 'Who's going with you?'

'Lucy and Nancy.'

'Hmm. The two people who've been trying to get you and Jack together.'

'Exactly. You see why I'm worried now.'

'Why don't I come with you as well? I can play your adoring boyfriend.'

'Would that help?'

'It might stop Jack making a play for you, just in case he's had second thoughts. Then you wouldn't have to worry about resisting his attentions.'

Em gave it some thought. Ben being there might be a good idea. 'We're leaving late Thursday morning, and we won't be back here until Friday afternoon. It's a big ask, expecting you to give up nearly two days of your time.'

'It's a good excuse for a trip to London. Most of my training clients have cancelled their sessions this month. They're all too busy stuffing themselves with mince pies and mulled wine now we're on the run-up to Christmas, which means I've got space in my diary for a night away with you.'

80

'We're 15 minutes late.' Em looked at her phone as the black cab slowly edged along the A40 in the evening traffic. 'I knew we should have left earlier.'

Nancy, Ben and Em had driven to London together that morning, and Lucy had caught the train down from Birmingham at lunchtime. They'd all met at Nancy's flat earlier in the afternoon, and now they were heading to the gallery.

'Relax.' Nancy put her hand out to still Em's twitchy leg. 'If you've won, they can't start without you, and if you haven't won, it won't matter.' The voice of reason, as usual.

Em's phone pinged. 'It's Jack.' She looked at the text.

    WHERE ARE YOU?

It wasn't surprising that he was wondering where she was. She texted back:

    Stuck in traffic. Will be there in 5 mins.

The reply was almost immediate.

We need to talk. Can we go for a drink
afterwards? Xx

Lucy peered over Em's shoulder. 'Wanting to go for a drink is an excellent sign. And he's put kisses at the end of it.' She looked thrilled.

'He might have done that without thinking.' Em was keen not to read too much into it.

'Ignore it,' Ben said.

'Is there something going on that I don't know about?' Nancy looked puzzled. 'Surely you want to encourage him?'

Em frowned. 'No, it's over between Jack and me. The last thing I want to do is give him the idea that I want us to get back together.'

'He might think you're just playing hard to get. Men enjoy the chase,' said Lucy.

Nancy raised her eyebrows. 'It's a bit late for chasing. He's already caught her once.'

'Nancy!' Em looked horrified.

'Well, it's true.'

They spent the next few minutes in silence. Em tensed as their taxi pulled up outside the gallery. There were so many butterflies in her stomach she thought she might be sick.

Ben got out of the cab first and held the door open as Nancy and Lucy emerged onto the pavement, and went inside. He leaned into the taxi and took Em's hand. 'We'll both go in together. That's what we agreed.'

'Yes. OK.' As she climbed out of the taxi, she could see Jack just inside the door. Had he had his hair cut differently? He looked smart in a suit with an open-necked blue shirt, the same colour as the one in the portrait. The one that made those eyes look so appealing. Stop thinking like that.

'It'll be fine.' Ben kissed her on the cheek.

'Was that for my benefit or Jack's?'

'Mine. You're a bag of nerves. Shut your eyes and breathe in for a count of five.'

Em's face started to turn red.

'You can breathe out again!' he laughed. 'Come on. It won't be that bad.'

Through the open door, Em could see Jack hugging Nancy, but he was looking at Em over Nancy's shoulder.

She held Jack's gaze as Ben led her inside. He still made her heart skip a beat. This was madness. *Hold on to Ben. Ignore Jack.*

'You must be Emily Gillespie.' A woman with a clipboard intercepted them as soon as they stepped over the threshold, blocking Em's view of Jack. 'I'm Elizabeth. I'm organising the event. Could you come this way, please?' She indicated a door off to the side. 'I'll take your coat.'

'Oh, but I ….'

'You can chat with your guests in a few minutes. If your partner wouldn't mind waiting here.' Elizabeth gave Ben an appreciative look up and down. 'We just need to brief the artists about the order of events,' she said to him with a smile.

Ben slipped his hand around Em's waist. 'See you in a minute, darling.' His voice was slightly louder than it needed to be, presumably so Jack could hear.

Em gulped. This felt uncomfortable. Jack valued honesty, yet here she was, conning him that Ben was her lover. She should be strong enough to hold her ground without using Ben as a human shield.

Her fellow artists were all in the side room already. They were a mixed bunch. The youngest woman looked like she was still at art college, but the remainder were older than Em. A man who was about Nancy's age was holding court, boasting about his previous competition wins. Em felt out of her depth.

Elizabeth interrupted him.

'I won't keep you long. Clara Benetti is here.' Elizabeth indicated the tall, blonde woman who had just walked into the room. Em froze. Jack's 'friend' from Italy. Of all the people.

'Clara will be presenting the prize this year. She's here with a camera crew. Clara, do you want to say anything?'

'Thank you. Congratulations to you all on being shortlisted. As you know, we're making a documentary about the prize, so I need to talk to each of you about your work. I believe you all signed and returned the consent form in your shortlisting letter. We've decided we'd also like to visit the winner at their studio next week to get some footage of them working. If you're the winner, Elizabeth will call you tomorrow to arrange it.'

The corner of Em's tiny living room wouldn't exactly wow the viewers. And the last person she wanted to be anywhere near was Clara. Em shook her head, trying to get rid of the image that had suddenly appeared in her head - Jack and Clara making out in Clara's swimming pool. Good job Em wasn't going to win.

Elizabeth was back in charge. 'We'll carry out the prize giving at 8 pm. Remember, the announcement won't be made public until Clara's programme is aired on December 28th, so I can't emphasise enough how important it is not to share the winner's name with anyone who's not here today. If you receive the prize, Clara will interview you and your sitter after the ceremony. You are all welcome to stay until we finish at 8.45 pm. Any questions?'

'But my sitter isn't here!' boasting man exclaimed.

'We'll worry about that later,' Elizabeth responded firmly. She didn't seem overly concerned. 'Anything else?'

Everyone shook their heads.

'Excellent. Please join your guests. There are drinks and

canapés at the back of the gallery. Enjoy your evening, and good luck.'

Jack almost pounced on Em when she emerged from the briefing.

'Hello, you.'

His normal greeting. Anyone would think nothing bad had happened between them. Where the hell was Ben? She looked around the gallery quickly. How could a six-foot-four man disappear so easily?

'You look fabulous,' Jack said, giving her a hug. She breathed in his aftershave, the scent taking her back to that beautiful summer evening in his secret meadow.

She desperately wanted to tell him how much she'd missed him. *Remember how horribly he spoke to you, how he thinks you lied to him?* She managed to restrain herself with a polite 'Thank you. I like your new haircut. It suits you.'

He smiled awkwardly. 'I've missed you so much. I wanted to say sorry about Connor. I should've believed you.' It was like he was following her fantasy script. Pity he hadn't done that weeks ago.

'What changed your mind?' she asked.

Clara appeared before Jack had time to respond. 'Hello, Jack.'

'Clara.' Jack looked uncomfortable. 'I didn't know you were going to be here.'

'It's lovely to see you again. Could I interview you about your portrait?' She was stroking his arm, with her back mostly turned towards Em, behaving as if Em was invisible. So rude!

'You should be interviewing Emily.' Jack looked apologetically at Em.

Em mouthed "Thank you" at him. Jack eased away from Clara's touch and put his arm around Em's shoulder.

'Oh yes, I'll be doing that too.' Clara looked at Em as if she were something she'd found stuck to her shoe.

'Can you interview me later, please?' Jack said. 'There's something I need to discuss with Em.'

'Of course.'

Em could tell from Clara's tone that she wasn't happy with Jack giving her the brush off, but Clara wasn't going to give up that easily. 'Perhaps we could go for a drink afterwards? Pick up where we left off on Tuesday?' Clara looked as if she was about to devour him.

Jack looked even more uncomfortable. 'No, sorry, not tonight.'

'I'll text you.' She walked off, giving Em another filthy look.

Did Clara say 'on Tuesday'? She wasn't referring to their summer dalliance in Italy then. Jack must be seeing her again. So he wasn't missing Em that much. What did she expect? It had been nearly four months since Jack had dumped her. Em felt disappointed, which was crazy. *Why do you care? No more Jack, remember?* Em slid away from him.

'I better go and talk to my other guests,' she said, quickly walking away.

81

Lucy looked at Em as she walked towards her. 'How did that go?'

'Where's Ben?' asked Em.

'He went to the gents.'

'I need to go somewhere quiet,' Em was trying to keep her composure.

'I'll come with you.'

They found the women's toilets at the back of the gallery. It was very plush with individual towelling flannels to use as hand towels and Molton Brown toiletries. There was an ornate chaise longue in the corner, perfect for sitting on while you were waiting for a friend or, in this case, being comforted by a friend while you were sobbing your heart out. Lucy did a quick check to make sure no one else was there.

'I'm so confused. I don't even know why I'm crying. I didn't want Jack back.' Em's tears were easing off now. 'I was coping until I saw him, and then it looked like he wanted to get back together. And I suddenly felt desperate to try again. And then Clara fucking Benetti stuck her oar in.' Em filled Lucy in on the conversation between Jack and Clara.

'It doesn't sound like he's that keen on Clara.'

'Keen enough to shag her again.'

'When did she say they were together?'

'Tuesday.'

'The day you posted that half-naked photo of Ben on the Dashford Grange Instagram account. It did get a lot of likes. With all that activity, Jack's bound to have seen it on his feed.'

'So Clara's my fault again? Is that what you're saying?'

'No. For all we know, he's been screwing loads of women.'

'What a comforting idea. Remind me why I'm friends with you?'

'Sorry, I'm trying to think.' Lucy looked serious. 'It might have been a reaction to seeing Ben. Clara seems to be his default revenge fuck. We ought to feel sorry for her.'

'So I'm supposed to see it as a sign he still cares? It's completely turned me off him, using another woman like that. It's such a mess.'

Nancy stuck her head around the door. 'They're getting ready to do the presentation. Elizabeth sent me to find you. Oh dear,' she said, seeing Em's face. 'We need to patch you up. I'll see if they'll postpone for ten minutes.'

'Do I look that bad?' Em asked Lucy.

'Right now, if you auditioned for a part as a zombie in The Walking Dead, you'd be a shoo-in.'

Five minutes later, Lucy closed her makeup bag and surveyed her handiwork. 'You'll do.'

'You've done wonders.' Em looked in the mirror again. 'I'm still a bit red around the eyes, but I don't suppose anyone will notice.'

They high-fived one another. 'Knock 'em dead,' Lucy said.

Which is precisely what Em thought Jack might be about to do to Ben as she and Lucy emerged from the toilets. She couldn't hear what Jack what saying, but he looked furious.

'Oh, my god.' Em rushed over as Ben started trying to placate Jack.

The security guard was also making a beeline for them as well. 'Gentlemen, please.'

His words seemed to break whatever spell Jack was under. He moved away from Ben. 'I'm sorry.' All eyes were on Jack as he walked quickly out of the gallery before Em could say a word. She needed to talk to him alone. Em started to follow him, but Elizabeth stopped her. 'We can't delay the presentation any further.'

'But I ….'

'You do need to be here. Emphasis on the "here".' Elizabeth gave her a meaningful look.

'I'll see where Jack's gone.' Lucy hurried outside.

'What was all that about?' Em whispered to Ben.

'Jack saw me messaging a woman on Tinder.'

Em closed her eyes. 'Did you have to do that here?'

'It's a cold night. I'll need someone to keep me warm later. And it's obviously not going to be you.'

Em looked puzzled. 'Were you thinking that you and I would ….'

'It crossed my mind. You were adamant you didn't want to get back together with Jack again. But I can see that's exactly what you do want. And I can safely say Jack still has the hots for you.'

'Why? What did he say?'

'He told me I was a fucking arsehole for cheating on you.'

'Did he really say 'fucking'?'

'Yeah, why?'

'He only swears when he's extremely upset.'

'When we're all ready,' Elizabeth glared at Em and Ben. Em felt like she was back in a school assembly. 'Clara Benetti will announce the winner.'

There was a polite round of applause as Clara took the microphone while Em tried to process everything Ben had said.

82

As soon as the award ceremony ended, Em grabbed her coat. She strode purposefully out of the gallery and around the corner into an elegant Regency square. She crossed the road and went through the gate that led into the garden in the centre of the square. A familiar figure sat in the middle of a bench illuminated by a street lamp, exactly where Lucy had said he would be in the text she'd sent Em a few minutes ago.

'Hello, you.' Em smiled at him.

'That's my line.' Jack moved up so Em could sit down. 'I am so sorry. I promised I'd be well-behaved, then I ruined your big night.'

'No, you didn't ruin it. It's me who should be sorry. It's my fault.'

Jack laughed.

'What's so funny?'

'It's just a phrase I never heard from Isabella. Hell would have had to freeze over before she would ever admit to being responsible for any problems.'

'I'm not Isabella.'

'I know. But seeing Connor standing half naked in your hallway made me think I'd misjudged you. It's hard to learn to trust again.'

'What made you decide you could trust me again after all this time? You didn't get a chance to tell me that earlier.'

'The portrait. You captured the real me - the vulnerable, lonely one. Not many people see that side of me. They only see a successful academic with a beautiful wife who appears to have everything. Isabella just saw me as someone she could use. But you ... you saw the lost soul inside.'

'Perhaps it's because I'm a lost soul too.' Em reached out and held his hand.

Jack squeezed it. 'I was so upset when I saw you with Karl, Ben, or whatever he's called now. It made me realise I wanted you back.'

'Lucy said she explained about me and Ben or, rather, that there isn't a me and Ben.'

Jack nodded. 'It didn't look like that when you walked into the gallery with him earlier.'

'I'm sorry. It seemed a good way to stop me from throwing myself at you. I didn't think you cared about me any more. '

'I thought it was the sort of trick Isabella would play. But Lucy explained. I guess I'm to blame for not being willing to talk. And I do care about you - a lot. I never stopped caring.'

She snuggled into him, feeling his heart beat faster. 'So does that mean I'm forgiven?'

'There's nothing to forgive.' He put his arm around her. 'Come on. I'm dying to know - did you win?'

'You weren't there, so I can't tell you. I'm sworn to secrecy.' Em had a mischievous look in her eye.

'But I would've been there if it hadn't been for the slight misunderstanding.'

'Is that how we're going to refer to that incident with Ben?'

'I'd prefer it if we didn't refer to it again. I promise I won't tell a soul the result until the TV programme's broadcast.'

'You could always ask Clara?' Em felt Jack's body tense. Before this went any further, she needed to know where he stood with Clara. Lucy's text had said it sounded like nothing was going on between them, but Em wanted to know for sure.

'I'm trying to avoid her.'

'It didn't sound like you've been avoiding her.'

'I promise I have.'

'But she said she saw you on Tuesday?'

'She did. At an event at the British Museum. There were lots of people there. She asked me to go for a meal afterwards, but I said no.'

'I thought you liked her?'

'I used to. But I didn't like her attitude to something that happened when we were in Italy. I've been keeping my distance ever since.'

He didn't look as if he wanted to elaborate further. Em decided not to push it. Jack hadn't been using Clara to take his mind off Em. That was all that mattered.

'So, did you win?' Jack was still eager to know.

'Yes - surprisingly.'

'That's brilliant news. You deserve it.' He laughed again. 'I was going to say your portrait was head and shoulders above the others.'

'That's a terrible joke.'

'Do you forgive me?' He kissed her hand.

'For the joke?'

'No. For calling you a liar. And for ignoring you for weeks. And for being abrupt on the phone. Have I missed anything?'

'Leaving me to cook for myself for three months.'

'Yes, that was particularly evil. I think you've lost weight.'

'Actually, I haven't. I'm just more toned now, thanks to Ben's fitness regime.'

'I can't properly tell with all those clothes you're wearing.'

'You better help me take them off then.' Em could see by the look in his eyes he was willing to assist. 'But not here!' she added hastily.

'I seem to remember you enjoyed a spot of outdoor recreation.' Jack pulled her closer.

'Not in the middle of London when it's two degrees!'

'It's a lot warmer at my new place.'

That cheeky look again. How Em had missed that. 'New place?'

'I needed a change. I'm renting a mews. I've had my eye on it for a while. One of my colleagues used to live there, but he's gone abroad. I only moved in last week. It's even got a loft conversion that would make a great studio if you know an artist looking for one.'

'I might be able to help you there.' Em shivered. 'I promised I'd go back to the gallery so the lovely Clara could interview me. Perhaps you can show me your new place afterwards?'

'I shall look forward to that,' Jack said. 'But there's something we need to do first.' And with that, he kissed her. A long, gentle, teasing kiss that took Em's mind off everything else.

'I've missed you, Jack.'

'I've missed you too, Em.'

Em smiled. What had she wished for? A mews property in London with a studio and a caring boyfriend who made her laugh. Perhaps Lucy had a point about the Universe delivering your wishes in unexpected ways. But there was one part of her dream that was still missing.

'Jack?' she said.

'Yes?'

'How do you feel about cats?'

MORE FROM SUZANNE LISSAMAN

Dear Reader,

Thank you for reading *Be More Octopus*. I hope you enjoyed it. If you did, please leave a review on Goodreads or Amazon - it helps other rom com fans discover my books, which means I can write more of them.

Talking of more books, if you'd like to find out what happened next to Em, Jack and their friends, the sequel *Be More Lucy* will be out later in 2023.

To get notified when it's published and get a freebie or two that I'm working on as well, sign up for my newsletter via my website: www.suzannelissaman.com

With love and laughter,
Suzanne x

Printed in Great Britain
by Amazon

29197248R00193